CROSSING PATHS

melanie stinnett

ISBN-13: 978-0-9898324-0-3

Cover Designer: Sarah Hansen, Okay Creations
Editor: Jovana Shirley, Unforeseen Editing
Formatting: Angela McLaurin, Fictional Formats

Visit my website at www.melaniestinnett.com

DEDICATION

To Fonty and Ms. J
You made a difference in my life,
and you still inspire me to follow my passion today.

1
June

SUNDAY

Standing in the driveway of my parents' home, I take in the scene from the end of the cul-de-sac. Two-story brick homes, manicured lawns, and friendly smiles line each side of the beautiful street. Our neighbors are most likely enjoying a late Sunday afternoon with their families today.

I reminisce about the times my mother and I would take walks down this street, waving hello to friends or stopping to admire the new landscape in a neighbor's yard. I loved those walks with my mother, like I loved the roses in Mrs. Harris' yard. I used to clip a few in secret and bring them to my mother on hot summer days. It was peaceful. It was quiet. It was full of love.

Most of our neighbors assumed the inside of our home matched the demeanor of the neighborhood. Unfortunately, this was not so. One member of our family strived to make sure our existence was anything but peaceful and quiet.

# # #

"Liam, put me down! Softly!"

My brother laughs with enduring triumph. Flying swiftly through the air, I think of ways I can smack the smile off his face before I remind him there's no trophy for scaring the crap out of me.

"I'm going to kill you!" I shout, brushing grass, dirt, and pride off my jeans.

"Not in front of Mom." He smirks as he jogs into the house.

As she slowly steps up from the curb to join me, Caroline can't take her eyes off the front door where my brother's presence graced its opening.

"No way, Caroline. My brother is off-limits. He can't even hold his own head on straight, much less manage a meaningful relationship."

"You never told me he was a Chris Pine on the hotness scale."

"Probably because he's my brother, and Texas isn't known for incest."

My best friend, Caroline, is having dinner with my family for the first time tonight. We met during our freshman year of college on the East Coast. Caroline's family lives near Seattle, so we were both far from home. Friendship came easily as we bonded over alcohol consumption, ridiculous roommates, and relationships with losers. We complemented each other with our differences.

Caroline—and I mean this in the best way—is completely full of herself. Of course, she has every right to be. She's tall, gorgeous, and a natural blonde with clothes and shoes that fit perfectly over her size two body. Caroline would never be caught out of the house in her pajamas with frizzy hair.

On the other hand, if she ever saw me putting on makeup or doing my hair, she would assume aliens had inhabited my body. Most of the time, my hair is a dirty-blonde mess. Someone once told me that I have dishwater blonde hair. I'm not even sure what that means, but it doesn't sound nice. I take every chance I get to throw my hair up in a ponytail or a quick bun. I wear worn blue jeans because they fit better than a new pair and simple tank tops or T-shirts with tennis shoes or flats in varying colors. I figure it's best to keep it simple, so the struggle is minimal.

After graduation in May, Caroline and I moved into our apartment in Texas, which is about twenty-five minutes away from my parents. It's far enough that I don't have to deal with them unless I want to, but it's still close enough to run home for the afternoon if Mom decides to fix my favorite dessert.

Before starting her job last week, Caroline went out of town with her family on one last vacation. They were in Hawaii for eight days, and Caroline's deep tan gives away how much time she spent on the beach. I don't think I'll ever figure out how to not be jealous of the way her skin turns to olive perfection from the sun.

As we walk through the front door into the main hall of our large but quaint home, I smell childhood and innocence, also known as the sweet scent of pot roast combined with a hint of chocolate cake. Caroline keeps step with me as we enter the kitchen. My mom is bent over, pulling out her beautiful creation of chocolate moist goodness from the oven.

"Hey, Mom. Caroline and I made it. Do you need any help?"

"Sweet little June," my mother says, "just take these potatoes to the table, and we'll be ready to eat. Hi there, Caroline. So glad you're here. I hope your first week of work went well."

"Sure did, Mrs. Derkert. Thanks for having me over."

Complete with a dollop of butter on top, the soft white mashed potatoes look heavenly. I hurry to the table, so I'm not tempted to make a pit stop at the kitchen island and eat them all.

The rest of my family is sitting around the dining room table. Made of dark wood and large oak planks, it's centered in the room and covered with a purple tablecloth that reminds me of the lavender growing in our backyard. Beneath the tablecloth, the wood is marked and stained from childhood incidents. Solid and sturdy, the table is held together by the love, tears, and laughter shared over the years. The chairs surrounding it are filled with a caring and close family. This is how I imagine my mother sees our dining room table.

After twenty-four years of having more meals than I care to count at my parents' table, I see it through a different set of lenses today. It is where my sister, Addison, can sit properly with her elbows off the table as she gloats about the perfection that is her life. It's a place my brother can lean back in his chair, balancing it on two legs, as he swiftly speaks about his great new job or a steady girlfriend we've never met. It's a space our father can lay down his rules on us kids while also giving our mother the much-needed attention and adoration she yearns for.

My father is a family practice physician, and he shares a clinic with two other doctors. He has worked in the same environment since before I was born. I remember sitting in an examination room with my siblings, playing with tongue depressors and trying to stick otoscope cones in each other's ears, while we waited for my father to finish with his last patient. It's a wonder none of us went into the medical profession.

My mother finished a degree in art, but she's never chosen to make money with those skills. After she married my father, they decided that they wanted to have kids right away. During our younger years, being a constant in our day-to-day lives was the most important priority to her. At this stage in her life, I think she's too accustomed to her independence to show up at an office and answer to a boss every day.

My parents loved us without respite throughout our childhoods. Of my two parents, our father was always the disciplinarian. He sat us in time-out, gave us a talking-to if needed, and spanked us when the offense was great enough. As a free spirit, our mother, on the other hand, gave us a creative outlet to cure us of our ornery attitudes. On weekends, we'd often lie in the grass with her, announcing the shapes of clouds, before we took nature walks to find rare plants.

Overall, I would say my home life was quite enjoyable.

My parents never sit on opposite ends of the table, like seen in movies when a couple gives loving glances or stern stares down the large expanse between them. My father seats himself at the head of the table with my mother on his right side. During my younger years, I distinctly remember them playing footsie under the table, like we didn't know what they were up to. Although their worship of one another was quite obnoxious at the time, it's now something I covet.

Sitting across from my mom is Addison, who has claimed the perfect child title. It really isn't fair since she was born first. Liam and I never really had a chance. Her hair, the color and shine similar to dark chocolate, is always in place, whisked away from her face with a sparkling pin or a quick braid. Her clothing speaks to her taste for designer brands and all the latest fashions. She married her high school sweetheart, Noah. He makes more money than all of us combined, and he's currently earning his paycheck overseas on business.

Although it might seem like I don't like Noah, I really do. He's a good match for Addison. Without him, she might have had to get a job and work for a living. *Heaven forbid.*

My brother, Liam, retreats from his seat next to our mother to get a cold bottle of water from the fridge. He's the consummate bachelor. All through our high school years, he would string girls along with his charm and good looks. I couldn't blame them though. My brother, as Caroline noted, is a handsome guy, and he can talk his way through any situation and come out on top, making a deadly combination for stupid girls.

Late one afternoon during his junior year, a girl came over without calling first. Like most girls, she thought she was in a committed relationship with Liam, so she was one hundred percent confused when she walked into the backyard and found him making out with one of her close friends. The next day, she told the whole school that he was a man whore. Even with that kind of reputation, the girls still lined up to ask him to the Sadie Hawkins dance the next month. Something about my brother makes him irresistible to the naïve ones.

Of course, there is the other side of my brother—the role of my protector. Although I appreciate the gesture, he single-handedly kept me from dating until he finally left for college, and even then, he would run off all my boyfriends when he came home during holiday breaks.

And then, there is me—sweet little June as my mother so affectionately calls me. I sit and quietly listen as usual, taking in all the latest information about my siblings' lives. Today, I have Caroline to lean on—at least in theory. I glance over at her, and she is still staring at my brother, like he's some kind of rare art exhibit. When I kick her under the table, she winces and looks to me as I emphatically mouth, *No!*

"Caroline, I hope you're enjoying the pot roast. It is one of June's favorites."

"Thanks, Mrs. D. A home-cooked meal is something I would never pass up. I don't even get that when I'm home in Seattle." Caroline smiles with a polite grin.

My mother turns her attention to me and gives me her

take-no-prisoners smile. *Here we go.*

"Maybe you can find new *friends* at work to spend some time with once you get settled in, dear."

To sum up the remaining details of the conversation, my mother takes the time out of her busy schedule to relentlessly harass my brother and me about our dating lives.

I dated a few guys in college, and although some of them were nice, none of them made the grade. My brother and I should blame our parents for our track records of indecisive dating. If they didn't have a seemingly perfect marriage, we wouldn't have set such a high bar for members of the opposite sex.

Liam shares my general disdain for this topic, so he quickly changes the subject. "So, Caroline, how do you like your new job at the design company?"

"So far, so good. I'm mostly familiarizing myself with everything right now, but I'm sure things will pick up in the coming weeks."

"You and June aren't far from where I work. Maybe we could all grab lunch one day this week?"

Oh no, you don't, brother of mine. "Don't you have a lot of lunch meetings, Liam? I'm sure taking time for lunch with us would put a big kink in your day."

"I'll see what I can do." Liam glares at me.

Caroline giggles.

I get up from the table. "Is everyone ready for cake?"

2
Liam

SUNDAY

Finally, a clear view of something other than my family at the dinner table. My sisters have had friends over for dinner in the past, but if their friends had looked like Caroline, I would have invited them over again myself. June has talked about her best friend Caroline before, but I've never had the pleasure of meeting her. If I had known how hot she was, I would have driven my ass out to the East Coast while they were in college.

During dinner, I tried to start a conversation with Caroline several times, but June was bent on intercepting my attempts. I can understand June's hesitation since she's well acquainted with my previous dating history, but she could give it a rest. Some days, I feel like my entire family still considers me an aimless bachelor with no intentions of settling down. I'm an electrical engineer in the airline industry, for heaven's sake. It's not like

I'm still working at the pizza place down the street. Maybe I still have a carefree attitude, but that doesn't mean that I'm not interested in a serious relationship.

At least June and I still have each other's backs when it comes to Mom's incessant need to discuss our opportunities to make new *friends*. A long time ago, the two of us made a deal to help each other avoid this topic. If Mom brings it up with one of us, the other sibling has a duty to change the subject. This is a serious pact. I would have sealed the deal with blood, but June is a little squeamish around bodily fluids.

Keeping in mind my mom's keen eye for matchmaking, I try to play it cool around Caroline. "You'll love my mom's chocolate cake, Caroline. It's a special family recipe."

"Mmm…anything chocolate is good in my book," she says, smiling at me.

Seriously, if she says "mmm" like that again, I might have to give June something to be pissed about. While many girls have smiled at me over the years, I don't know that any of them have done it while holding their eyes closed and humming with pleasure—at least not in front of my parents. I know she's humming about the cake, but I bet I could give her something more to hum about.

I can't take my eyes off of her as she gives me another small smile while putting her chin into her palm with her elbow resting on the table. Something about her grin keeps my eyes locked in place. It's bright and draws me in. *Not too big. Not too small. Just right.* I sound like I'm quoting the three bears or some nursery rhyme. *What the hell is wrong with me?*

At that moment, June walks back in, places the cake in front of me, and hands me a knife. "Would you like to cut the cake, brother?" she asks, attempting to guide my attention away from her friend.

"Why not?" I give June the most counterfeit smile I can offer.

She rolls her eyes and takes her seat, blocking my direct view of Caroline. *Damn it.*

"So, Liam…" Addison begins.

The signature high pitch in her voice tells me she's about to ask for something.

"How is your job going?"

"The job is great. What do you want?"

"Liam, be kind to your sister." My mom slaps my hand, the very hand sliding a piece of chocolate cake toward her.

Isn't there some kind of saying about that? Something like…don't slap the hand that passes you cake.

I glance back at Addison, and without a doubt, I know I'm right in my assumption. Her grin oozes sisterly love even though I know she could do without me on any given day. Ever since she found out about my flight perks and general travel discounts, she's been trying to plan a trip for her and several of her girlfriends.

"Spill it, Addison," I say, wanting this conversation to be over five minutes ago.

"If I was planning a trip to, say, Australia, would you be able to get a great deal on a ticket?"

"If you mean free, then no, I can't help you there. If you

mean, watch for sales, then I can shoot you an email when something comes up, but you'd probably be better off calling a travel agent."

"Are you serious? You can't do anything for Noah and me?"

I don't know how Noah deals with her constant whining. It's grating on my nerves already.

"Yes, I'm serious. I've told you before that I can only get major discounts within the continental U.S. And if you really want to know how I feel, I think you and Noah can afford your own vacations."

"That's enough," my dad states with a stern tone.

"Thank you, Daddy," Addison says, batting her eyelashes in his direction.

Was she adopted or just dropped when she was a baby? She can't seriously think he is on her side. We all drop the conversation and move on to eat our cake. I catch a few more glimpses of Caroline's smile as she talks to June about their new apartment and the excitement this week will bring.

After everyone is finished with their cake, I stand and start collecting plates. Mom tilts her head in confusion as I walk backward through the swinging door to the kitchen. I place the plates in the sink and look out the window into our backyard. Actually, I'm looking into everyone's backyard. My parents' neighborhood has wrought iron fencing, which I have always found annoying. I watch as a little boy and his dad are playing catch at the house directly behind us. Just a few houses down, two little girls are running in circles, trying to catch one another.

Their parents are sitting in lawn chairs with smiles on their faces. I never thought I would say this, but I feel a little bit jealous.

"Can I help?" Caroline asks from behind me.

"Oh, hey. Sure. Grab a towel, and you can dry."

We stand at the sink in silence as I wash the dishes and hand them over to be dried. She doesn't make much eye contact with me. I notice the way she presses her cheek against her shoulder, like she's nervous about something, and it's cute as hell. I'm about to ask her what she's so nervous about when the swinging door opens. June falls into the kitchen, tripping over her own feet, before she steadies herself against the refrigerator. *Thank God I didn't get the clumsy gene.*

"Caroline, you don't have to do that," June says.

Caroline places the dish towel on the counter. "Just trying to help."

"You ready to go?"

"If you are," Caroline says, glancing my way out of the corner of her eye.

As June walks back into the dining room, I begin drying my hands. Caroline looks up at me, still seemingly nervous.

"Nice to meet you," I say.

"You, too."

When she leaves, the kitchen feels empty. I want to follow after her, but I'm not sure why. I finish the dishes alone and say good-bye to my parents.

On the way back to my apartment, I call a few friends to see if anyone wants to catch the game and grab a few drinks at a local bar. Everyone is busy, so instead, I turn on the TV and pull out my laptop to do a little work.

I'm surprised no one took me up on my offer to meet at the bar. Generally, I don't enjoy the smoke-filled taverns unless a good game is on the big screen. Plus, I stopped drinking a few years ago. It wasn't for any particular reason. I don't know anyone who has been involved in a drunk-driving accident, and I haven't experienced any horrific incidents related to drinking. I didn't have a problem with limiting my own alcohol consumption. It just didn't seem fun anymore.

I watched my friends drink too much, and I paid my inflated tab one too many times, I guess. So, I'm the sober friend now. That title is about as awesome as being the pooper-scooper at the dog kennel. For about a year, at all hours of the night, I would get calls asking for rides home. At first, I thought of it as my duty to help my friends in need. Then, I just got tired of it.

Since I stopped frequenting the bars, it's been tough getting dates. It's not like the women from the bars were my type, but at least I got to go out and have a decent time a few nights each month. I've dated a couple girls from work, but that gets messy quickly. So, lately, I've put dating on the back burner while I try not to worry about my lonesome existence.

I toss my laptop down at the end of the couch and head to my bedroom. Falling onto the bed with my eyes closed, I find myself thinking about Caroline. I know June might kill me if I pursue anything with Caroline, but I don't think I care. I'm tired of considering how other people might feel about my decisions. The only problem is that, outside my parents' house, I'm not sure I'll see her again, and asking her out on a date with June sitting between us during Sunday dinner doesn't sound like a good idea. I guess I'll have to play it cool and see what happens.

3
June

MONDAY

Four weeks ago, I started my dream job...or so I thought. So far, I feel like my Media Planner title should be changed to Personal Assistant for Paul Hargrove. In all honesty, I shouldn't complain too much. To most people, sitting in on important meetings and fielding phone calls for the head Media Supervisor would likely be counted as a great learning experience. It's just that I don't want to sit and listen and take messages. I want to be a part of the action. I want to present a design and carry out a media campaign.

The lessons learned in college are utopian ideas of how the real-world marketing system functions. Here—in the land not filled with lollipops and gumdrops—people disagree, clients get angry, and marketing executives choose stupid ads to make high-paying clients happy. And it's all in the name of the almighty dollar.

Late last week, Mr. Hargrove came out of his office and dropped a plane ticket on my desk. "Pack your bags, darlin'. I need you to go to a meeting."

He later informed me that I would be sharing his input regarding media options for a new client's advertisements. At first, I was quite proud that he was sending me and only me to accomplish this task. *How awesome that he believes in my abilities after only a short time on the job.*

Later that same day, I overheard him discussing his vacation plans for the coming week, and then he commented on the lack of appropriate education for recent graduates. I realized then that my previous elation might have been premature.

Whatever his motivation might be, I'm leaving my sweet Texas existence today and heading to New York City where I can almost guarantee that it will be anything but sweet. Here I am, two hours early, waiting for my plane to arrive.

I hate flying! I'm sure the passengers sitting near me are enjoying the look of dread on my face while my fingernails are constantly tapping on the plastic armrest. The special part about today is that I have the joy of not only one but two flights. I know I'm being a big baby about the whole ordeal, but I abhor situations that involve giving up control of my life to someone else. This includes things like sitting in the passenger seat of a car, allowing a new barista to make my drink at the coffee shop, and flying, of course.

Caroline wanted to come with me, so she could keep me company and make sure I didn't have a panic attack on the plane. Unfortunately, she wasn't able to leave work behind since she only started a week ago.

While sitting at the airline gate, I stare through the wall of glass, watching as large planes drop to the ground. Each gigantic plane plummets toward the runway, scoots along the asphalt, and then begins a smooth roll toward its assigned gate. Passengers filter off the plane, appearing to be happy as they have reached their destination, but they lack that look of salvation from death. After witnessing this same scene repeatedly, I should have a little more faith in the flight industry. However, my brain keeps telling me that it couldn't possibly go that well for everyone.

Waiting near the large windows allows the bright sunlight to warm me. My eyelids begin to feel heavy. I should have gotten more sleep last night, but the terror of flying kept me tossing and turning.

Looking up, I meet the eyes of…*wait, this cannot be happening. What is Gavin doing at the airport?* There's no way he's on the same flight. I slide down in my chair and turn away, doing my best to avoid any form of contact.

Unlike most of the guys I dated in college, Gavin was the one I thought might make the cut. He's tall with dark hair, and he has an amazing body, molded by all his time spent training for our college's swim team. We met during a party at a mutual friend's house, and he was pretty much perfect from the start. Along with his good looks, he was a gentleman. He opened doors for me, paid for dinner, and gave me his jacket on cold nights. He would even call me after his swim meets to make sure I made it home safely. He seemed to be the total package, and after a year of dating, I was preparing myself for forever.

Then, on a foggy night during my junior year, I made a plan to surprise him. He liked to swim alone once a week to clear his head, and on that particular evening, I figured he wouldn't mind a little poolside action. Dressed in a tank top and sexy shorts with a new bikini underneath, I entered the pool area, tiptoeing my way across the tile floor. As the pool came into sight, I noticed no one was swimming. Although it seemed odd, I kept walking, thinking that maybe he needed to go to the restroom. It turned out to be much more than a simple potty break. I found him in the shower room with his Speedo around his ankles and one of his teammates on his knees. Evidently, our lack of sex life had less to do with my restraint and more to do with his gender preference. Over the following few months, he attempted to apologize several times, but after that night, I chose to boycott him and all things related to swimming.

"Hi, sweetheart," Gavin says as he leans over to kiss me on the cheek.

In what alternate universe does he think it's okay to touch me? "What are you doing here?"

"Just thought you could use some company. I heard that you haven't dated anyone since…well, since you and me."

"And you thought you could help with that situation?"

Sitting on the armrest of the chair, he places his hand on my shoulder. "Your mom was just worried about you."

Suddenly, in the background, I see my family and Caroline walking toward us with a banner. It's crisp, white, and spans at least five people wide. The bright red letters bluntly spell out, *Intervention*. I cower into my chair, hoping that it swallows me whole before passersby realize what's happening.

My father reaches me first. "We love you, June. We just want you to be happy."

To his right, Caroline and Addison nod in agreement with solemn looks across their faces. Liam is absent from the censure, which is not a surprise since they'll probably make it a two-for-one sign when they move on to his pathetic love life. To my father's left is my crazy mother. She reaches for my hand, and just as she is about to speak—

I open my eyes.

Gavin is not sitting on the armrest of my uncomfortable airport chair, my family is not present with an Alaska-sized banner, and I do not need to disown my best friend. *Oh crap, did I fall asleep and miss my plane?* Glancing at my phone, it looks like boarding should start in about five to ten minutes. *What a horrible dream.* Apparently, my mother has been really getting to me lately.

When my phone rings, I see that she can't give it a rest in real life either. "Hey, Mom."

"Honey, are you on the plane?"

"If I were on the plane, I probably wouldn't be answering my phone."

"Yes, you're right. Well, sweetie, I was just calling to wish you luck in case you don't have time to talk tonight."

"Why wouldn't I have time?"

"I just thought you might run into some colleagues or

maybe make some *friends* on your flight."

Is she trying to make me hang up on her? Lay off, Mom! Instead of feeding her need to constantly intrude in on my life, I change the subject. "I'm looking forward to our trip next weekend."

"Oh, me, too! I hope the weather holds out."

Mom, Addison, and I take a trip to the lake at least two or three times a year. I am pretty sure Addison dreads leaving her perfect life with its daily routines behind, but I have missed these trips. Since I was away at college, this will be my first time back to the lake in two years.

"Well, I better get going. I think they're calling for my flight."

"Alright, sweet June. I love you."

"Love you, too."

The employee checking us in at the gate is spouting off numbers so fast that it sounds like we're at an auction. *I wonder if she's had special training or maybe her dad sold cattle at the livestock circuit when she was young.* Either way, she might have chosen the wrong career. I end up last in line to check-in since I missed the moment when she called out my section on the plane.

I walk down the dull long hallway lined with advertisements for the airline I have obviously already chosen. When I reach the open door of the plane, I pause briefly before taking a measured step inside. I may or may not have caught the stewardess laughing under her breath as I walked by.

I brought one piece of carry-on luggage since I will be in New York for only a night. Heaving the luggage up over my head, I fit it snugly between a Big Bird backpack and a pink suitcase that I am sure is too large to qualify as a carry-on.

Glancing to the window seat, I meet the bright blue eyes of an older woman.

She looks at me with a sweet smile. "Hello."

I ease into my seat as I return the greeting. *Friendly conversation should pass the time.* Instead, the woman proceeds to crochet, not speaking another single word to me. *I need to stop by one of the expensive newsstands and buy some reading material for the next flight.*

The takeoff feels like a slingshot is hurling me with no regard for the fact that I'm human and not a bright yellow tennis ball, and when we land hours later, it feels very much the same. Although the flight wasn't the worst I have ever experienced, I still had to work hard to not grab the white paper sack in the seat pocket in front of me.

Once off the plane, I take in my first deep breath in more than two hours, allowing the cool air to enter my lungs and calm my body. Unlike most travelers, I'm thanking God for my layover.

To save myself from boredom, I walk the short distance to an airport store to buy a magazine. Looking across the covers, there isn't much that draws me in. I glance over so many words that take up useless space in my head—J-Lo's new love interest, VP hopeful thinks too much about his looks, brown bear saves child's life before killing other family members.

I walk over to the book section. It seems childish, but a Dr. Seuss book catches my eye. I have loved Dr. Seuss since I was a little girl. His books are so catchy and fun. I decide to purchase the book along with a trashy gossip magazine, and then I place them into my bag.

After I walk back to the gate and sit down, I pull out my book. When I glance up from my bag, I meet a set of piercing hazel eyes. The man looks away, and he stands quickly, but he's unable to walk because of the crowd of people around him. For once, I'm thankful for unruly children who pay no mind to their surroundings. My eyes scan over his body, taking in every inch of him. His chestnut hair becomes messy as he runs his hand through it. Clean lines of muscles are apparent through his crisp light blue button-up shirt, and his dark jeans fit nicely in all the right places. When the sea of children parts, he strides away down the corridor. It's a good thing because I think I might need a cold shower after taking in that view. Returning to my book, I peruse the funny and unworldly mind of Dr. Seuss.

Before long, an employee, who does not sound like an auctioneer, announces it's time to begin boarding. I complete the same routines as earlier today. I hand over my ticket, trek down the hallway, place my carry-on in the overhead bin, take my seat, and freak out.

I close my eyes and attempt to calm my nerves. Someone's leg brushes gently against my hand. I open my eyes, and there he is. His backside is directly to my right as he stores his bag away. I tell myself to look somewhere else but it isn't happening. He turns and takes his seat across the aisle, two rows ahead.

When I catch the hazel-eyed stranger glancing at me, I attempt to drag my eyes away from his without success. Another group of passengers board the plane, and as they walk between us, they break my trance.

I pull out my magazine and pretend to read about the demise of another celebrity marriage. *Did he mean to touch me? Surely not.* In these tight, confined spaces, it's easy to accidentally bump into people.

Within a few minutes, we are getting ready for takeoff. I put down my magazine, clench the armrests tightly, and close my eyes. As the plane speeds up, I tighten my grip. The ride smooths as we climb higher, and I open my eyes only to meet his again. I think I see a hint of a smile before he turns away.

I return to reading my magazine.

Later in the flight, I notice the stranger unbuckling his seat belt. *Is he coming to talk to me? What will I say?* The seat next to me is empty. *What if he asks to sit with me? Should I say yes if he asks me to dinner? What the hell? June, get a grip!*

While he's walking down the aisle toward me, I look at every small stitch of the seat in front of me. I reach for my drink, forgetting about the open magazine resting on my lap. In slow motion, my hand strikes the spine of the magazine, and it begins flying through the air. I reach for the magazine, and it slips out of my hands, gaining momentum upward. The pages seem to fan out in all directions, and then each page appears to smack him in the face one at a time before the shiny magazine finally falls to the floor.

He leans down to pick it up, and when he meets my eyes, he gives me a smile as he places the magazine on the tiny tray that still holds my untouched drink. As he draws his hand away, his soft fingertips touch my arm, and then he continues his trip to the restroom.

I am frozen in place. *That did not just happen. How could I have made a fool out of myself without even letting a word come out of my mouth?* I close my eyes and pretend to be asleep for the rest of the flight. During the landing, I convince myself to continue the charade even though I want to hold on to something for dear life.

As I start to exit the plane, I keep my eyes focused on my toes. I take my time getting off, hoping not to make anymore contact with a particular person. Once in the terminal, I rush to find the restroom. I'm not sure how long I need to stay for the coast to be clear, but whatever amount of time I have to serve in this restroom stall is what I deserve for the absurd amount of embarrassment I caused myself on that flight.

# # #

When I arrive at the hotel, I'm exhausted. I dread going to sleep in fear of another awkward meeting with an ex-boyfriend intertwined with a family intervention or worse. Lying on the surprisingly comfortable bed, my mind wanders, thinking about the past few years. *It can't be my fault that I haven't found Mr. Right.*

After the situation with Gavin, it was difficult to find a date. It wasn't because I didn't want to date. It was that every guy I went out with or even had a simple conversation with wanted to know what happened. I was shocked at the gossipy nature of their questioning. Were we having sex? Did I see any warning signs? Was I really surprised? One guy actually made a joke about how I had the "special key to the closet," like every guy I touched would turn gay. I honestly wondered what that said about him since he was one of the only guys who called for a second date. Needless to say, dating became a challenge my senior year. It was easier to spend time focusing on graduation and hanging out with Caroline.

Since I returned to Texas a month ago, my mother has been set on getting the dating train rolling again. Two weeks ago, she invited Barry, a childhood friend, over for our Sunday dinner. She spent the entire evening going on about how he became a doctor and was practicing in the same area as my father. She was so talkative that Barry was only able to speak a sentence or two in the midst of her praise. When he left that evening, I apologized on the front steps of my house. We both agreed to give my mother a show, and I allowed him to kiss me full on the lips, softly and tenderly. He smiled at me with a knowing grin as he turned to walk toward his car. Neither of us felt anything in the kiss. My mother, on the other hand, was sure there would be a wedding by this time next summer.

One thing my mom doesn't understand is that I don't go for men like Barry—men who never want to leave their hometown, who are happy to join the family business, and who live life as usual for as long as usual will allow. It is part of the reason I went to college on the East Coast. I wanted adventure. I wanted something different. Although I have moved back to Texas and it will always be considered home, I do not feel the same sense of obligation to the great state.

Closing my eyes, I picture the stranger from the airplane.

His eyes drew me in so easily. Although he looked a bit older than me, I'm sure he's probably still in his twenties. *What insight could be gained from a close-up view of those eyes? What would it be like to touch his face, gently run my fingers through his hair, and feel his lips against mine?* His hands would fit nicely around my hips or on the soft skin of my face. *I'm crazy. I don't even know the guy.*

It's probably a safe bet to assume he's unattainable. *Maybe he has a girlfriend or likes to sleep around? He could be a self-made billionaire who doesn't trust women. A guy that good-looking has to be out of reach.*

I turn on the TV to a late show I've never watched, and I drift off to sleep, thinking about the impossibility of a stranger.

4
Caroline

MONDAY

"June, have you seen my gray pencil skirt?" I yell out while searching through my closet. "June?" *Damn it, she isn't here.*

I forgot she's on a plane headed for New York City. She should be back late tomorrow afternoon, and I might just kill her if she comes back with the exact piece of clothing I can't find.

My best friend, June, and I have lived together for the last three years, and we're now renting an apartment together while we dive into the real world. During college, I spent most mornings making fun of her drab attire while she laughed at my brightly colored dresses and high heels. I guess the saying "opposites attract" can be true for friends as well. The only major similarities we have are we both speak English, and our dating history is a little spotty.

We met at a party. Although, I'm not sure June knew what it meant to party. We were college freshmen taking it all in. That particular night, I was making my way to the kitchen to refill my drink. Sliding my back along the stairway railing, I tried to avoid interrupting a couple with their tongues so far down each other's throats I was worried they would stop breathing. As I came to the bottom of the stairs, I tripped on the last step, launching the remainder of my drink onto the back of a guy's shirt, and then he spilled his drink on someone else. This domino effect continued for about four or five people until June got a plastic cup full of beer directly in the face. I apologized profusely as she wiped the liquid away from her eyes. When she looked up at me, she was smiling, laughing even.

"That's okay. I was looking for a reason to get out of here anyway," she said through her laughter. "I think I'll just leave and get something for dinner. It's still pretty early."

"Can I join you?" The party was lame, and I had already embarrassed myself enough for one night.

With that, our friendship began. We left the party, got a change of clothes at June's dorm room, and headed to Denny's. Breakfast for dinner—I don't think there is a better meal. June and I were both thousands of miles away from home, and we were beginning to miss our families. At one point, I told a stupid joke, and June laughed, spitting her drink all over me. We called it even, and from that night forward, we were inseparable.

After freshman year, we rented a two-bedroom duplex and lived there until graduation. We saw each other through general education courses, many more parties, and some crappy relationships. During the holidays, we went our separate ways to visit family, but when we returned to school, it was like no time had passed.

As graduation neared, we started to look at job options. On the same day, we both got calls about job offers in Houston, and we accepted without hesitation. We had already talked about how perfect it would be to get a place together as we started our careers.

I would have loved to go with her to New York today. I am sure it would have been fun even though the visit would be for less than twenty-four hours. I've heard the shopping and spas are amazing. I had already planned out where I might get a full massage and the stores I would need to hit first.

It's too bad my job requires that I actually show up. I work for one of the top interior design firms in Houston. I've known I wanted to be an interior designer since I was five years old. When I was supposed to be napping on a Sunday afternoon, I was usually rearranging my stuffed animals, holding up paint samples against the wall, or flipping through the many design magazines that were always lying around. A room was never complete in my eyes. There was always room for improvement, especially when your decor options were limited to your mother's fashion choices.

I love my job, but when I enter the office today, I'm hoping the day flies by quickly. With my best friend out of town and no other friends yet in this new town, life is pretty stale.

Dinner at June's childhood home yesterday was great. Since I officially moved in with June after my family vacation had ended a little over a week ago, dinner away from the apartment was the first interesting thing I did. *See? My life is lame.* June's family was simply precious. Her parents showed enough PDA to make Cupid vomit. Addison, her sister, seemed nice even though she was a little quiet. And their brother, Liam...*well, he is just hot.* I can't believe I haven't noticed him in any of June's pictures. Before we left, her parents gave me huge hugs, and it felt like fresh air being breathed into my lungs.

On the way back to our apartment, June kept saying how pissed she was because her mom had brought up the fact that she hasn't had a serious relationship in over a year. Honestly, her mom could have easily been talking to me, too.

While June had at least a couple of longer relationships in college, I tried to steer clear of the guys who seemed too serious. I just wanted to have fun and enjoy myself. For the most part, I accomplished my goal. I dated constantly—from football players to debate team members and from musicians to library workers. I didn't really stick to a type.

June had a hard time keeping up with my dating pace. It was hilarious to watch her struggle as she tried to recall the names of my dates from the previous weekend. One night, when I came home with a different guy than the one who had picked me up earlier that evening, June literally fell off the couch in shock. The guy I brought home happened to be a study partner from one of my classes, but I wasn't about to tell her that.

"Good morning, Caroline." My boss' voice brings me back to reality.

"Hi, Audrey."

"We have a lot to do today. Mr. Thorne's wife will be here this afternoon."

"I'll get right to work then."

Audrey smiles, and with her coffee in hand, she heads into her office.

The morning goes by quickly as I work on the presentation boards. When lunchtime arrives, I set out by myself to grab a quick bite. Last week, June mentioned a small Italian place around the corner that has great lunch specials. Heading that way, I walk down the large sidewalk, trying to avoid the mass of lunch travelers. *Mental note: Don't take lunch at noon ever again.*

As I enter the front doors of the restaurant, I hit a wall of people dressed in varying levels of business attire. I hear the hostess tell a customer standing at least five groups ahead of me that the wait will be forty-five minutes. Since I only have an hour for lunch, I decide I'll have to try this restaurant out another day or maybe call ahead with a to-go order next time. *I should pick up something quick, so I can get back and finish up the presentation boards.*

As I turn to leave, I hear someone call out my name, but it couldn't possibly be for me, so I keep walking.

"Caroline!"

As I hear my name again, I turn around and run right into Liam's chest. Liam's hands firmly grab my upper arms. I am thankful he is steadying me because I don't think I could handle standing on my own with his hands touching my bare skin.

"Hey, are you here to have lunch? The food is really great,"

Liam says with a wide grin as he slowly releases me.

"I would love to try it out, but I can't wait forty-five minutes to be seated. Maybe another day." I look down at my hands, avoiding eye contact. *What is wrong with me? I'm not shy.*

"Well, why don't you come sit with me? I have a table for two, but the guy I was meeting for lunch couldn't make it."

This probably isn't a good idea, but I agree because I'm hungry…and because Liam is, as I established earlier, hot. Today, he's dressed in casual business clothes. Dark slacks fit snugly at his waist, and the short sleeves of his green polo shirt show off his muscular arms. I can only imagine the muscles hiding underneath. I shake my head, trying to dislodge any other inappropriate thoughts from my head.

June was pretty clear that her brother was off-limits, but it's not like he would actually be interested in me. He pulls out the chair opposite from where his food sits. The waiter stops by the table, looking a little confused, but he takes my order just the same.

"So, do you like your job?" Liam asks before he puts a bite of chicken into his mouth.

Wow, I could definitely kiss those lips. They look so tender. I bet he's a really good kisser. When I catch Liam's eyes, I notice his whole face is smiling along with that beautiful mouth.

"Are you still trying to decide if you like your job or not?"

Oh crap, I didn't answer him. "No. I mean, yes, I like my job. It's exactly what I was looking for. Thanks for asking. What type of work do you do?"

"I work in the airline industry."

We go on and talk about his work, my work, his family, my family, the new apartment I share with June, and June's crappy love life.

"Did you date much in college?" Liam asks, looking down at his mostly empty plate.

"Some but nothing too special. Most of the guys June and I met weren't worth our time. At this point, I figure I'm better off spending my energy focusing on my new job."

"Probably a good idea. Speaking of work, I need to get back to the office. Hey, before I leave, can I get your phone number?"

My heart flutters, and I choke a little on my water.

"I feel like it would be a good idea to have a backup way to get in touch with June if she isn't answering her phone." Liam slides his business card along with a pen across the table.

"Sure, that definitely makes sense. After all, June is well-known for misplacing her phone or leaving it on vibrate all day." I smile and write down my number on the back of the card.

"Here's my card. Keep my number with you in case you need anything." Liam hands me another card with his name, office number, and cell number.

We part ways with a quick awkward wave and head back to work.

The afternoon goes by just as fast as the morning. After I put the finishing touches on the presentation board, I have a few minutes to spare before the afternoon meeting. Everything goes smoothly. The clients are happy, oohing and aahing during the entire presentation. They assure Audrey that they will let us know their final decision by tomorrow afternoon. It's such a relief to be done with my first major project. Hopefully, we'll get good news tomorrow. If so, June and I will have to go out and celebrate.

I leave work and decide to do a little shopping. This coming weekend, the interior design society in Houston is having a fundraiser to benefit a local children's charity. Although my closet already looks like a high-end department store exploded inside of it, I feel the need to buy a new dress for the occasion. I might even splurge and buy some new shoes and accessories. On my way to The Galleria, my phone rings.

"June! How was your flight?"

"Horrible. You wouldn't believe the crappy day I've had. I'm on my way to the hotel now."

"I won't even ask, but I'm glad you made it there safely. Are you ready for the meeting tomorrow?"

"Yeah, I think so. Mr. Hargrove gave me all the notes, and I made a few of my own before I left, so I would be prepared."

"I wouldn't expect any less from you." June was always the one on top of things in college. I'm not sure how I would have made it through without her. "I better get off here. I need to park and do a little shopping."

"You…shopping?"

I can hear the sarcasm in June's voice as I imagine her smiling. "Alright, alright. Good luck with your meeting tomorrow."

"Thanks. Bye."

I head into The Galleria and make my first stop at Neiman

Marcus. I try on about twenty dresses before sitting down in the dressing room. I'm completely worn out from my indecision. I find myself being hypercritical about the way the fabric lays, how low-cut the neckline is, or whether the length of the dress is appropriate. I just can't make up my mind. Usually, this is so easy for me. Most things look good on me, so it's normally a simple matter of finding the color or style to suit the occasion.

This time though, I keep thinking of Liam, wondering what he would think of each dress. *Would he find it attractive? Would he think it was too revealing?*

I need to stop this crazy train. Not only is he not interested in me, but he's also my best friend's brother. *I'm probably not even his type.* There's also the fact that my best friend just so happened to forbid me from dating him. I enjoyed spending time with Liam today. Talking with him felt so easy and comfortable even if he didn't act overly interested in anything more than a friendly conversation. *Maybe the Liam I met today was on his best behavior…or maybe his true self is different than what June thinks of him.*

I shouldn't be worried about impressing Liam. He'll never see this dress. As I finally choose a blue knee-length dress with a bow neck that shows off my collarbone, my phone trills. I search through my purse, thinking it is probably June calling to tell me how her hotel room is amazing.

Enjoyed lunch today. Thanks for the company. —Liam

Well, that was nice. Maybe June's brother isn't the big jerk she thinks he is. *Should I respond?* If I don't, he might think he has the wrong number.

Me, too. The food was great. —Caroline

It's official. I'm an idiot. *The food was great? Ugh.* I just sent him the awkward pat-on-the-back of text messages. If he was interested before, he definitely isn't interested now.

5
June

TUESDAY

I wake up feeling rested and ready to face the challenges of the day...as long as those challenges only involve one meeting and two flights back to Texas. I jump into the shower and stand under the constant hot water. Thoughts of airplanes brings back memories of the handsome stranger I managed to maul with a magazine. As I run my soapy hands over every inch of my body, I think about how it would feel to have his hands on me instead. I imagine leaning my head against his naked chest while running my hands down the sides of his body. His kisses would make my insides melt.

I open my eyes and bring myself back to reality. Rinsing my body, I step out of the shower and onto the cold tile floor. *Maybe I should take Mom's advice and start dating again.*

I need to clear my head before this meeting. This is my first chance to make an impression during my professional career. I have to make a positive you-could-really-be-something impression today. I know from experience how a bad impression can leave a lasting image.

My sophomore year of college, I sat in the front row of my advertising class, trying to make a good impression. Sitting in the back or even middle rows had never worked for me. It had proven to be too much distraction for my fidgety mind. Just before class began, a woman casually dressed in a college logo T-shirt and worn-looking dark denim jeans took a seat next to me. She asked if she could borrow a pen even though I noticed she didn't have a notebook. Although it seemed odd that she needed a pen, I handed one over just the same.

"Have you heard much about this class?" she asked, settling into an easy slouch in the uncomfortable wood chair.

I watched as she rolled my pen back and forth between her fingers. "Not really. From looking over the course's web page, it seems like the teacher thinks we have no other classes or much of a life outside of this course."

"I wonder if your first boss might have the same opinion when you're working on the biggest advertising proposal of the year," she responded matter-of-factly before leaving her front row seat to stand behind the lectern at the head of the classroom. "My name is Professor Moore. Welcome to Advertising 201."

She never let me live down that first interaction. She would often ask me if my nose was numb from being stuck in my homework. *Lesson learned: Always ask for names and credentials before beginning a conversation.*

For today's good impression, first on my checklist is a killer outfit. I stole a few pieces from Caroline's closet. I doubt she would ever miss such a miniscule slice of her wardrobe. I slip on the beautiful green top and knee-length pencil skirt. After pairing the outfit with some killer black heels, I survey myself in the mirror. *This will definitely turn heads while still looking professional.* It's nothing like what I normally wear, even to work, but I need to stand out for this meeting.

Second, I have to be prepared for absolutely any scenario. Along with the pages my boss gave me, I have a few notes of my own. Of course, my thoughts are a last resort since my boss made it clear that his ideas sold the company on letting us have a seat at the table.

Finally, I need to make lasting contacts. I brought a handful of my new business cards with all the necessary contact information.

With these three things in place, I'm sure someone will take notice and remember me when I walk out the door.

My boss emailed a map with walking directions from the hotel to where the meeting is being held. With plenty of time to spare, I leave the hotel, walking at a steady pace. I take in the noises of the city—cars honking, people yelling, and many of my sidewalk companions huffing as they push through to reach their destination quickly. Overall, this city does not give off a friendly feeling, but it's different, and I can appreciate the unique atmosphere.

Right before I reach the address of the office building, I

notice a construction site blocking not only the road ahead but also the sidewalks leading to the building where my meeting is being held. Batting my eyelashes, I give a sweet smile to a construction worker.

"Hi, there. Any way you could let me through? I have a meeting in the building just past that fence," I say, pointing.

He groans under his breath, obviously annoyed by my presence, and then he spouts off a line that sounds as rehearsed as a Broadway play. "I'm sorry, ma'am," he says with no regret on his face. "You'll have to walk around the block. This area is too dangerous for pedestrians."

Ma'am? Do I really look that old…or unattractive? Now, I only have ten minutes until the meeting begins. My feet are already aching from faltering in these heels, and the sun is glaring down on the pavement. *Place a big fat checkmark in the unfriendly city column.*

When I take off down the block at a quick pace, I realize that construction has also blocked off the next two cross streets. I become aware of the fact that if I don't start running, I'm going to be late to this meeting. Regretting my decision to wear heels, I take them off and start a slow jog with the sunlight hitting my face.

After I finally come around the block, glad to have the sun on my back, I start up the steps to the front doors of the Truman building. All of the sudden, I run smack into the back of a man in an expensive business suit. I fall awkwardly against a railing to the side of the doorway. Feeling a sharp pain around my ribs, I know I'll have some serious bruises later today.

"I am so sorry. I'm running late, and I just didn't see you." I peer up at the man, but I can't make out his face. The glare of the sun reflecting off the glass door behind him is making it hard for me to keep my eyes open.

"No, no. It's my fault. I stopped too quickly as I came up to the door. Let me help you." He gently moves toward me, his body blocking the sun's reflection and bringing his face into view.

When I see his beautiful hazel eyes, I know he has to hear me gasp.

"I thought maybe you wouldn't recognize the stranger you threw a magazine at." He laughs gently. "By the way, my name is Cohen."

Although my face is already heated and likely red from my last-minute jog, I feel it going another shade deeper.

"Um, I'm so sorry. My name is June." Placing my hand in his, I allow him to pull me back onto my feet.

"Well, June. Are you here on business?"

"Yes, I'm going to a meeting in the Rousch conference room."

He tilts his head slightly, grinning down at me. "Let me show you the way. Maybe we can discuss your frequent need to assault me after the meeting, but first, you might want to put on your shoes."

Embarrassment doesn't even begin to cover the emotion I'm feeling right now. I pay careful attention to make sure my heels end up on the right feet. Placing his hand on the small of my back, his touch is slight but present as he leads me through the large glass doorway and then over to the elevator. Looking up at him, I smile timidly.

When we reach the conference room without further assault, I turn to say good-bye.

"Thank you for showing me where to go. I'm running a little late, so I better get in there," I say, pointing at the doorway behind me.

"Oh, I'm not leaving. I'm attending the meeting, too." He walks through the door, heads over to the refreshment table, and pours himself a cup of coffee.

I take my seat, which happens to be the only empty seat remaining, and then I watch as Cohen takes his place in the front of the room. This situation is getting worse by the second. My sophomore year experience was trivial compared to the fool I just made of myself.

Cohen leads the meeting without any hint of awkwardness. I shamelessly stare at him although no one notices because they are all staring, too. Thank God staring is normal when intently listening to someone.

I force myself to pry my eyes away for a quick review of my notes. Throughout the meeting, I gather myself at the appropriate moments, and I respond based on the guidance my boss has given me, using a couple of points from my personal notes along the way. And then, too quickly, the meeting is over.

I take off for the restroom, which seems to be my hiding place lately. When I look down at my feet, I notice a few scuff marks on the side of the left shoe. Taking it off, I can see that the red interior of Caroline's shoes is covered in black. Taking off the other shoe, I notice that the bottoms of my feet are also black from running down the streets, and they've ruined the interior. *I have no idea how much these cost. Caroline is probably going to kill me when she sees these shoes.* I exit the stall, and I wet a few paper towels to clean the bottom of my feet.

I clean the shoes as best as I can and then peek my head out the restroom door. I can't see anyone in the hallway, so I leave the restroom and take the elevator downstairs. When the elevator opens on the ground floor, I exit and look toward the lobby doors, preparing myself for the push and shove of the foot traffic on the sidewalks outside.

"June, wait."

I am halfway to the front doors when I turn and see him. I want to run away like I used to run in high school track—without abandon and with stamina. I bet he wouldn't chase me, not with all these people around. They'd probably think he was trying to hurt me, and they'd stop him from reaching me. Instead, I smile and put my shoulders back. *This should be good. He probably wants to talk to me about my unprofessional behavior during the plane ride and on the building steps. I'll be lucky to have a job when I get back to Texas.*

"Let me take you to lunch."

He smiles when my brows furrow in confusion.

"What?"

"Let me take you to lunch. We can eat at the airport if you're flying back today."

"Um, I'm not sure that's a good idea."

"Why? Are you planning to beat me with a spoon?" He

smirks. "Listen, I'm flying out later today, so I just thought if we're going to the same place, then maybe we could grab a bite together."

I give in, and we agree to have lunch at the airport.

Two hours later, I exit the cab at the airport and roll my luggage behind me. I enter through a set of sliding doors and I see Cohen sitting on a bench near the check-in desk. I catch his attention with a small wave hello, and he smiles. We both check in at the kiosk and make our way through security. Being a gentleman, he lifts my luggage onto the security belt, not allowing me to put forth any effort. I catch myself staring at him as he bends to take off his shoes. I linger on his messy dark hair, his shoulders, his arms, his hands, and his shoes. Every part of him is interesting.

We reach the first busy restaurant, and I stop at the hostess stand.

"June, would you mind if we ate somewhere else?"

"Sure."

He leads us to a small sandwich shop tucked in a quiet corner. We make our food selections and choose a table in the back of the seating area.

"Is this against company policy?" I ask.

"What? Eating lunch with a business associate? I don't think so." He smiles.

Right, June. You are just having a business lunch. Stop taking yourself so seriously. I smile back with some reserve.

"So, June, do you make a habit out of throwing things, including yourself, at other people?"

I feel my entire body heat as embarrassment washes over me again. "Not usually. I believe you've caught me at a bad time."

"Oh, have I? What would it have been like if I caught you at a good time?"

"First of all, I would have said hello instead of throwing my magazine at you, and then we would have had a wonderful conversation about some mutually interesting topic. Second, the stupid construction worker would have let me through, so I wouldn't have run into you on the steps. I would have beaten you to the conference room, and then I would have impressed you with my knowledge of media accounts."

"I guess I would have been okay with the hello and the conversation, but I rather like the fact that you ran into me." He pauses, looking down as he twirls his fork between his fingers. "And I was still impressed with you."

When he glances back up at me, my heart stutters as I catch a light in his eyes.

We continue talking about his life back home and our college years. I try to avoid any topics that might bring up awkward stories, which is pretty challenging for me. I'm amazed at how easily our conversation transitions from here to there. He begins telling a story about his dad and a runaway golf cart. About halfway through, I laugh so hard that I have trouble catching my breath.

A man who can make me laugh—now, that is an important trait.

*Here we go again, June. An important trait for what? A friendship?
A business relationship?* Obviously, this could never be any other
kind of relationship. He is a business associate from another
company who lives across the country. Of course, he also
happens to be really good-looking, and he seems to have every
trait on my secret perfect-man checklist. *Maybe I should look on the
bright side.* At least I am making friends in the industry, which
couldn't be a bad thing.

After we finish eating with about thirty minutes left until
my flight leaves, he walks with me to the gate.

"It was really great having lunch with you, June."

God, I love the way he says my name. "Thanks. I enjoyed it very
much."

"Here's my card. Call me if you're ever up in the Seattle
area."

I take his card, reach in my purse, and then give him my
card as well. We smile at each other, not knowing how to part
ways.

"Do you text?" I sound stupid, but I want to linger in the
conversation.

He nods.

"We can keep in touch then."

He nods again with a slight smile this time.

"Okay, bye." I turn and walk toward the gate with my
carry-on in tow. It feels much heavier than it did before as the
weight of possibilities to come presses for me to stay in this
moment.

After a few more seconds, I turn to watch him walk away. Instead, I find him still facing me, standing in the same spot. He pulls his hand out of his pocket and waves. I return a small wave and head back in the opposite direction with a huge smile on my face.

When I make it to the gate, I take out my phone and save his number before my clumsiness finds a way to lose his business card.

6
Caroline

Sleep didn't come easily last night, and as always, morning came too quickly. Still lying in bed, I stare at the ceiling, going over my current work project. *Who am I kidding?* I'm not thinking about work. I'm thinking of Liam—sexy, funny, and incredibly off-limits Liam.

I've been trying to think of anything other than him since I got his text message yesterday. I grab a magazine off my nightstand and flip through pictures in the "Sexiest Man Alive" article to try and get him off my mind. It doesn't work. Unfortunately for me, Liam is hotter than most of these guys, and he doesn't come with a bunch of celebrity baggage.

How am I going to face June when she gets home? She knows me too well to think I would be worthy enough to date her brother. I mean, we are best friends, and she loves me, but she knows my dating record. She wouldn't believe for a second that I could be serious about a real relationship.

Truth be told, I'm vain and sometimes selfish. I want a guy's life to revolve solely around me. I can't cook, I hate to clean, and I have always maintained that it would take one hell of a guy to convince me to have children. I've seen what a kid can do to a woman's body in less than a year. I'm not even sure why I am worried about it. There's no way I am going to tell June about my lunch date with Liam. His text last night had to have been out of kindness to the new girl in town. *Wait, did I just say date? Oh well, I don't think inner monologue counts.*

After wasting precious morning minutes by wallowing in bed, I convince myself to stand up, get ready, and head to work.

# # #

As the day goes by, it continues to be fairly uneventful. Normalcy seems to be back in full swing. Around two o'clock, my phone vibrates from the inside of my purse, which is tucked neatly underneath my desk. Since my boss is out for the afternoon, I dig it out to see who's calling.

"Hi, Mom."

"Caroline, I didn't expect you to answer."

"Well, it's your lucky day. What's up?"

"Nothing, sweetie. I'm just sitting in the waiting room at the doctor's office."

Did she just call me sweetie? That's strange. "Is everything okay, Mom? Why are you at the doctor's office today?"

"Oh, um…just a normal check-up. They told me I might be waiting a little while, so I thought I would give you a call. Are you enjoying Texas and your new job?"

"Definitely. It's all great. On Sunday evening, I went to dinner at June's parents' house, and it was really nice. Her family is great. Don't say anything if you happen to talk with her, but her brother is so gorgeous that I can barely keep my eyes off of him. I can't believe I never noticed a picture of him before."

"Uh-huh. Well, I'm glad you are enjoying things there."

As her voice cuts out a little, I hear my mom sniff a couple of times.

"Mom, are you crying?"

"Heavens, no." She laughs gently. "I just have a little cold. I'm sure the doctor will give me something to knock it down. Oh, Caroline, they're calling my name. I need to go. I love you, sweetie."

"Love you, too. Bye."

As the afternoon wears on, I'm distracted. That one simple phone call was the strangest conversation I have ever had with my mom. She didn't laugh loudly, causing me to pull the phone away from my ear. She didn't haze me, attempting to make me feel embarrassed about my attraction to my best friend's brother. And she called me sweetie—twice!

Although my family is nowhere near as close as June's seems to be, I have always been able to read my parents pretty well. When my favorite aunt, Karen, passed away, I took one look at my mom's face and knew something was wrong. When my dad got me crazy awesome seats to the Justin Timberlake concert in high school, I started screaming in excitement before he even pulled the tickets out of his back pocket. Looking back, I guess it was always easy to read their facial expressions. Now, I know something is going on, but the specifics are fuzzy.

My mind begins to review the worse-case scenarios. Maybe my stepdad, John, is getting laid off. I know the economy has been down, and earlier this year, they were a little worried. Surely, we wouldn't have gone on that huge vacation if they were still concerned. I'll have to remember to call John later to do a little more snooping.

# # #

Leaving work, I head to pick up June from the airport. I can't wait to see her smiling face. I pull up to the curb and watch as June practically skips to the car. *Hmm, she seems happier than usual. June is normally happy, but skipping? What happened to her in New York?* It looks like I have more snooping to do than I realized. I jump out of the car and throw my arms around my best friend.

"I'm so glad you're home."

"Thanks, friend. It's good to be back."

"What's with the million-dollar smile?"

"What are you talking about?" June blushes a shade of red that can only be mimicked by the most brightly colored roses.

"Okay, seriously, something is going on. Did you get the contract already?"

"No," she answers simply as she cheerfully hops into the car.

I don't think I've ever seen someone cheerfully get into a car. It's a very strange sight, especially when she should realize we're about to hit a wall of traffic worse than standing in line for a new iPhone release.

"Let's get out of here before you get a ticket for loitering or something," June says.

"Hey, if that hottie cop over there wants to give me a ticket, I will gladly take his card with the number to his office." *Wait, what am I saying?* If I keep acting like this, June will never be okay with me dating Liam. Then again, I probably won't be seeing him again anyway. "He looks our age. Do you want me to get his number for you?"

"No! Just drive, Caroline." She giggles.

Did June just giggle? This day is getting weirder by the second.

As we pull on to the highway, a great idea hits me. "What do you say we cook dinner at home and drink some wine tonight? We can talk about your trip, and maybe the alcohol will get you a little more loose-lipped about whatever happened in New York."

"Ha! I doubt that, but some good pasta sounds wonderful. Stop at the Epicurean Market, and we'll grab what we need. I think we need some See's Candies to go with our meal, too."

"You speak to my heart. Italian food, wine, and chocolate. If you were a man, I would marry you right now."

June laughs loudly, throwing her head back. She seems so cheerful. Even if I don't find out what happened in New York, I know something has altered her mood in the best way possible.

When we get home, June cooks dinner while I pour glasses of wine. After I open our See's Candies, she asks me to grab her phone, so I can play a new song by some British girl. She gushes about the song, telling me how the lyrics are so great. If June wasn't in such a good mood, I would tell her that a song about dancing at discos and eating cheese on toast is not exactly enlightening. Just as I'm about to suggest a song change, my phone chimes to tell me I have a new text. I walk to the other side of the couch and turn away as if the back of June's head could read the screen on my phone.

Are you busy Friday evening? I have this event to attend, and I was hoping you might be available to join me. —Liam

Did I read that right? Crap! This can't be happening. I am not supposed to get involved with June's brother. *Wait, I have the perfect excuse to avoid him on Friday night.*

Would love to, but I actually have a charity event to attend for work.
—Caroline

It doesn't happen to be for the Boys & Girls Club, does it? —Liam

Yes, that's the one. —Caroline

There is no way he is attending the same event!

Sounds like we're headed in the same direction.
Could I convince you to let me pick you up? —Liam

Well, I had plans to go with some girls from work, but I'm sure they
wouldn't mind just seeing me there. —Caroline

Great, it's a date. I'll pick you up at 6:30 on Friday night. —Liam

Okay, thanks. See you then. —Caroline

A date! He definitely said it's a date. With the strangeness of today, I reread the text a few more times to make sure it's not a mirage to my weary eyes. *What am I thinking? You know what? I don't care.* It's not like I'm pursuing him. He asked me. My smile has already spread from ear to ear as I walk back into the kitchen. I'm trying in vain to hide my excitement, but June sees through me with one glance.

"Who was that?" she asks with a knowing grin.

"A guy I met at work. He wants to go to the charity event together on Friday."

June's mouth drops open. "I was only gone for one day. You must have really wowed him. Is it the one you told me about last week? The hot guy from the office down the hall?"

I hesitate, thinking about my answer. I don't want to lie. "No, it's a new guy I just met. I don't know much about him, so there isn't much to tell." *A certain level of vagueness isn't considered lying, right?*

Thankfully, June leaves it at that. "Dinner is served," she announces as she places our dinner on the bar place mats.

The food and wine are wonderful. The See's Candies are otherworldly. And, of course, the company is the best part. I am so glad to have June home even though I have to hide the fact that I'm lusting over her brother.

Thinking forward to the rest of the week, I know Wednesday and Thursday will pass in a blur. Things are going to be crazy at work as we get ready for client meetings and prepare for the charity event. Since my boss is head of the committee in charge of the event, I'll be running around, arranging flowers, setting tablecloths, and making sure everything looks beautiful. As the date gets closer, I know there will be last-minute additions to make sure my life does not survive without chaos. Up to this point, the details appear to be falling into place. If I can just keep myself from falling into a relationship with June's brother, I'll be doing alright.

June

WEDNESDAY

Driving to work, I'm blaring music through the speakers with my windows down. I'll do anything to keep my mind off that crazy business trip. I'm resolved to the fact that I will turn down any further opportunities to embarrass myself or the company in out-of-state adventures. This was simply an indication that I should keep my feet planted firmly in Texas.

Honestly, I don't know why I'm letting it all get to me. I was awake for what felt like hours last night. If I told anyone in my family that small fact, they would take me straight to a doctor. A normal sleep routine for me consists of changing clothes, laying my head on the pillow, and falling fast asleep in two seconds.

While answering text messages from her new boy toy last night, Caroline seemed oblivious to my distracted mind. It was impossible for me to stop thinking about Cohen. I should have asked for Caroline's advice, but truth be told, I don't want advice. I want the whole experience with him to disappear. It was humiliating. It was frustrating. Although he was amazing, I don't want to dwell on that.

"Good morning, Mr. Hargrove. How was your vacation?"

"June, it was wonderful. I think I should leave more often if this is the outcome." He jogs toward me, which is quite a sight by itself as he's not a small man. He tosses a single sheet of paper, and it floats onto my desk.

Mr. Hargrove:

We sincerely appreciate you sending your bright assistant to our meeting on Monday. Her ideas and suggestions were a breath of fresh air. Our official letter of contract for the job will be emailed this afternoon. I look forward to working together.

~ Cohen

I blink my eyes several times. My vision must be playing tricks on me. *Oh my gosh! I did it!* I made an impression—and a good one at that. My boss is still lingering over my desk, waiting for some kind of response.

I peer up through my bangs, still blinking my eyes. "Wow! Mr. Hargrove, I am so glad that I was able to present your ideas in a way that impressed them."

"Oh no, you don't." He practically jumps across my desk, lifts me to my feet, and gives me a tight hug.

Over his shoulder, several of my coworkers are reacting to his awkward display. A few are laughing while others are trying to pick up their jaws from off the ground.

Pulling me back by my shoulders, he looks me in the eyes. "After receiving his note, I called Cohen this morning to discuss a few things. The ideas he was impressed with were yours. I had never heard them before, and they were brilliant. I had no idea what kind of talent you were hiding in that brain of yours," he says while tapping his finger against the side of my head. "Keep up the good work, and you'll be moving up the ladder in no time."

I know the smile on my face has to look ridiculous, but I don't care. *This is unbelievable!* Mr. Hargrove gives me a quick pat on the shoulder before walking back into his office. I sit back down in my chair and pick up the phone to call Caroline.

"You aren't going to believe this!" I quickly tell her about what happened, and I almost lose my hearing when she starts squealing on the other end of the phone.

"Well, that definitely calls for a celebration. More wine and See's Candies?"

"Sounds wonderful to me. I need to go, but I'll see you after work."

"Alright! See you then."

The rest of the day flies by, and I see Caroline as I'm walking into the apartment building. She has wine and candy in hand, and she's striking a goofy pose. She looks like a cross between Vanna White and one of *Charlie's Angels*.

"Geez, Caroline. Could you be any weirder?"

She laughs. "Don't tempt me, June Bug. Let's get inside, and start this dance party."

Our celebratory dinner consists of grilled cheese sandwiches, wine, and chocolate. We spend the entire evening dancing around the kitchen, through the living room, and then into our respective beds. *I think tonight ranks up there as one of the best nights of my life.*

"Hey, June?"

"Yes, Caroline?"

"You rock!" she shouts as one of our favorite songs begins to stream from the speakers in her room.

I smile to myself, hugging my pillow. *Now, that's what friends are for*

♯ ♯ ♯

THURSDAY & FRIDAY

The week continues to go by quickly. Mr. Hargrove gives me more projects and asks for my opinion on several new jobs. I feel like I am soaring above the atmosphere, looking down at the earth. My life has a good view at the moment.

Friday afternoon, I walk into my office, focused on filing away some papers and grabbing more information before my next meeting. A smell catches my attention, and I glance up to the table by my doorway. Beautiful pink and white peonies greet me. They must be in the wrong office. Pulling off the card, I read the handwritten words.

Congrats on the new contract! See you Monday.
Try to keep your hands to yourself, so you don't assault me. ~C

No freaking way! He's coming here? What will I say to him? What will he say to me? What will I wear? I need Caroline! It's time to spill the beans about my trip and get some advice.

# # #

When I get home, Caroline is cleaning like a mad woman.

"What are you doing?" I laugh loudly. She looks ridiculous with cleaning gloves pulled up to her elbows while dirty paper towels are littered throughout the living room.

"My brother will be here tomorrow, and I don't want him to tell my mom what a slob I am."

"You are being crazy. You know you could always blame the mess on me."

"My mom would never believe that."

"Well, at least let me help you."

# # #

Within two hours, the whole place is spotless, and it smells lovely. We plop down on the couch together, and Caroline catches her first glimpse of my flowers.

"June?" A grin forms across her face. "Where did the flowers come from?"

I blush instantly, feeling a heat spread throughout my entire body.

"Don't be mad at me—"

"But?" Caroline pulls her legs up, sitting Indian-style, and turns to face me on the couch. "Where did you meet him?"

"In New York."

"What? I thought we were friends. You met a guy in New York, and you didn't tell me?"

"Well, he doesn't actually live in New York." I give Caroline the full recap of my horrible encounters with Cohen—from the flying magazine to the office building steps to our airport dinner. "Oh, it was horrible!" I throw my head into my hands. Sitting still for a second, I expect Caroline to cover me with her arms and hug me until I don't feel like a total idiot anymore. Instead, I hear her burst into uninhibited laughter.

"That has to be the funniest thing I have ever heard. So, you threw your magazine at his head on the plane? Then, you chose to run smack into his backside before your meeting?"

"I didn't choose to run into him. It just happened."

"Wait a minute. He's the one who sent you flowers? What did you do? Kiss him as he helped you up?"

"No, I didn't kiss him. You are impossible! After the meeting, he found me and asked if I was going to the airport. He was flying out, too, so we ate at a little sandwich shop in the airport. Nothing happened. He's practically my boss."

"So, what does the card say?" She reaches out to snatch it before I can catch her. "Oh my gosh, he likes you! You better get a tan while you're at the lake this weekend."

"Just shut up. I am totally freaked out."

"You are so silly. Is he hot?"

"Yes."

"Did he seem nice?"

"Yes."

"Does he have money?"

"Caroline!"

"Alright, well, he passes my test. Did you get his number? I think you should date him. Maybe you should even consider bringing him to Sunday dinner, so your mom can start planning your wedding and how many babies you should have."

"Sure, that sounds like it'll work out just fine since he lives on the opposite side of the country. I thought you would feel sorry for me and help me pick out something nice to wear for Monday. See if I ever bare my soul to you again."

Caroline stares at me, waiting for the answer to the only question in her approval speech. I don't want to get into this right now. She raises her eyebrows and motions with her hands to indicate that she's waiting.

I raise my hands in surrender. "Fine. Yes, I got his number."

She jumps up from her seat on the couch, clapping like a child too full of energy. "You should text him. You should text him right now!"

"And say what?"

"Anything. Come on, June! He obviously likes you. Give it a chance."

I involuntarily smile, but before I can put my smile back where it belongs—off my face—Caroline starts poking at my sides with her Twizzler-like fingers.

"See, you like him, too! Just do it."

"Okay, okay, but you have to leave me alone about it after this."

"Pinky swear," she says, not offering her pinky.

I draft several different text messages, trying to figure out which one would sound like I'm interested and grateful but not desperate.

~~Got your flowers. That was nice.~~

~~Thank you for the gift.~~

~~Come to Texas and be with me.~~

I finally settle on one.

The flowers are beautiful. Thank you. —June

I hit Send, and shortly after, my phone vibrates, showing a new message.

You're welcome. —Cohen

"Let me see it," Caroline says, lunging toward me.

I pull my phone away before she can reach it. "Stop it. He just said, 'You're welcome.' That's it, so don't worry about it."

She shakes her head and sits back down on the couch.

"Fine."

I can't believe she gave up that easily.

Caroline glances to the carpet and then peeks back up with a strange look on her face. "I need to ask you a favor," she says.

That's an odd change in attitude. "Sure. Anything. What do you need?"

"Can you help me pick out a dress for my date tonight?"

8
Caroline

FRIDAY

"You want my help picking out something to wear?" June questions, looking at me like I just asked her to build Noah's ark.

She's right. I would normally ask anyone before asking for her help, but since it is her brother, I thought her guidance might be good. Of course, I can't tell her the reason behind the request.

"I don't really need much. Just tell me if you think I should wear this dress..." I hold up the blue dress I just bought in one hand. "Or this one." My other hand lifts a black dress that shows a little more skin. "Now, remember, I'll be on a first date with a professional guy."

June laughs. "Do you really like this guy or something? I thought you said you didn't know much about him."

I give her a glare.

"I would pick the blue one," she says, holding her hands up in surrender.

"Thanks, June." I run over and hug her.

# # #

I take a quick shower and settle in at the bathroom mirror. June walks in and hops up onto the counter. Her legs are swinging back and forth as I put on my makeup and then do my hair.

"Don't you have to get going? What time are you supposed to be at your parents' house?" I ask.

"Oh crap." She hops off the counter and rushes out.

I can hear her running through the apartment. I lay my hands flat against the counter, taking in a deep breath. The sooner she is out of the apartment, the sooner I don't have to worry about her running into Liam.

"Have fun tonight, Caroline, and don't do anything I wouldn't do."

I can tell she is smiling as I hear the sound of the door closing behind her.

Suddenly, I am alone and nervous as hell. *I am going on a date with Liam. What if he is meeting some other people there, and he doesn't pay attention to me? But then, why would he want to pick me up and spend time alone with me in a car?* This whole insecurity thing is driving me nuts. I have never acted this way before.

I finish putting on my last coat of mascara before I go and sit on the couch. The bright red digital numbers of the clock read 6:17, but I know it is a few minutes fast. I need something to pass the time. I turn on the radio, but nothing good is on at the moment. I switch on the TV and find nothing good there either. Walking to the kitchen, I grab a bottle of water, come back, and sit on the couch. *Only 6:21?*

At six thirty precisely, I hear a light knock on the door. Standing in front of the closed door for a short moment, I take in several deep and even breaths. I thought deep breaths were supposed to be calming, but apparently, the MythBusters need to do some investigating on that one.

I open the door slowly, and Liam is standing there. He looks amazing in a light blue button-up shirt with a jacket and dark dress slacks. His hair is short but still long enough to be messy although I am sure he took some time to style it that way. His smile brings warm light into the room. My deep breathing routine was pointless because I suddenly feel like I can't catch my breath. My heart is pounding. I can't swallow. *Breathe, damn it.*

"Caroline, you look…" He pauses and takes a breath. "Beautiful."

Liam stands casually with one hand in his pocket and the other hand held out to take mine. *Did he just say beautiful?* I touch my hand gently to his, and immediately, the breath rushes back into my lungs. If his touch has this impact on everyone, he should look into a job at the ER. He could save lives with that kind of superpower.

"Let's go enjoy some charity fun," he says pulling me into the hallway.

We walk to his car, his hand rarely leaving the small of my back. His touch feels strong, and when he moves away, I find my body wavering in its absence. He opens my car door, and I sit, impatiently waiting for him to get to the driver's side door. I don't want to waste a moment of time with him tonight. I watch in the mirror as he walks to the other side of the car. *Damn, his butt looks good in those pants.*

The drive feels relaxed and easy. We talk about our work week and listen to music filtering through the car speakers. As we get closer to the event, my heart starts to race. I feel nervous, hoping everything has turned out well.

We arrive right on time. The warm night air is perfect as we walk through the doors. Tables with bright yellow tablecloths are scattered throughout the room. Each one features a different item up for auction. Surrounding each item is a masterpiece of colorful tulips entwined with greenery and woven into curly willow branches. The centerpieces, designed by Audrey and me, will be sold tonight as spring wreaths. I take a few seconds to marvel at the beauty that Audrey and I have created. *The charity is sure to benefit from our efforts.*

"Everything looks wonderful," Liam whispers into my ear.

"You think so?"

He nods once as he smiles down at me. We mingle and take a look at the silent auction items. For the rest of the evening, we have little alone time. He leads me to the bar several times to ensure our drinks are full. Each time, he orders water for himself and whatever drink I prefer. I watch him as he talks with others. Although he engages them in meaningful conversations, he never leaves my side. Throughout the night, I can feel his touch. Sometimes, his hand rests across my back or on my upper arm. Other times, he lightly touches my shoulder or grips my waist. I find myself longing for his touch to linger, but he never keeps his hand steady in one place.

Audrey, my boss, catches a glimpse of me from across the room, and she heads over with her husband to say hello. Her eyebrows rise in approval as she sees Liam with his hand placed at my waist. I introduce them to one another, and Liam says hello as he shakes her husband's hand.

"Caroline, do you think we could talk in private for a moment?"

I look to Liam who is already sharing stories about fishing with Audrey's husband. He gives me a quick glance, and he nods.

"Sure, Audrey."

As we walk away, I begin to worry that something has gone wrong. *Did I remember to mark each auction item? What if someone thinks the colors are too bright?* We walk into a nearby hallway, and Audrey turns to me, grabbing me by my arms.

"He is so good-looking. Are you two dating?" She smiles.

"Oh, Liam?" I ask, confused.

"Yes, Liam. Oh my gosh, if I wasn't a married woman, you would have to fight me off. You better get your claws in that one!"

I begin laughing. "You scared the crap out of me, Audrey. I thought something was wrong."

"No, everything is perfect. No one has said anything

negative about the event. They love it all. What I really want to know is if you are dating that little bit of hotness out there."

"No, but maybe," I answer, laughing again.

"Well, turn that maybe into a yes soon. Wow!" She swipes her hand across her forehead, wiping away the fake sweat apparently caused by Liam's hotness.

"Okay, okay. Sheesh. Settle down, girl."

"Let's get you back over there before some piranha snatches him up."

When we walk back into the room, Liam and Audrey's husband are still talking. I am in awe of Liam's ability to converse about nearly any subject as he presents himself with such charm.

Audrey slips her arm around her husband's waist and gives him a small hug. "Honey, don't you think Caroline did a wonderful job?"

"It's better than wonderful. I know the charity is appreciative of all your work," he says.

"I think we should head over and buy a wreath for my mom. She'll love what you've designed," Liam comments.

I feel my face begin to blush as Liam takes my hand in his and leads us away. This is the point in the evening when I should remind myself to be careful. Unfortunately, my mind seems to be on the losing end of this tug of war as my heart leaps from my chest when he whispers into my ear.

"Caroline."

I look up at him with my mouth slightly agape.

"They said they'll deliver it to the house. Are you ready to head home?"

What? It's time to go already? "Whenever you are," I answer.

"I'm really more curious about what would make you happy," he says, his hand lingering on my waist. His eyes are fixed on mine, and we stand silent, staring at each other.

Eventually, he turns and leads me to the car. We drive to my apartment without a word to one another as music plays softly. I can't help but wonder what he's thinking. *Did he have a good time? Did he wish we could have talked more? Did he think I talked too much?* By the time we pull into the parking spot, my mind is going nonstop.

We walk together to my apartment door.

"Thanks for tonight," I say as I turn the key to unlock my front door.

Leaning back against the door frame, I look up and meet his gaze. His deep brown eyes are trained on me, and my glance does little to deter him. As if in slow motion, his hand reaches up to my chin, and his lips touch my cheekbone. I have never felt a kiss so soft. It's as if he uses only the weight of feathers to touch my tender skin. His lips linger on my cheek as his hand squeezes my arm lightly. When he pulls away, I realize I've been holding my breath. When he lightly brushes his thumb across my cheek, the air rushes back into my lungs. *There is that lifesaving power again.*

"Are you busy tomorrow?" Liam asks, leaning in closer with his hand now at my waist.

"Work project...I mean, no, um...no. I have a few finishing touches to put on a work project, but it won't take long," I say.

"I have an extra ticket to the baseball game tomorrow afternoon. A buddy and I are going. You could come along if you want."

I see what looks like a little glint of hope in his eyes. *How am I supposed to say no to that?*

"Sure. What time should I be ready?"

"Noon. We can grab some food at the ballpark if you're okay with a late lunch."

"Okay."

Liam gives me a sweet smile. "See you tomorrow. Tonight was fun." He slowly turns and walks toward the stairs.

I watch him as he walks away until his figure disappears behind the glass door leading to the stairwell.

I dance straight to my room. I kick my legs and thrash my arms in an uncontrolled fashion, squealing, before I throw myself onto the bed with a ridiculous grin on my face. *I can't believe this is really happening. Am I falling for June's brother?*

I need to find a way to tell her before this gets out of hand.

9
Liam

FRIDAY

Caroline's sweet blue eyes had mesmerized me all night long. If we hadn't been in a crowded room full of other professionals, I would have given her a real kiss hours ago. But standing at her front door, I froze. I couldn't decide what I should do. I knew my sister would be pissed if she knew we were spending time together.

In the end, I kissed her. I kissed my sister's best friend. Granted, it was only a kiss on the cheek—not that I didn't want to do more, believe me. That kiss, although brief, was one of the sexiest experiences of my life. She just stood there in that beautiful dress, looking up into my eyes when my lips left her skin. I have no idea if she was waiting for me to kiss her on the lips or just waiting for a good-bye, but next time, I don't think I'll be able to hold back.

What's even more unbelievable is that I invited her to a baseball game, and I don't really have an extra ticket. I'll have to ditch one of my friends to take her along. Eli wouldn't be a good choice. He would never let me live down the fact that I shoved him off for a girl. James would be the more logical choice since he has a wife and kids. Maybe he won't harp on me too much.

I pull out my phone and lean against my car. I call James, dreading the conversation.

"Hey, Liam. You already ducked out of your charity event?"

"Yeah. You know those rich people. They don't stay out too late."

"Well, why don't you meet us over at Eli's? We're going to play some pool and have a few drinks."

"Pool sounds good. See you in a bit."

Crap! Now, I'll have to bring up Caroline in front of all the guys. I make the quick drive home, change into something more appropriate for a game of pool, and head to Eli's house.

Walking through the side gate and to the back door, I can hear the music blaring and the guys laughing. At least I'll have a good time before I get reamed for liking a girl. I swear that sometimes I feel like I'm back in high school with these guys.

"Dude, Liam! What's up, man?" Oliver slaps me a quick high five.

From the look in his eyes, I can already tell that he's drunk. *Guess he'll be staying here tonight.*

"You guys ready to get your asses beat?" I pull a cue stick

from the wall and rub chalk against the end.

"Oh, sure. The expert has arrived. Please show us all how it's done," Eli jokes.

We play a few games, and I school them for a while. Then, I sit back and let them berate each other. The more they drink, the more they bicker back and forth about the rules. It's actually quite humorous. After a couple of hours, I'm debating on whether I should head home when James speaks up.

"Alright, Eli. You win, but I've always been a loser at pool, so I'm not sure how good it should make you feel that you can beat me." He places his cue stick in the holder on the wall. "Listen, guys, I gotta head out. Lindsey is expecting me to be home soon."

"Lindsey makes my lunch. Lindsey wants me to take over the kids' car pool for a day. Lindsey—" Eli starts harassing James.

I tune him out. *This is exactly what I'm trying to avoid.* "I'll walk out with you. I'm beat from this week."

"You guys are such losers," Oliver says, sitting on the couch.

He's so drunk by this point that I'm not sure he'll be awake in two minutes. I bet he won't even remember this conversation.

James and I walk across the paved stones, retracing our steps to the driveway.

"Guess I'll see you tomorrow then," James says, walking toward his gray van.

"Actually, I need to ask you for a favor."

"Sure, what do you need? Is everything okay?"

Man, he is such a good guy. He's always worried about everyone else, and he would do anything for anybody. I'm grateful for friends like him. *This really sucks.*

"Oh, yeah, everything is fine. It's just…well, I met this girl, and I sort of gave away your ticket to the baseball game tomorrow."

"You did what?"

"Listen, if you still want to go, I can just buy us tickets and sit with her somewhere else."

"You're serious! Who is this girl? Do I know her?"

"Just a girl I met last weekend."

"You must think a little bit of her to start ditching your friends."

"I know, it's a dick move. I took her to the charity event tonight, and when we were saying good night, it just came out. I didn't mean to invite her."

"Let me guess. You were just trying to figure out another time you could hang out with her, and the baseball game was the first thing that came to mind."

I look up at him sheepishly.

"Hey, I understand. When Lindsey and I met, you guys wouldn't lay off, but I didn't care. I knew she was it for me, so it was all worth it. I hope she's it for you, man." He gives me a pat on the back and begins walking away toward his van. "I do expect some payback though. Tomorrow's game is supposed to be good."

"The tickets for the next game are all yours!" I shout after him.

Although it'll be rough not having James around to corral Eli at the game, I definitely made the right choice. Sliding into the driver's seat, I lean my head back against the headrest and think about having another few hours with Caroline. I didn't even ask her if she likes sports. With her beautiful body and bright eyes distracting me, I know I won't be paying much attention to the game. The big question is, *How will Eli react when I show up with Caroline instead of James?*

10
June

FRIDAY

Standing in the driveway of my parents' house, I wonder how to get these flowers to my bedroom without being noticed. It reminds me of playing Mario Brothers with my brother when I was little. He always knew all the tricks, and I was stuck running right through the middle of every trap and disaster. Now, the only difference is that instead of losing fake lives, I'll lose my sanity if my mother finds out a guy sent me flowers.

I should have left them at the apartment since we'll be at the lake until Sunday, but I wanted a chance to enjoy these beautiful peonies even if it is just during the brief ride between here and my place. And, okay, I'll admit that a little reminder of the hot guy who sent them isn't such a bad thing either.

Grabbing my weekend bag in one hand and the vase of flowers in the other, I head for the side door. I somehow avoid interactions with human beings, but when I reach the stairs, I have to concentrate as our pet horse tries to plow me over. *Okay, so he's not a horse, but geez, could my parents have chosen a bigger dog?*

I climb the stairs to my childhood room and struggle to turn the doorknob. While trying to open my bedroom door, I realize that I probably should have left my weekend bag at the foot of the stairs. Using my hip along with the heel of my hand, it finally pops open.

This room has changed many times over the years while I was growing up, but since I left, it's become my mom's personal shrine. Pillows are propped up against the headboard, framed pictures from high school are scattered on every available surface, and my desk chair is set askew as if I'm about to sit down and begin my homework.

I set the flowers down on my nightstand and step back to admire them for a moment. As I let a smile spread across my face, I hear the front door open followed by the sound of Addison's heels. *Why can't she wear sensible shoes?* I close the door to my room before I head back downstairs, lugging my bag out to Addison's car.

Soon after, we're on the road, driving through the winding curves that lead to the cabin near the lake. As we pull in, I catch a glimpse of my favorite spot—a blue-and-white hammock in the shade. I brought my e-reader full of new books, so I can relax and enjoy my time. Funny enough, these weekends typically consist of the three of us doing completely different things, and we usually come together only for meals. The quiet time between us is something I treasure.

When we arrive, everyone seems tired, so we eat a quick sandwich and head off to bed.

SATURDAY

Early in the morning, I hear my mom outside. Slipping on some comfortable jean shorts, worn flip-flops, and a graphic tee that says something about being a Texan, I head straight to the hammock. Mom pulls out several pallets of flowers from the back of Addison's car, and then she begins planting them in the gardens around the cabin. A few minutes later, Addison heads down to the lake with a towel, wearing a bright pink designer cover-up over her swimsuit and some flip-flops.

This moment is perfection.

I get situated in the hammock, starting where I left off on my most recent read. About a chapter in, I'm caught in the middle of a really steamy scene. Feeling a little awkward, I look over to make sure my mom is still tending to her flowers, and then I keep reading. These two random strangers have never met before, and over the span of two days, they can see into each other's souls, feeling what the other feels. He can completely destroy her resolve with one touch of his fingertips to her cheek. *Do scenes like this actually play out in real life?* It sounds insane, but it also sounds beautiful. I want a beginning like that. I want powerful emotion and genuine desire. Just as the scene is starting to reach its climax, my phone begins to ring.

"Thanks for ruining my reading moment, Caroline," I say, faking disdain.

"Oh, shut up. You know talking to me is more exciting than reading one of your love stories."

"Alright, are you trying to piss me off or what?"

"He asked me out again."

"What are you talking about? Oh, the guy from work who took you to the charity event? He must really be into you. So, are you going out with him next weekend?"

"No, he wants to take me to a baseball game today."

I laugh so hard that I almost fall out of the hammock. "You're going to a baseball game? That'll be a riot. Wait, what about your brother?"

"I already called my brother to tell him that I'll have to see him tomorrow. This guy is seriously hot, June. I can't turn him down. I know I have hated sports in the past, but surely, I can get through one baseball game. And, you never know, maybe I just haven't given sports a fair try before. Maybe I'll have fun."

"You crack me up, Caroline. Just go and have a good time. Be ready to spill it when I see you at my parents' on Sunday night. I want serious details."

"Alright. Think peaceful thoughts about me today."

"Okay, weirdo. See you tomorrow."

I hang up the phone, laughing to myself. My best friend is nuts, but it's kind of nice to see her nervous about a guy. *Maybe she's finally found someone who can settle her wild side. Maybe we'll both find love.* I finish reading my steamy love scene, and eventually, I fall asleep in the shade of the trees.

11
Caroline

SATURDAY

There's no way I'm getting any work done before the game. I resort to working out because I need something to do while I wait for noon to roll around. I'm hoping exercise will relax my nerves. I spend an hour and a half swimming in the pool. Then, after changing my clothes in the locker room, I head home.

My legs feel like Jell-O as I walk up the stairs to the apartment. I wonder how much walking I will have to do this afternoon. I have never been to a baseball game, so I don't have a clue what the ballpark is like. I didn't mention to Liam that I'm not into sports at all. Hopefully, he won't pick up on the fact that I know nothing about baseball.

Just like yesterday, Liam is punctual to the nanosecond. His friend is going to meet us at the ballpark, so we head out, just the two of us. We arrive at Minute Maid Park, and I'm not sure what I was expecting, but it is freaking huge. I don't know if my poor legs will even make it to the gates.

When he takes out our tickets from his back pocket, I have to remind myself not to stare at his butt. As we begin to walk, Liam grasps my hand in his, locking our fingers together. He smiles down at me, and we walk hand in hand to our seats. When his friend appears, Liam drops his hand away from mine.

"Hey, Eli."

"What's up, Liam?" his friend says, giving me a questioning glance.

"James told me last night that he couldn't make it to the game. This is Caroline. She decided to spend a little time with us today while we enjoy some good ol' American pastime."

"Well, nice to meet you, Caroline. I'm not really sure how he convinced you to hang out with us two losers." Laughing, he slaps Liam on the back before he takes his seat.

"Me neither. I've never been to a game before, but I think it'll be interesting." I smile broadly.

They both look at me as if I told them aliens just landed on the field. As they're staring at me, I take in a little more of Liam's good looks—tall, tan, and a smile worth keeping in my memory just to have around for a bad day. I can't believe it's possible, but he looks just as good in a casual shirt, jeans, and a ball cap as he does in business clothes. The casual look might even suit him better.

"Never been to a game? What a shame that you've missed out on this until now," Eli says, shaking his head. "We'll be sure to give you the entire baseball experience."

Liam chuckles under his breath. From that point forward, every time a vendor came by, offering peanuts, beer, popcorn or anything else, Eli and Liam would tell me I had to have one to complete my experience. By the fourth inning, I was wondering how I could fit any more into my stomach. Although I think the guys realized my fullness, Eli continued to buy beer after beer after beer for me. During the seventh inning stretch, I think I just needed a stretcher.

"Are you doing okay?" Liam asks, leaning in closely.

I can feel his breath on my neck. With alcohol coursing through my system, I feel the urge to wrap my arms around his neck and pull him closer to me. Somehow, I fight off the request of my body and answer with words instead. "Sure, I'm just a little tired." Although my words sound fine to me, I'm quite sure that I'm slurring.

In the middle of the ninth inning, Liam whispers something to Eli. He simply nods and pats Liam on the back.

"Let's get you home, okay?" Liam says softly as he takes my hand to help me stand.

He lets me walk up the stairs, but when we're about halfway to the car, he lifts me into his arms, carrying me the rest of the way. Thankfully, we're not parked too far. Resting my head against his chest, I want to take in his scent, but even the act of breathing deeply is too difficult right now. After Liam gently places me in the passenger seat, he reaches across my lap to buckle my seatbelt, and then he slightly reclines the seat.

# # #

When we get to the apartment, I'm able to walk although not very well. Liam unlocks the door and leads me to my room.

"Are you going to be okay?" he asks with concern in his eyes.

"Yeah, I'll sleep it off. Do you want to sleep with me?" *Ugh.* I close my eyes for a moment, cursing beer and baseball for turning me into a blubbering lunatic.

Liam grins, turning his head away from me. I think I hear him laugh.

He looks back toward me. "You should get some sleep. I'll see you at dinner tomorrow. Mom, June, and Addison will be back from their trip." He brushes a stray hair away from my face and kisses my forehead. Then, he's gone.

I am definitely an idiot. My second date with the guy and I get drunk to the point of not being able to walk on my own. He didn't even kiss my cheek before he left. He obviously didn't want his friend to know we were together since he barely touched me during the game. *Maybe he's realizing that I'm not quite his type. Maybe he sees me more as a friend. Or maybe he thinks I'm not even worth that.*

12
Liam

SATURDAY

Thinking about the last twenty-four hours, I walk through the glass door of the apartment building. As I rest my body against the brick wall, I lean my head back, look up into the darkening sky, and smile. The Caroline I saw last night was amazing. She was smart, funny, beautiful, and sweet. She interacted with people from all different professions, and she held her own in every conversation. When my kiss landed on her cheek at the end of the night, it was like fire melting my resolve. I was lucky to have made it back to my car without turning around to knock down her door.

Today, she showed all those traits again but with a carefree demeanor. She got along with Eli like they had been friends for years. Throughout the game, she cheered for both teams even though people around us were giving her funny looks. I knew she was starting to get a little tipsy, but I had no idea she wouldn't be able to walk when we left. As I carried her to the car, I could feel her warm breath on my neck. Again, I don't know how I put her in my car without taking her lips in mine. I know it was the alcohol talking, but when she asked if I wanted to sleep with her, it took all my strength just to walk away.

Tomorrow, we'll all be having dinner at my parents' house again. I was hoping to talk with Caroline tonight about telling June that we had been on a couple of dates. I don't want things to get weird when we're around my family. *Maybe we'll get the chance to talk before June gets back from the lake.*

13
June

SUNDAY

In general, our trip to the lake is uneventful and wonderful—minus my constant thoughts of Cohen and my dread for what might happen on Monday.

Sunday morning, we pack up and head back home. Mom has been fawning over me a little too much this weekend, and I know she and Addison are ready to pounce.

Mom glances back at me over the passenger seat. "June, are you sure you're okay? You were in the sun all weekend, and you still look a little pale."

"Mom, I'm fine. I'm tired, but it's nothing to worry about."

"How is Caroline? Are you two still getting along? What did she do this weekend? Any dates lined up this week?"

"Geez, Mom. Could you ask any more questions without taking a breath? As a matter of fact, Caroline went on two dates with the same guy this weekend."

"Well, I wasn't really asking about Caroline's dating lineup, but good for her."

I just need to make something up, so she will lay off. "If you absolutely must know, I met a guy at work, and we might be going out on a date soon. We just haven't picked a day yet." *Who knows? It could end up being true.*

"Oh well, that sounds promising." She grins from ear to ear.

Addison chimes in. "You know, if you want him to really notice you, you should wear more of those short skirts you have. I could let you borrow some of my expensive jewelry, too."

"No, Addison, I think what I normally wear along with my own jewelry is just fine."

"I think I'll set you up to see George when we get home today. He'll do wonders for all that built-up tension you have," Mom adds.

George is my mom's masseuse, and he's also her answer to the world's problems. According to my mom, if someone can't figure out how to alleviate the stress from life with an herbal remedy or a long walk, then George is the guy to see. Whether I was experiencing heartache from a major breakup, stress from preparing for a big test, or nerves while waiting for college acceptance letters, Mom would make an appointment for me with George. No offense to George, but sometimes, I'm more stressed after I leave his office than when I walked in. Having a random hot guy rub all over my naked body doesn't spell relaxation to me like it does to my mom and sister.

"We have Sunday dinner planned, and Caroline is coming over when we get home. I'm not going to leave to see George while my best friend is sitting alone at our house."

"With four other people at the house, I doubt that she would feel alone." Mom glances over to Addison, giving her a look of frustration.

Suffocating, she is absolutely suffocating. I have never been so glad to see the entrance to my parents' subdivision. It's amazing how all the relaxation of the weekend is washed away by a short drive home. I can't get out of the car fast enough.

"Hey, June Bug," my dad says cheerfully from behind the side fence.

"Hi, Dad! Are you grilling dinner?"

"Just getting started. Steaks and pork chops. I hope you're hungry."

"Actually, I'm starving. Let me take my things in, and then I'll come sit with you."

I walk to my room and immediately collapse onto my bed. Turning to face my nightstand, I gaze at my flowers. *Am I crazy?* This guy sent me flowers, wrote a note that sounds like he's excited to see me tomorrow, and I am terrified. *How could he possibly have any interest in me after my clumsy introduction times two?* It's not that I'm uninterested in getting to know him, but he lives really far away. I just started a new job, a job that happens to kind of make him my boss.

Reaching over to the flowers, I pluck the card off the holder where it sits between a white and pink peony. I run my fingers over the handwritten words. Surely, he couldn't have written these words himself, but the words did come from him. I close my eyes and see his face, his smile, his casual walk, and the way the light glints off his dark hair. *Is it too much to hope that he actually does like me and that things could work out?*

"June? Are you in here?" My mother bursts through my thoughts as she opens my bedroom door. "Are you feeling okay? Why are you lying…" Her voice trails off as she trains her eyes on the flowers in front of her. "Did you get these at the market? They're beautiful."

I slip the card under my pillow, so she doesn't ask to read it. It's funny how her concern for my well-being is eclipsed by her curiosity. She knows good and well that I didn't get these flowers at the market. *When was the last time she saw peonies like these at our local market? And when would I have had time to go to the market?* My mother is the queen of asking illogical questions in an effort to obtain information. I've seen this tactic in action so many times that I don't even take the time to argue with rational thoughts.

"Just a congratulations from work for that new contract I was telling you about."

Only time will tell if this answer will appease her need for juicy details.

"How nice! Well, in that case, I'm glad we bought the good steaks."

I stand and allow my mother to embrace me in a warm hug.

"Thanks, Mom. I think I'm going to run out and sit with Dad while he finishes grilling."

"Alright, dear. Addison and I are going to be sorting through some fall decorations. Come join us if you get bored."

"Sounds good, Mom."

Sorting through decorations sounds like a new form of torture I have no interest in submitting myself to. I step out the back door and pull a chair up close to where my dad is focused on the grill. Bear, the dog-horse, trots over and lies across my feet, his favorite spot. I lean forward, place my head in my hands, and sigh.

"What's wrong, June? You look a little down. You feeling okay?"

"I guess so. Just a stressful week."

I tell my dad about my business trip and the new contract, leaving out any information about Cohen. Leaving his post at the grill, he leans down to grasp both my shoulders. I swear he looks like he's going to cry. He is always so proud of me.

One time, after I came in fifth place in a spelling bee at school, he took me out for dinner at my favorite restaurant, and he even bought me dessert. He didn't care that I didn't get a medal or ribbon, and he breezed right over the fact that I came in fifth out of only six kids.

"June, that is absolutely wonderful. I am so happy for you. I knew you would be great at whatever you chose to do."

I bring my finger up to just below my eye and wipe away a fake tear. "Dad, it's all because of your parenting skills and exceptional encouragement over the years," I joke, trying to break out of this awkward moment.

He laughs and goes back to the grill.

"Dad, did you ever embarrass yourself when you first met Mom?"

"Sure, I did. The first time we ever went out on a date I dropped her ice cream down the front of her dress. Then, I did the classic move, trying to clean it up with a napkin, before I realized I was rubbing my hands all over her chest. It was extremely embarrassing, but it turned out to be a great story to tell at dinner parties." He chuckles to himself as he flips a pork chop.

"Did you worry that she wouldn't like you after that?"

"I guess, but I was too smitten with her to not give it a try. A couple days later, I asked her out on another date. I promised I would keep my hands to myself, and I'd let her get her own ice cream from then on. Why do you ask? Did someone make a fool of himself, trying to impress you?" He winks.

"Not exactly. It's actually the other way around. My first impression wasn't the best. I basically attacked him with a magazine. Then, I literally ran into him when we were walking into a business meeting. Later that day, he asked me to spend time with him. I don't know if you would call it a date, but we ate lunch together, and then he sent me a note at work the other day."

"It sounds to me like he's interested. I wouldn't worry about *attacking* him. I am quite sure he wouldn't mind a sweet girl like you getting his attention in whatever way you choose. If you want to continue getting to know him, just be yourself."

"Thanks, Dad. As always, good advice."

"I do what I can. You know, being a family doctor lends

itself to a lot of counseling," he says, laughing. "Go let your mom and Addison know that dinner is ready."

I go back inside to find them sitting in the middle of the foyer. It looks like a giant pumpkin threw up around them. I don't envy those people who work at Hobby Lobby. *This is ridiculous.* Not wanting to get caught up in all the mess, I don't say anything, and I walk back outside.

"They're ready when you are, Dad." Turning to walk back inside, I hesitate. "You know, you really are the best, Dad."

"Don't make me blush, June Bug," he says, smiling. "Oh, before you go in, could you turn off the sprinkler?"

I walk over to turn off the hose, and then I brush a quick kiss against my dad's cheek.

"Love you," I say as I push against the door to the kitchen. Nothing happens, and I end up banging my shoulder into the door. I try again. Nothing. When I try the doorknob, it turns, so it's not locked. "Dad, have you been having trouble with this door?"

About that time, I give one more big push. The door flies open, and I fall flat on my face. Looking up toward the ceiling, my brother comes into view. He has a huge grin spread across his face. *I should have known.*

14
Caroline

SUNDAY

I get up Sunday morning, go through my usual routines, and then proceed to stress out. This weekend could not have been more embarrassing. I'm trying to think of any excuse to avoid going to June's house today, but nothing is coming to mind. *Did I really let Liam carry me? Was I that pathetic? How could I go from charity event beauty one night to drunken baseball spectator the next?* There is absolutely no recovery from this shame.

To top it all off, I can't even talk to my best friend about the situation. I am now certain a reality show should be made about my life. It could be called *Undercover Idiot!!!* And yes, there should be three exclamation points along with loud horns that blast for emphasis as each one shows up on the screen.

I mope for about twenty more minutes until my phone chimes. Glancing at the screen, I see that I have three new text messages.

> *Save me. We'll be home around 3:30 this afternoon.*
> *Please don't leave me alone. —June*

Ha! It's funny to watch June squirm under the influence of her mom and sister. I don't know how she grew up in the same house but ended up being so different from them. I guess I should support my best friend despite hoping to never enter their beautiful home again. I send her a quick text back.

> *Late lunch with my bro at 1, and then I'll head your way.*
> *You shall be saved. —Caroline*

> *Thanks is not enough. Chocolate of any kind will be rewarded*
> *upon your arrival. —June*

I scroll to the text below.

> *Caroline, this is your mom. Call me when you can. —Mom*

She always sends text messages like she is leaving a phone message. Scrolling to the last message, I hesitate to open it. Of course, it's from Liam.

> *Hope you are feeling okay today.*
> *See you for dinner at the fam's house. —Liam*

It would be more gentleman-like of him if he would stop contacting me. There's no way he could be interested in a train wreck like me.

I dial my mom's number and wait for her to answer.

"Hello?" Her voice sounds hoarse, and her normal cheery tone is gone.

She doesn't sound good. "Hey, Mom. I got your text. What's up?"

"Just wanted to say hello to my sweetest baby girl, and I wasn't sure if you had to work on the weekends."

"Mom, you know you can call me anytime. I always have time for you. How are you doing? You sound down."

"I'm okay, just feeling tired. I think I might have caught some kind of bug that's going around."

"Well, take care of yourself, Mom. I don't want to have to call John, or better yet, fly up there and put you in line."

"I doubt you or anyone else could put this woman in line."

When she laughs lightly, it makes me smile.

"You're probably right."

"Will you be seeing your brother while he's in town?"

"I'm actually headed out the door soon to meet him for lunch. It sounds like he has a pretty busy schedule while he's here though."

"He really needs to slow down."

"I'll tell him you said so, Mom, but he'll probably want me to call you back and tell you the same thing."

"Alright then. Well, you two enjoy your lunch. You should really think about coming home to visit soon. We would all love to see you."

"I'll try, but I'm not sure when I'll get time off work."

"I love you, Caroline."

"Love you, too. Are you sure everything is okay?"

"Yes. It's fine. Just enjoy yourself."

"Okay. I'll call you soon. Bye."

"Bye."

After we hang up, I still feel like something is off with her. Maybe my brother will have some insight. If he doesn't, I'll have to make sure and call John tonight.

Growing up, my brother and I were always really close. Much like Liam was for June, my brother was protective to the extreme, but he was also my biggest cheerleader. I'll never forget the time I decided to run for student council in elementary school. He had to have known that my opponent was the most popular girl in school, so I had no chance of winning, but he still stayed up all night with me, making posters for my campaign. We agreed to hang them in the hallways at school. When he realized just how dismal my chances at winning were, he cut holes in the tops of two signs, attached them with rope, and wore them on the front and back of his body all day. I still lost the election, but it felt good to know I had his support.

After my downer of a weekend, it will be nice to see him.

We decided to meet at a diner near his hotel, and when I walk in the door, his huge grin greets me instantly. Taking quick steps toward his open arms, I accept his embrace like it's the air I need to breathe. There's no one in the world that can infuse joy in my heart like him.

We laugh through the entire meal. I take time to ask him about Mom, but he says he hasn't noticed anything different when he talks with her. I should have known that a man probably wouldn't have picked up on the subtle attitude changes of his mother. Plus, he has his own issues to deal with back home.

We talk about nothing of importance, and it feels nice to let go of all the stress I've been feeling over the past few days.

Before I'm ready, it's time for me to leave and head to June's house. My brother and I agree to try and catch up later this week before he heads back home. He gives me one more solid embrace before we both get into our respective cars.

Flipping on the radio, I begin my drive across town to meet June at her parents' house. As I pull into the neighborhood, I slow down when I'm just a few houses away. I park against the curb, and lower my head down to the steering wheel.

I begin to talk out loud, going through the situations that might occur once I walk up the steps into their home.

"What if he ignores me? Should I say hi to him first or let him approach me? If he says something about us in front of his whole family, I might die. Then again, at least it would be out there, and we could move on, right? June would totally freak out. I'll have to come up with a way to explain—"

A loud knock startles me.

I jerk my head toward the window and see Liam. He's on the other side of the glass, grinning down at me. His muscular arms are crossed above his head, shadowing his face from the sun, as he leans on my car. I can see that his gray T-shirt is half-soaked in sweat, and his hair is glistening in the sunlight. I remind myself to close my mouth, so it doesn't appear as if I have lost complete control just from the sight of him.

"You doing okay in there?" he asks with a slight laugh through the glass.

I lower my window. "Uh, yeah. Listen, I need to apologize about yesterday."

"No need. I had a good time. See you at the house. You do remember which one is ours, right?" He's still smiling as he leans further into my window.

"Yes, I remember."

"Okay then, I'll see you in a few." He jogs away into the sun.

I watch him jog down the sidewalk, up the walkway, and into the front door. I replay our short conversation as I slowly drive up to their house. He basically dismissed my apology, but he wasn't very specific about why he had a good time. *Did it have anything to do with me? Maybe he just enjoyed the game.*

I walk up to the front door and knock as softly as possible. I'm hoping no one will hear it, and then I can pretend I thought no one was home, so I can leave. I hear a faint, "Come in," and I open the door into an explosion of fall holiday decor strewn across the foyer floor.

June's mother smiles. "Hi, Caroline! June is out back, supervising her father's grill work. Get yourself something to drink in the kitchen on your way out."

"Alright, thanks," I say, trying to fake a smile. I glance up the stairway and around the corner as I head to the kitchen. *No sign of Liam.*

As I push open the door, he is leaning against the counter, just finishing off a glass of water. His head is tilted back slightly, getting the last drop, before he swallows. I never knew drinking water while covered in sweat could look sexy. I close my eyes to limit the visual stimulation as I try to ward off the blush I feel creeping into my cheeks.

"You took your sweet time getting in here," he states.

When I open my eyes, he is standing closer to me with his hip resting against the kitchen island.

I walk toward the door that leads to the backyard and pause briefly to face him. "Um, well, I had to traverse the mountain of holiday decorations in the entryway."

Laughing, he steps toward me and places one of his hands against the door just above my shoulder as his opposite hand takes hold of my hip. Before I know what's happening, my back is pressed tightly against the door.

"I was hoping we could talk tonight," he says softly.

My heart begins beating quickly, and it feels like it's in my throat. "Really?"

He nods and leans in closer to me, his nose brushing against the skin just below my ear. "Have you told June?" he whispers, touching his lips to my neckline.

Goose bumps rise all over my body, and I feel certain that I might faint at any moment. "No," I respond in a voice so hushed that even I have trouble hearing it.

His lips trace the line of my jaw. Each time he moves to another place on my skin, the prior space feels numb and neglected. When I feel his hand tighten on my hip, my body tenses in response. Just as he is about to reach the corner of my lips, the doorknob turns, and the door jolts against my back. My eyes widen in concern, and Liam hangs his head, sighing in what seems like frustration.

He looks into my eyes as the door continues to shake, and then he nods his head toward the other door. Continuing to hold his weight against the door, he releases his body's pressure from mine, and I walk slowly backward through the opposite doorway.

I hear a loud thud as the door closes behind me. As June begins yelling something unintelligible, I hold my hands over my mouth, attempting to stifle a laugh. Liam runs through the door at lightning speed, closely followed by June.

Although she stops when she sees me, she's still yelling loudly. "One day you're going to regret playing all these nasty jokes on me. I could have gotten a concussion! You are such a buffoon!" She clenches her teeth and stomps her foot like a small child. "Hey, Caroline. I didn't know you were here."

"Just got here a few minutes ago," I say, trying to act nonchalant. Glancing up the stairway to the wooden railing across the upstairs loft, I catch a glimpse of Liam smiling.

"I'm thirsty. Let's get a drink," I say, giving Liam a small smile in return before I walk out of sight.

# # #

About twenty minutes later, we are all gathered around the table.

The only difference from last week is that Liam is sitting opposite his father at the end of the table. This places him catty-corner to me, and it makes me nervous. I assumed by his actions at the baseball game that he wasn't interested in more than a friendship with me, but based on what happened in the kitchen, I'm now feeling confused.

One thing is for sure—I'm going to have a tough time keeping my eyes off him with his just showered look complete with wet hair. When he walked into the dining room, I caught a glimpse of his crisp blue T-shirt and his gray sweatpants hanging low on his waist, and I came to the quick conclusion that this guy would look sexy in just about anything.

"Liam, are you trying to avoid my wrath by placing Caroline between us?" June asks, pointing at him with her fork.

"No, sis, and there's no need for violence. I'm just practicing for adulthood, trying out the head-of-the-table business."

"Well, it looks good on you, son," Mr. D., responds, effectively ending the discussion.

Liam rests his foot against mine. His constant touch keeps me distracted throughout dinner, earning questioning glances from Addison. June eventually clues in to my unusually reserved nature.

"Are you feeling okay, Caroline?"

"Yeah, I'm fine," I state simply.

"Are you sure? You're really quiet tonight."

"I'm okay. Just a little worried about my mom. I talked to her earlier, and I could have sworn she sounded like she had been crying. She said it was just a cold, but she was acting weird. I asked my brother about it, and he said he hasn't noticed anything different about her."

"Oh, it's probably nothing to be too concerned about. Maybe she just misses you and didn't want to tell you," June's mom suggests.

"Maybe," I say before taking a drink of my water.

Liam sneaks in a quick squeeze of my knee as we are getting up from the table. I trip over the leg of my chair, barely keeping the contents of my plate in place. I swear that I have never acted like this before, and it has me out of sorts. As much as I want to spend time around Liam, I'm glad to join June upstairs as she gets her things.

"Hey, can you grab my flowers?" she asks, pointing toward the nightstand.

"Sure." As I pick up the vase, I notice the card is missing from the plastic holder. "Did you throw away the card?"

"No," she says, pulling it out from under her pillow.

"Even if you slept here last night, it would be strange to sleep with that under your pillow." I smirk.

"Oh, shut it. I had to hide it when my mom walked in. I didn't want to explain who they were from."

She hands over the card, and I read it again as I slip it into the holder. "Who signs their name with an initial? Even rappers put forth more effort than that."

"First of all, I wouldn't have much insight into the way rappers sign their names. Second, the card is sweet, so I don't care how he signed it." June sticks out her tongue.

I laugh, and then we head downstairs to say a quick good-bye. Liam and Addison are nowhere in sight, but June's parents are waiting at the bottom of the stairs. Her mom gives us each a hug and steps out onto the front doorstep as we walk to our cars.

"See you girls for dinner next week."

"Alright, Mom. See you then," June says loudly as she gets things settled into her car. I walk toward the street, and my phone chimes in my purse. Digging it out, I see Liam's name, and I can't help but smile.

"Is that a message from your boy toy at work? I expect full details when we get home!" June shouts from her driver's side window.

"Yeah, yeah. Whatever," I reply.

I tap on the message.

I don't think I'll be able to keep my hands off of you at the table next weekend. Are you going to tell June we've been seeing each other? —Liam

Not sure. It didn't seem like you were too keen on informing Eli at the baseball game. —Caroline

We should talk. Let me know when you're available. I'll make time. —Liam

As I drive home, I think about the implications of telling my best friend that I am kind of, sort of dating her brother. I am beyond "Hey, do you think this would be okay?", and I'm pretty sure I'm not to "It doesn't matter what you say because I'm in love with him." This is going to be tough, and I will have to tread lightly. Maybe I can test the waters tonight when we get home.

15
June

MONDAY

I'm beginning to worry about Caroline. Last night, she mentioned something at dinner about her mom, and I'm hoping everything is okay.

A few years ago, we had a scare with my mom when she had some weird pains in her stomach. When the doctor ordered scans, there were spots they weren't sure about, so they ordered a few more tests. The process took several weeks, and of course, the entire family was throwing around the word *cancer* in hushed voices. That made the situation much more stressful. We were relieved when everything turned out normal.

I think Caroline is doing the right thing by trying not to worry too much—at least until she knows more. Although, I'm sure it's weighing on her more than she wants to admit.

Last night, I tried to brighten her mood and get details

about this new boy she's went out with a couple of times. She all but blew him off as nothing, but I can tell it's more than nothing. When she gets messages from him, she smiles and laughs like a giddy schoolgirl, making me think she might actually be into this guy. The only weird thing was that in the middle of talking about him, she asked me if we could meet Liam for lunch one day this week. I know how commitment-phobic she can get, so she better not try to avoid this new guy by making plans with me. I'm going to encourage this relationship even if it only lasts a few weeks. Considering the longest she spent with the same guy in college was a weekend, anything would be an improvement.

Alright, back to the task at hand. I shouldn't be thinking about Caroline this morning. I'm sitting in my office, typing and retyping a document. Every two seconds, I look out my door toward the entrance, waiting for a glimpse of Cohen. *I know, I know. It's ridiculous.*

This morning, Mr. Hargrove told me the three of us would be having lunch together, and it's almost eleven o'clock already. *Oh crap!* I forgot to text Caroline to let her know that I can't meet her for lunch today. Leaning down under my desk to retrieve my phone from my purse, I notice a slight scuff on my shoe. I rub my finger gently across it, but I'm only making it worse. *That's awesome.* Now, I have officially caused a wardrobe malfunction. *Oh well, at least my hair cooperated this morning.*

"June?" a familiar voice says.

It's a voice I didn't realize I had memorized.

I lift my head too quickly and bang the back of it on the

edge of the desk. "Ow," I whine, closing my eyes.

"Are you okay?"

Before I see him, I feel Cohen's hand on my arm as I open my watering eyes. His hands are gentle and reassuring, but I curse myself for letting this be our reintroduction—and for possibly messing up my hair.

"I know I told you not to attack me, but that didn't mean you should attack yourself," he says while smiling down at me.

"I am so sorry. I should probably go to the restroom and take a look at this."

"Here, let me. You probably won't be able to see that far back on your head."

He laughs, and I roll my eyes at him.

"Is it tender?"

"A little," I say, wincing as his hands work their way through my hair to the spot where I hit my head.

"I think a little knot is coming up. If you start feeling tired or dizzy, you need to let me know. You might need to have it checked out."

"Oh, I'm sure that won't be necessary," I say, trying to dismiss my clumsiness. *Is it ridiculous that I want to throw him onto my desk right now? Maybe I do have a head injury.* "Let me see if Mr. Hargrove is ready for lunch."

I pick up the phone and dial my boss' office number.

He answers after half a ring. "Yes?"

I'm taken aback by his abruptness. "Uh, Mr. Hargrove, Cohen is here. We were thinking about leaving soon for lunch."

"I'm sorry, June. I won't be able to make it. I've got an

overseas conference call that's been rescheduled for twelve thirty. Go on without me."

"Oh, okay. We'll see you this afternoon," I say before hanging up the phone.

"Well, it looks like it's just the two of us," I say, turning to Cohen.

"Great! What'll it be?"

"Hmm…do you like Mexican food? There's this amazing Mexican place just a block or two away."

"Perfect." He smiles.

"I'm just going to step into the ladies' room for a quick second."

I walk into the restroom, pull out my phone, and dial Caroline's number.

She picks up after just one ring. "Hey, are you busy for lunch?" she asks.

"Yeah, sorry, and I'm going to be late for dinner tonight."

"Business crap?"

"Well, remember that guy I got the flowers from?"

"Uh-huh."

"He's here, and he's hot. We have to go to lunch alone because my boss is busy. I'm freaking out."

"No big deal, June. Just be yourself, and try to relax."

"Right…relax. I can do that."

"Sure you can."

I hear her laugh, and I roll my eyes, knowing she probably thinks my high-strung personality will make lunch pretty awkward.

"Try to find something in common with him, and talk about that," she says.

"Okay, I can try that. I need to get going, but I'll try to text you later and let you know how it goes."

"Have fun and do lots of things your mother would disapprove of."

"You are almost as bad as my mother."

"I know. Bye."

"See you later."

# # #

The restaurant is within walking distance from the office, so we make our way while we briefly talk about his company's contract and the new media campaign taking off this year. Even though our discussion is short, I can hear the passion he has for his company's products and services. His enthusiasm excites me for the ongoing project we'll be working on together.

We enter the restaurant, and the hostess seats us at a booth by the window. Sitting across from one another, we scan the menu in silence for a minute or two. I've been trying to think of a way I can bring up the flowers without making a big deal about them. I don't want him to think that I thought more of them than he had intended. Since he hasn't mentioned anything and the text message reply wasn't quite the response I was looking for, I'm sure they were purely congratulatory in nature. As much as that disappoints me, I still feel that I should express some sort of gratitude for the gesture.

"Thank you for the flowers," I blurt out, peering at him over the top of my menu.

He doesn't move his menu, but I swear he begins to smile as I see wrinkles forming at the corners of his eyes.

"You're welcome," he states simply. After a short pause, he lowers his menu to the table and makes eye contact with me, holding my stare. "Listen, June, I need to tell you—"

The waiter chooses this moment to stop by the table and collect our drink orders.

"Can I get you something to drink?" the waiter asks.

Cohen looks to me, offering me the chance to talk first.

"I'll take a sweet tea," I say.

"And I'll have a water," Cohen adds.

When the waiter walks away, I continue our conversation.

"You don't need to say anything. I feel like I should apologize for being so unprofessional in New York," I say.

About that time, another waiter arrives at the table to take our food order, and we give him our entrée choices in quick succession.

"Unprofessional? Don't be crazy. I just wanted to say that your suggestions at the meeting in New York were refreshing, and your input on this project so far has been outstanding. Your company is lucky to have you."

"Oh." I push a smile through the disappointment I'm feeling. *I knew I was reading too much into our shared meal in New York and the flowers last week. Things like that must be typical in the business world.* "Thank you." It's all I can say without allowing my voice to falter.

From my point of view, the remainder of our meal is a little awkward, but I go ahead and try to make small talk about work and family. Cohen is kind, but he doesn't seem overly engaged. I guess I can move on—to what, I'm not sure. *Past the hope that Cohen had any level of interest beyond business, I guess.*

# # #

On our way back to the office, our conversation becomes more casual.

"Have you ever been to the Museum of Fine Arts?" he asks, his eyes focused on the sidewalk. "I was thinking of going to view one of their exhibits while I'm in town."

"Sure, I've been a few times. I don't think it's too hard to find. It's over on Bissonnet. I can show you a map when we get back to the office."

"Actually, I am pretty directionally challenged. Do you think you could come with me? I mean, if you're interested in seeing the exhibit."

"That is a strange thing for a man to admit." I laugh. "Sure. I don't mind. It sounds like something I would like to see."

We part ways at the office as he goes into a meeting with Mr. Hargrove for the afternoon. I head back to my office and begin working on another project. Within a few minutes, my computer trills softly. Seeing Cohen's name come across my email excites me in ways that it shouldn't. *I'm going to have a nervous breakdown if I don't get these stupid emotions in check.*

June,

*I'm staying at the Omni Hotel at Four Riverway.
Why don't you pick me up at 6:30? See you tonight.*

—Cohen

I'm certain he has no romantic interest in me at this point. Asking the girl to pick up the guy is business-friend territory for sure.

# # #

That evening, I pick him up, and we enjoy the museum together. Cohen's laughter and smile are a common occurrence throughout the night. I laugh until my stomach hurts and my cheeks burn. In fact, the museum staff asks us to keep it down at least three times.

I know I shouldn't torture myself, but I keep thinking about what it would be like to spend more nights with him. Instead of being holed up in the apartment, watching television shows or eating take-out from the same tired restaurants, I could be with Cohen, enjoying culture and art.

I feel a connection with him, but it's obvious he doesn't feel the same way. At different times during the night, I purposely stand close to him, but he never once reaches for my hand or touches me in any way. He's a perfect gentleman. He opens doors for me, and as we walk through the museum, he even offers time for me to sit and admire the exhibits.

Instead of being bummed that I won't get a shot with this funny, gorgeous guy, maybe I should be positive. *At least guys like this are out there, right?*

I get the feeling his charm and wit have been in place since birth. I catch myself wondering about what his father and mother might be like. *His role models must be kind and gentle people.* I toss these thoughts aside like the lunacy they are, and I remind myself that I will never know the influences that have made him so desirable.

# # #

I feel a tug of sadness as I pull up to his hotel. "Thanks for inviting me along. I really enjoyed it," I say, hoping for a little more than a smile and a wave in return.

He sits, hips angled toward me, and stares at me as words tumble from his mouth. "I would have never found my way without you."

Looking into his eyes, I feel like there is some deeper meaning I should understand, but before I can explore my thoughts with more conversation, he begins to get out of the car. We part ways with a polite nod and wave, but I know I caught sight of those wrinkles at the sides of his eyes as he turned away.

16
Caroline

MONDAY

I have read the last few text messages from Liam over and over again. Trying to interpret their meaning is giving me a headache. *Does he think we need to talk because I want too much too quickly? Or does he think it's time we gave a real relationship a try?* Either way, he is driving me to bad habits. I have ingested far more chocolate in the past few days than I have in the past year.

When I think of him, I am giddy and nervous at the same time. I have been laughing at jokes that aren't funny, feeling all mushy inside when I see old people holding hands, and daydreaming about the way his lips will feel against mine. After just one week and a few tense moments, I am envisioning myself in a relationship with Liam. It is a strange and foreign feeling.

My most recent relationship lasted for only a weekend

when I went out with the same guy on consecutive Friday and Saturday nights. The following Sunday, he sent me two text messages and called my phone three times before one o'clock in the afternoon. I guess I should have been flattered, but instead, I was annoyed.

June repeatedly told me that my commitment button was broken. To me, it felt as if this so-called button was yanked from the wall, disconnected, and covered over. It wasn't dysfunctional. It just wasn't there. Every time a guy came remotely close to finding that button, an annoying alarm would sound off in my head, and I would run the other way. So many guys were either too sweet or too rude. They paid too much attention to their looks, or they appeared too ragged around the edges. Jocks were too involved in sports or other activities while geeks were too lazy, living life as a couch potato in front of a television or computer screen. I could never find a happy medium—until now.

Liam makes me want more. He's carefree without being careless. He's the perfect mixture of messy short hair and neatly pressed clothes. I thought I would die when he came down for Sunday dinner after just taking a shower. His hair was still heavy with wetness while his body was covered with crisp clean clothes. Although it's obvious he spends some time on presentation, his appearance always has a take-it-or-leave-it look, and I will definitely take it.

Working through this Monday morning is going to be tough while carrying around images of Liam all day.

June called me earlier to say she can't do lunch, so I send a quick text to Liam.

Busy for lunch? —Caroline

Have a meeting. Can we get together after work? —Liam

Sounds good. What were you thinking? —Caroline

How about a movie and then a quick bite? —Liam

Sure. —Caroline

I'll see what's playing and text you later. —Liam

I'm slightly disappointed about not having lunch with him, but a movie could be fun. Two hours in a dark room while sitting next to a hot guy doesn't sound too bad.

Since I'm not heading out for lunch, I try to take the time to get ahead on some new projects. Audrey and I order in lunch and work diligently through the afternoon. The day goes by slowly, but I don't mind. It gives me an opportunity to linger on thoughts of Liam as I imagine what our relationship could be. Of course, these thoughts are also interspersed with ideas of why it couldn't work out. I push the latter option to the side and try to stay positive.

I get home from work and change into my best jeans and a sexy green tank top. I'm pulling a cardigan around my shoulders when I hear the front door open.

"Hey, June. How was lunch?"

"He asked me to take him to a museum."

"For lunch? That's a little weird."

"No, tonight!"

"What kind of date is that?" I ask, walking into her bedroom as she throws some clothes onto her bed.

"It's not a date. He wants to see this exhibit, and he doesn't know how to get to the museum."

"Sure," I say sarcastically.

"Shut up! He said that I'm a good employee, and my company is lucky to have me. Does that sound like a pick-up line to you?"

"Alright. Geez, settle down. What are you going to wear?"

"I'm thinking this blue skirt and white top. What do you think?"

"I think you're hoping it turns into a date."

"Ugh! Get out! I can't talk to you right now."

I laugh as I head back toward my room. When I walk into my bedroom, I notice my phone light is flashing. *Crap, Liam must have texted me.*

What do you think about seeing the new Bruce Willis movie? —*Liam*

Action sounds perfect. —*Caroline*

He's a man after my own heart. I think I would have cried in utter disappointment if he had recommended a chick flick or some other sappy story.

Was beginning to think you were backing out on me.
Is June home? —Liam

She's leaving soon, but I don't know what time.
I could meet you there. —Caroline

Okay. Meet you there at 6:30? —Liam

See you then. :) —Caroline

I finish getting dressed and say good-bye to June. She is seriously stressing out about this guy. I know she likes him, but he must be some really good eye-candy or make some really great money. She is tied up in knots. I hope he's good for her. She deserves someone really wonderful.

# # #

As I walk up the steps to the theater, I see Liam standing with his back to me. I give myself a couple extra seconds to take in the view, and then I make myself walk up beside him. He looks down at me with a sweet smile as he places his arm around my shoulders. It feels comfortable and easy, like he has touched me this way a million times before. It's like nothing I have ever experienced. I don't want to squirm away or make an excuse to go to the restroom. Instead, I fold myself into his side, and I enjoy the feeling of his arm tightening around me in response.

"Hey there. If there's something else you'd rather see, just let me know."

"No, I like Bruce Willis. This movie should be good."

We walk together to the ordering kiosk, and I watch as he chooses the movie and pays for our tickets. He takes my hand and leads me into the theater lobby.

"Do you want something to drink?"

"Sure. Do you mind if I grab something to eat here? I don't want to ruin your dinner plans," I say, wondering what he'll think.

"Are you kidding? You're not ruining anything. I love theater food. What do you want?"

"Popcorn and a hot dog?"

"Are you okay with sharing a drink?"

"Sure. Whatever you like is fine."

We order our food and drink, and then make our way into the theater. We're about thirty minutes early, so we have our choice of where to sit. Liam picks seats toward the top and in the middle of the row. We finish eating before the movie starts. As the previews begin to play, Liam's arm finds its way around my shoulders again. His arm stays there throughout the movie, and his fingers gently caress my upper arm every few minutes. He makes no attempt to touch me in any other way, and I sit in total stillness, not wanting to ruin the connection we have.

As the plot wraps up, I realize I wouldn't be able to tell

anyone what happened during the movie if my life depended on it. I know that Bruce Willis kicked some ass, but that happens in just about every movie he is in. When the theater lights begin to brighten the room, Liam pulls me against him in a quick side hug before he gets up to leave.

As we exit the theater and round the corner at the bottom of the stairs, he takes my hand in his. I feel butterflies kicking up in my stomach. This is the part of the night when we go our separate ways. We walk into the parking lot and the unknown ending of our date is driving me crazy. My body is shaking, and I hope he doesn't notice it as he holds my hand. I need to get in control of myself.

"So, do you know what time June will be home?" he asks.

"No, she was going to a museum, so I imagine it won't be too late."

"I was planning on dinner, but since we already ate, would you like to come back to my place?"

Don't act too eager. "Sure. That sounds fine."

"Alright. Do you want to follow me there?"

I nod in agreement as he opens my car door. I slip in and give him a quick smile before he closes the door. All the way to his apartment, I'm thinking of what I will say. I know we should talk about what we want from all this, but I'm not sure if I'll be able to resist kissing him if he touches me in any way. I resolve to keep my emotions in check, so we can discuss the important issues we need to work out. Not to mention, a kiss after eating a hot dog for dinner could be disastrous.

It only takes a few minutes to reach his apartment complex.

We pull into the parking lot and park side by side. Meeting on the sidewalk, we walk down a short hall to his door. He pulls his keys from his front pocket and unlocks the door. My mind is racing, and I can't seem to contain my body's response to his. He swings the door open wide and motions for me to go inside.

His apartment isn't a complete bachelor pad. There aren't any big posters of sports stars or hot models. His television and furniture are modest, but I do see a couple of different gaming systems in the living room. I watch as Liam reaches into his back pocket to take out his wallet, and I begin to wonder how it would feel to have my hands in his back pockets with my body pressed against his. I'm lost in thought when Liam's voice interrupts me.

"Come here," he says, holding out a hand. "You look worried. Is everything okay?"

"Sure. I just know we need to talk," I say, stepping to him.

His arms encircle me and pull me closer into his chest. I breathe in the scent of his cologne. When I close my eyes, I feel his lips against the top of my head.

"We don't have to talk tonight. Let's just relax."

He must be oblivious to how he affects me. There is no way I can relax in this moment. He leads me to the couch, and we sit, our hips touching. His hand caresses my face, and I smile hesitantly. I lean toward him, knowing I should just give in now because my willpower has no chance. He presses his thumb against my chin, turning my face away from him. I feel his lips against my neck. Prickling specks of energy rush down my arms and through my torso. He continues to the hollow of my neck, and moving my face the opposite direction, he traces an imaginary line up the other side of my neck. I take in a breath and close my eyes. *Maybe I can relax.*

The world stops. There is no sound more important than the breath leaving his body and moving toward mine. As Liam rests his forehead against mine, I wonder how I will hold myself back if our lips touch. I don't want to push things too far if he doesn't want more, but I don't want him to think I'm a prude. I push aside my worry and take a small breath.

Then, gently, as if not wanting to interrupt my personal calm, he kisses my lips. There's no pressure to deepen the kiss. I let his hands warm my cheeks as I try to let go in this moment. I tell myself that all my worrying is pointless because I don't have to be in control when I'm with Liam. I can let him take the lead and allow a little piece of myself to become lost in him. When his lips leave mine, I sit with my eyes still closed.

"Relaxed?" he asks.

I open my eyes. "Very."

This is the point where I would normally leave the guy's house. I would make some excuse about needing to get some work done or having to go to the grocery store. Instead, I pull my legs underneath me and get comfortable on the couch beside him.

We spend the next hour or so watching sitcoms and laughing our asses off. Then, someone knocks on the door. Liam stands, walks to the door, and then looks through the peephole.

"Holy crap," he whispers in my direction.

"What?"

"It's June!"

My eyes widen in surprise, and I jump up from the couch. I haven't been to any other room in his apartment, so I don't know which direction to go. Liam points to what I assume is his bedroom, and I run to it without question. I shut the door behind me and lean my body against it. June's voice is soft as she enters the apartment, and I stand with my ear to the door, straining to hear their conversation.

"Geez. What took you so long, Liam?"

"Um, I was in the bathroom."

I silently laugh to myself.

"Do you need a prescription from Dad to take care of something?"

"Shut up, June. Why are you here?"

"I need to talk."

I listen as June describes her evening at the museum. She asks Liam if this guy might be into her. I had no clue that she came to him for advice like this. I thought I was her go-to person. I feel a little pang of jealousy, but I know what it's like to have a brother who loves you enough to listen to your girlie gossip and your need for relationship advice. To be honest, it sounds like this guy likes her, so I don't understand what the problem is.

After about thirty minutes of sitting alone in Liam's room, I start to wonder if she will ever leave. Walking toward the bed, I begin to look around his room in the dim light of his bedside lamp. Just like the living room, it doesn't scream bachelor. His bed is made with a dark gray comforter and pillows with white-and-gray patterns. Although the remaining furniture—a dresser, bedside tables, and a chair with an ottoman—is all made of dark wood, his room has a light feel. Two large framed black-and-white airplane images hang above the headboard of his bed. A few small model airplanes are also scattered on his dresser and one bedside table. A single framed photo is present on the opposite bedside table. The photo is a candid shot of him with his family.

My ears perk to attention when Liam's voice begins to get louder from the living room.

"June, I hate to cut this short, but I have a huge meeting in the morning. It sounds like you need to be patient with this guy and give him time to tell you how he feels. Some guys like to build up to the big reveal."

I can sense the smile in his voice at the last sentence, and I know June must be rolling her eyes.

"Alright, brother. Have a good night. Love you."

"See ya, sis."

The door closes, and within a couple of seconds, Liam opens his bedroom door. "Well, I didn't expect to have you in my room tonight."

"Yeah, about that, I better get going, too."

Liam laughs and hugs me. "Alright, just wait a few minutes to make sure she's gone."

With that, I realize that we are definitely keeping this a secret from June at least a little while longer. *What would have happened if she had found me in his apartment?* There's no way I can tell her I was with him tonight.

Liam lowers me back to the bed in his arms, and I find that relaxing place again.

17
June

TUESDAY

After my talk with Liam last night, I feel much better about the Cohen situation. I have decided to avoid him at all costs. I know Liam said to give him time, but I thought space would be a good idea, too. As I'm getting my things together to leave for the day, Cohen pops his head around the corner of my doorway.

"June, I haven't seen you much today."

"Well, I am a busy lady." I motion over my cluttered desk as if I'm hosting a game show.

Cohen laughs. "I hope you aren't too busy to grab a bite to eat tomorrow evening."

"Sure. I can make a reservation at Julianna's downtown. How many should I tell them?"

"Just two, and we might have to work a little late, so we'll probably just head out from here." He gives me a quick grin, and then he's gone.

I know I've had this discussion with myself before. In fact, I'm pretty sure the discussion was just last night, but this guy is really confusing. *Why does he want to go to dinner with just me?* I start running through scenarios in my head, and finally, I come to a conclusion that seems plausible. *Maybe his company is interested in hiring me. Maybe I should do some research about them before meeting with Cohen tomorrow night. What would I say?* I haven't even worked two months at my current job. *Would I have to move to Washington? What about my apartment with Caroline?*

I'm beginning to find it difficult to breathe. *That's enough. Just go and see what he has to say.* I should pretend like it's just a meeting about the current contract and enjoy myself. After all, it isn't very often that I get to sit across the table from a guy who could cause supermodels to faint in adoration.

# # #

WEDNESDAY

Cohen was right about staying late. The next workday is brutal. Between meetings, phone calls, and going through 215 emails, I don't even have time to eat lunch. By the end of the day, I'm dying for a good meal and a drink. If I were being honest, I would like to put on my pajamas and slippers, but the sexy black dress and heels I brought to work will have to do. As I unlock my office door and step out, Cohen is leaning against a desk directly in front of me.

My eyes scan his body. From head to toe, there is nothing out of place. His hair is even a mess of perfection. *Damn it. Why does he have to be so endearing?* I'll have to remind myself to look past him while we're at dinner tonight. That should make for some good conversation. *Hey, June. Are you having a stroke? You seem to be looking to my right instead of directly at me.*

"Hey, you look great!" he says.

"Thanks."

"You ready to head out?"

"Sure."

Maybe if I limit my responses to only one word, I'll keep from making a fool out of myself tonight.

Cohen drives us to the restaurant. We don't say much and awkward silence fills the space between us. I'm not sure what to talk about since I don't know what this dinner is all about.

We're seated, and the waiter takes our drink order right away. I am looking over the menu when Cohen starts to speak.

"June, I need to be honest with you. I didn't ask you to dinner to discuss the contract with your company."

Point one for me. At least I was right about that.

"I've needed to talk to you about something else."

The waiter brings our drinks just as Cohen opens his mouth to continue talking. *Looks like we're in for round two of mealtime interruptions.* Cohen shoots him a glare.

As the waiter walks away, I say, "I have been so grateful for the opportunity to work with Mr. Hargrove. He's someone I have followed in the industry since I began college."

"I am so glad that you are somewhere you feel you can

excel and succeed. You deserve it all. You're bright and outgoing. You amaze me."

I know my smile has spread across my whole face by this point.

"I've researched your company in Washington and the needs they fill. I am particularly impressed with their involvement in the community as well as how they monitor the appropriate use of resources to maintain a healthy environment." I'm hoping I don't sound like a sound bite taken from their website.

As the waiter comes by to take our order, I notice Cohen seems more than a little nervous. His face appears flushed, and he's rubbing his napkin between his fingers over and over again. Once we're done ordering, I begin mentally preparing for the interview that I'm sure is coming.

I'm reviewing key points about the company in my head when Cohen reaches across the table, placing his hand on top of mine.

"June, before we get interrupted again, I need to finish. You might think I'm crazy when I tell you this. You might even ask me to take you home, but I have to tell you."

My heart begins to pound in my chest. *What is he talking about? Why does he look so concerned?*

He takes a breath. "You are all I've thought about since the moment my eyes caught yours at that airport last week. I felt your presence during the entire flight, and I walked out of the airport, thinking I had lost a chance to meet someone who could have been important to me. Then, you ran into me on those steps at the Truman building." Pausing, he shakes his head slowly as he looks down into his lap. When he looks back up, his eyes capture mine, and I see purpose behind their hazel hue.

Words begin to tumble quickly from his lips. "I knew I couldn't let you walk away again. You might not believe it, but I know you crossed my path that day for a reason. I wasn't sure what it was about you, but I had to get to know you. My life has been so hectic over the past few years. I haven't been in the market for a real relationship in a long time. I'm not even sure where to begin when it comes to dating, but after seeing you, I do believe that it's possible again. I know that when I looked into your eyes, I saw something that made me believe in taking a chance. If you didn't feel it and if you don't feel it now, I will walk away, but I couldn't go another minute without telling you that I want you in my life."

I stare at him, wide-eyed. I talked myself into thinking that he had no interest in me and that our airport meal had just been a business interaction. I was talking myself through an interview when he was actually preparing to pour out his heart to me. *What do I say to that?*

"Um, to be honest, I'm not sure what to say."

"Say you'll let me take you out while I'm in town. Just give yourself some time to get to know me and explore your own feelings. If you have no interest in seeing me after I leave town next week, then we'll drop it, and you'll never hear me mention it again. It's just that I haven't felt this way in a long time. When a woman has a talent like throwing magazines at lightning speed, I know I can't let the chance pass me by."

Feeling the heat of a blush reaching my cheeks, I cover my face with my hands. Before I can stop it from happening, I'm laughing so loud that I'm sure the valet outside can hear me. "Well, when you put it that way..." I peek through my fingers to his side of the table.

His grin reaches from ear to ear, and those damn wrinkles at the sides of his eyes make me smile even more. I could never mistake whether he is happy or not. I think I already found my favorite thing about him.

The rest of dinner is more relaxed. I start giving over to the emotions I've been feeling for Cohen.

After dinner, we go back to the office parking lot, so he can drop me off at my car.

"June, I've enjoyed tonight so much."

"Me, too," I say, looking down to my feet.

I watch as his hand slowly reaches up to my chin. He lifts my head, so our eyes can align again.

"I know I'm leaving soon, but I would like to see you again...outside of the office."

"Okay," is all I can say as I study each colored specks in his eyes.

When his hand moves to cup my cheek, I lean into his touch. Reaching for his face, I touch the wrinkles that are forming at the corners of his eyes.

"Can I kiss you, June?"

"Please," I whisper.

Wasting no time, he places his lips over mine. With one hand on my cheek, his opposite arm encompasses my body, leaving me no need to hold my own weight. I feel my muscles relax, giving in to his embrace. He kisses me with soft small pecks over and over again. It's as if all the emotion he releases transfers to my body, overwhelming my senses.

When we pull away from each other, I wipe at my eyes and feel a slight wetness, realizing his caress has caused tears to form. *What have I gotten myself into?*

Cohen walks me to my car, opens the door, and guides my body as I sit down. He stands, looking down at me with a look I can only describe as adoration. When his eyes scan over my body, I feel as if he is memorizing every inch of me along with every small moment of this experience.

"I'll see you tomorrow morning," he says before pressing his lips to my forehead.

"See you tomorrow."

We are both still for a moment, smiling at one another, and then he slowly brushes his closed hand across my cheek before he shuts the door. As he walks away, I wrap my arms around myself, not willing to let the warmth escape from me. Eventually, I come to terms with the fact that I have to go home, but at least I have comfort in knowing that I'll see him again tomorrow.

18
Caroline

TUESDAY

Today passes by without seeing Liam. He texts me early in the day to let me know he has meetings through lunch on Tuesday and Wednesday. I'm feeling a little down about not seeing him or having the chance to talk through anything. I still haven't given June any clue about us, and it is killing me. It hasn't been too difficult to keep our secret though since I haven't seen her at all. She's been spending time with her new lover boy from work.

# # #

WEDNESDAY

Tonight, June is out to dinner for work, so I decide to be

bold and call Liam. After the phone rings several times, I'm about to hang up when I hear his voice.

"Hello?"

"Hi, Liam. It's Caroline."

"Caroline! This week has been murder. How are you doing?"

"Well, I'm okay. I was actually calling because June is out tonight, and I don't have any plans. I was wondering if you might want to come over and have that talk?"

"That would be great. Give me twenty minutes."

"Okay. See you soon."

"Bye."

What was I thinking? Do I have enough time to shower? What should I wear? I know this talk needs to happen, but what will I say? What do I want? I feel like one of those annoying toys stuck in the plexiglass box, running its head into the sides over and over again. I need a reset button. I decide not to go overboard, and I put on some purple sweatpants and a college logo T-shirt.

Punctual as always, Liam is knocking at my door twenty minutes later. I comb my fingers through my hair, straighten my shirt, and then open the door. Liam is standing a few feet away, looking down at his phone. He's through the door and hugging me before I have a chance to react.

"Well, hello," I say, laughing.

I walk into the living room and sit on the couch when I notice Liam isn't following. He's stopped off in the kitchen, gotten a glass, and is filling it with water.

"Make yourself at home. I guess you know where the

glasses are."

"I should since I moved all this in while you were on a great Hawaiian vacation with your family." He smirks as he heads toward me, plopping onto the opposite side of the couch.

"So, the other day, you said we should talk?" I ask with caution in my tone.

Liam takes a drink of water, looking at me over the rim of his glass. "Sure, um...I just didn't want you to get the wrong impression."

I feel my heart sink into my stomach.

"I enjoyed taking you to the charity event. I had a wonderful time. The baseball game was great even though I wish I would have told Eli to back off on the alcohol consumption."

I begin to panic, watching him stare intently into the bottom of his glass. *Did he come over just to tell me he's not interested? What about Sunday at his parents' house and Monday night at his place?*

"Listen, Liam, I am so sorry about the baseball game. I don't normally drink that much, and I don't know anything about sports. It wasn't Eli's fault. I should have been more responsible. I completely understand if you don't want me to tell June about any of it."

"I think that not telling June would be a good idea for now," he says with a serious look on his face.

"Okay, but what do you mean by 'for now'? I mean, I understand if you don't think I'm your type."

"Not my type?" Liam's brows furrow. He reaches across the couch and takes my hand. "The only reason I don't want to tell June is because I'm afraid she might steer you away from me. My family seems to believe that the high school me has never grown up. I'm almost certain that June thinks I ruin every girl I touch."

My lungs begin filling with air again as my breathing returns to normal. "I feel the same way. I don't have the best track record with dating, and I don't think June would approve."

"Let's enjoy some time getting to know each other and not worry about June or the rest of my family for now. Would that be okay?"

"I think that would be alright."

"Are we done talking?" Liam asks as he moves his body closer to me.

"I am."

"Good," he whispers before he places his lips against mine.

I move one hand to where his hand is on my thigh. His hips rest on mine, and he deepens the kiss, placing my back softly against the couch. The feeling of his body on top of me is intoxicating. He places my hand to his chest, and then he slides his hand to my waist, caressing the skin just above my sweatpants. I can feel his muscles flex as he holds his upper body above me. I'm struggling to keep my breath even, not wanting to make any desperate sounds. As our tongues meet, my phone begins to vibrate on the coffee table.

"Leave it," Liam says before he takes my lower lip between his teeth.

Reluctant to break free from this moment, I wrap my arms around his waist, drawing him even closer. The phone vibrates again. "I can't." I grab it and tap the screen to see the message.

You better still be up! He kissed me!
I'll be home in 10 minutes. —June

I jump up from the couch, dumping Liam onto the floor. "Crap. I'm sorry. It's from June. She's going to be home in ten minutes. You better go if you don't want to tell her about us."

Liam gets to his feet and wraps his arms around me. "So, you're really okay with not telling June?"

"I'm not sure I can keep it a secret for long, but I think it'll be okay for a little while."

"Alright."

He leans in to kiss me, but I turn my face for a kiss on the cheek instead.

"If you keep kissing me, we won't have a choice but to tell June."

"You're probably right. I'll call you tomorrow. Maybe we can go out this weekend?"

"Sure, that sounds great."

We walk to the door, and I wave as he heads down the hallway to the stairs. After closing the door softly, I run to the bathroom to make sure I don't look like a mess.

Five minutes later, June steps in through the door. I'm beginning to wonder if their whole family is this punctual. She stalks straight to where I am standing and hugs me until I'm scared I won't have any breath remaining.

"You are not going to believe my night!" she squeals.

She recounts dinner and his confession of having feelings for her. She tells every detail of their kiss that brought her to tears. It is all so beautiful. I'm beginning to get a little jealous that she can talk so freely about her budding relationship, but then she says something that stops my thoughts in their tracks. She says his name—*Cohen. Did she really just say Cohen?*

Trying to hide my shock, I get up from the couch and move to the kitchen for a glass of water. "Where is he from?"

"He lives in Washington."

Alright, Caroline. Be cool. Don't freak out. "That's awesome. Where does he work?"

"The Bushing Company."

Oh my god! This can't be possible! What does she know about him? Should I tell her? This could get really bad. I'm feeling sick to my stomach.

"Why do you ask?" June says with concern in her eyes.

"No reason. Listen, I need to get to bed. I have an early day tomorrow. I'm so glad you had a good night." I give her a tight hug.

"Are you okay?" June questions.

"I'm fine. I'm just tired."

As I walk down the hall to my room, I grab my phone and text my brother.

What the hell are you doing with June? —Caroline

What are you talking about? —Cohen

June is my best friend. How did you not put two and two together? Or did you just not care? We need to talk. You can't do this to her. —Caroline

I can't talk right now. Just found out I have to leave Friday morning to head back home. Please don't tell her. I'll explain soon.
I promise. —Cohen

Everything is getting more complicated by the minute. Thirty minutes ago, I agreed to keep lying to my best friend about dating her brother. Now, I have to lie about knowing she is dating my brother even though every part of my being wants to tell her to run in the other direction. I want to rewind my night to around thirty minutes ago and push pause, so I can enjoy a little more bliss instead of this chaos.

19
June

THURSDAY

I show up for work on Thursday with a huge smile plastered to my face. This week has been perfect. The only time in my life that consisted of this many exciting days in a row was when my parents took me to Disney World at the age of eight. I shouldn't have to explain how a theme park vacation pales in comparison to my last three days.

I replayed my kiss with Cohen a million times before I fell asleep last night, and then I dreamed about it while I was sleeping. I am fairly certain no kiss will ever replace the space in my mind where this one resides.

I am trying to be careful of placing my emotions for Cohen into a box where they don't belong because I've had so many letdowns in the past. He is so wonderful though. Not only is he handsome and sweet, but he's also always professional. I still can't believe that he had all those feelings for me, but he was able to play it off as nothing while at work.

Although I know that our physical connection will have to be minimal today, just thinking about seeing him gives me a jolt of electricity. *Maybe Mr. Hargrove will have to back out on lunch again today.*

After grabbing a cup of coffee from the office kitchen, I get started on some projects I need to complete before the weekend. My happiness makes it easy to work, and before I know it, the clock says two o'clock. I haven't eaten lunch or seen Cohen today. *That's odd.*

My stomach growls so loudly that I'm sure the entire office thinks I've deprived myself of food for days. I get up from my desk, walk out of my office and into the mass of cubicles. Cohen is talking with one of my coworkers at a cubicle across the large space. He looks up at me and gives me a small smile. I know we have to keep things under wraps since we are working on this project together, but a large part of me wants to jump over these desks and tackle him to the ground. Instead, I follow his example of professionalism, and I decide to feed my hunger with a trip to the kitchen to heat up a frozen meal. *Should be tasty.*

On my way back to my office, Cohen joins me.

"Hey, I'm sorry I haven't been able to see you today. I have lots to get done before the weekend."

"No, don't worry about it. I understand. I've been buried all day, too." I smile and touch his arm.

"Alright, well, I better get back to it. I'll see you later."

"See you later," I say with my brows furrowed as he walks

out the doorway.

That was a strange conversation. I figured he would ask me out for a date tonight or at least sit and talk with me for a little bit. I guess he really is busy.

I don't see Cohen for the rest of the day, and when I get ready to leave work for the night, he is nowhere to be found. Checking out with Mr. Hargrove, I have this sinking feeling that something isn't right, but I try and put the feelings aside. *I'm being paranoid because of past relationships. I need to give this a chance.*

I go home, and feeling beat from my busy day, I eat a quick dinner and then head straight to bed. I take out a book and read until my eyes feel too heavy to keep open. I close the book and turn out the lights. I'm glad when sleep comes quickly.

FRIDAY

The next morning is all sunshine as the light streams into my car windows on the way to work. I feel happy despite my minimal interaction with Cohen yesterday. Since it's Friday, there's not much to be unhappy about.

After I walk into my office, I sit at my desk and notice a folded piece of paper lying across my keyboard. My name is written in sloppy writing across the front. With curiosity, I open the paper.

June,

I'm sorry I couldn't stay to say good-bye. I had to return home. I hope to call you soon. Please know that the last few days have been beautiful— much like you.

~C

My eyes begin to water as I look down at the rough paper. I try to gather myself together and sweep my emotions behind the curtain of my closed eyes. *I'm overreacting. He's just a guy.* I knew that he would have to leave soon. I never even asked him when he had to head back home. From our conversation the other night, I assumed that we would see each other again outside of work before he left town. *He must have had something come up with his company back home. He'll call.*

As I work through the day, I check my personal phone, office voice mail, and email account too many times to count, and I've received no calls or messages from Cohen. *Of course, he is flying across the country today. Who knows how many hours he could be stuck in airports and on airplanes?* I shouldn't worry about it.

By the afternoon, I've moved through the sad stage, straight past the worried stage, and into the irritated stage. *Cohen hasn't called. He hasn't texted. He hasn't emailed.* During a meeting today, Mr. Hargrove mentioned that a different associate would be handling Cohen's phone calls for the next few days.

He could have at least had the decency to tell me that he was simply looking for a few fun nights out on the town. *Why in the world would he tell me all those things and then leave without a word?* I guess I should give him credit that he left a note, but that note left me more confused than if he wouldn't have said anything at all.

It's a good thing I didn't tell my mom about our few dates. She would have relentlessly asked me about him, and I would have to tell her that he used me. I'm sure she would blame it on some unappealing quality I have, and then she'd suggest ways to *hold on* to the next boy that comes around to take a chance on me.

Frustrated, I pick up my phone and text Caroline.

Girls' night tonight. Guys are ridiculous. —June

What? Are you okay? —Caroline

I guess. See you tonight. —June

I'll pick up some take-out. —Caroline

I go back to wrapping things up with my emails. After I put a few finishing touches on a spreadsheet, I'm out the door. As I'm riding down the elevator, my phone trills. The sound is so quiet that I don't hear it at first. It must be shoved in some invisible space. I put down my workbag and try to dig out my phone from the dark cave that is my purse. Of course, I can't find it.

I'm still searching when the elevator door opens on the first floor, and three gray-haired men in business suits look at me like I've lost my mind. My workbag has fallen over, and part of its contents has emptied out onto the floor. My purse is half-slung over my shoulder with my opposite hand stuck deep inside. I swear that I'm normally more put together than this. One of the men walks into the elevator and presses the button to hold the door. After thanking him with a sheepish look, I gather my things and haphazardly toss them into my bag before exiting the elevator. *This day could not get any worse.*

When I get to my car, I search through my purse again, and I'm still not able to find my phone. I think I might be hallucinating. I could have sworn I heard it ring three more times between the elevator and my car.

As I'm pulling out of the parking garage, a car flies into the entrance, causing me to brake quickly. My workbag falls to the floorboard, scattering papers and folders everywhere. In between a few of the papers, I see a green flashing light. *My phone!*

I throw my car into park and dive toward the passenger seat. It's not that I'm desperate, but it could be a text from Cohen. Grabbing the phone, I quickly flip to my messages screen. It's not from Cohen.

Don't forget about the baby shower tomorrow at 2. Mom is expecting you.
—Addison

Well, that sucks. I did forget. One of Addison's close friends is having her first baby, and I really like her. I'll have to convince Caroline to come with me. As much as I want to wallow in my disappointment about Cohen, maybe a baby shower will keep my mind off the whole situation. Cupcakes and party mints have a way of cheering me up.

20
Caroline

FRIDAY

Ever since Wednesday night, I've been trying to avoid June. I can't believe the guy she met in New York is my brother. *What a freaking small world.* I tried to call him on Thursday, but he blew me off. His text said something about having to leave town. Next time I talk with him, I'm going to threaten him within an inch of his life if he hurts her. I know he's in a hard spot, but he's going to have to decide if he's ready to put everything out there.

Unfortunately, I don't think he understands the predicament he has put me in. Not only do I have to omit this particular truth from my best friend, but I also have to hide the fact that I'm dating her brother. *This situation couldn't get any worse.*

I've been trying to figure out how neither of them recognized the other. I mean, she's been my best friend for about four years now. Then, I realized how it happened. I never referred to him as Cohen when I talked about him. Although his friends and many other people refer to him by his first name, my parents and I call him CJ most of the time. With our last name being Smith, it's easy to overlook a definite connection. I also think about the vacation pictures I kept in my dorm room and the ones I now have on display at our apartment. Although my brother and I have always been very close, we didn't take family trips together.

We were young when our parents divorced. I was eight years old, and Cohen was ten when it all came to a head. Truth be told, our parents probably should have never gotten married. I remember they argued a lot, and I don't recall many smiles in my house before the divorce was finalized. At the time, I had no clue what was going on, and I was confused about our parents living in different houses. About six months later, my confusion turned to frustration and fear when our dad got a new job out of state. Being a ten-year-old boy, my brother wanted to have someone to play baseball with, so he decided to go live with our dad. I, of course, was scared to leave our mom's side, and then my brother and our dad left.

I'll never forget the night before Cohen moved eleven hours away.

"Care, don't worry. We'll still get to see each other."

"No, we won't. Why does Dad have to be so mean? I don't want you to go." I pouted with tears welling up in my eyes.

"He said I can come visit a bunch, and you'll come see us, too."

"But I don't want you to go, CJ. If you stay, I promise I won't spit in your baseball glove, and I won't hide your books anymore."

"I don't care about that," he said, shaking his head. "What if I promise I'll call you all the time? Will that make it better?"

"No," I said, my tears turning into sobs.

"Come here, Care. Go to sleep. Like Mom says, everything is better in the morning."

That night, my brother held me in his arms until my tears turned to dreams.

When I woke up the next morning, he was sitting on the edge of the bed, waiting for me to open my eyes. I didn't feel better, but I knew I didn't have a choice in the matter. I helped Cohen as he finished packing a few things, and I made sure to slip a couple things into his suitcase—my favorite Barbie doll and a handmade card detailing how much I loved him and would miss him. I was so scared he would forget me.

Looking back, it's funny to me that I wasn't concerned about my dad leaving, but I couldn't stand the thought of being without my brother. Even back then, my brother was a caring person who could draw anyone in with his gentle spirit.

Through the remainder of elementary and most of middle school, Cohen and I stayed close. We wrote letters, sent pictures, made frequent phone calls, and visited each other whenever we could. When he started high school, things began to change. Cohen started playing baseball, he made new friends, and he even had a steady girlfriend. When I needed something that he could provide from a long distance, he was still there for me, but our visits with each other dwindled considerably.

When I was a junior in high school, Cohen and Julie, his high school sweetheart, got married and moved to Seattle. Although he lived nearby, we still didn't see much of each other since he was struggling through college courses, and Julie was starting up her bakery.

By the end of my senior year, we were living our own lives, only running into each other every now and then. I don't think either of us wanted life to take over that way, but we were both so busy that it had to be okay for the time being.

When I left for college on the East Coast, I knew I would be cutting my ties to home even further, including my connection to my brother. It was a hard decision, but I felt it would help me grow into a better person.

Cohen and I still talked on the phone a few times a week, but after everything happened with Julie, he changed a lot. It was tough to know what he was going through but not be able to be there for him. I told my parents I thought he should move on, but it makes me nervous that he is using June to get back in the game.

June walks into the apartment and looks nothing like her normal cheery self. Her shoulders are slumped, and the red splotches on her face tell me she was crying on her way home. I know that whatever she's worried about has to do with my brother.

"Bad day?" I ask, trying not to let on that I know anything about her situation.

"You could say that," she says, slouching into the large

comfy chair in our living room.

"Anything I can help with?"

"Not unless you can tell me why guys say one thing and then do another."

"Oh, June. I'm so sorry. Guys are brainless sometimes. This guy is foolish if he doesn't want to hang on to you."

I grab our take-out off the counter and bring it into the living room. I feel like such a hypocrite. We eat our food while listening to some funky indie music that doesn't help her mood, and then we decide to go to bed.

"Oh, hey, I forgot to ask you," June calls out from her bathroom. "Do you think you could go with me to a baby shower at my parents' house tomorrow?"

"I don't have any plans, so I don't see why not."

"Thanks. We need to leave around one fifteen or so. It's supposed to start at two."

"Sounds good. See you in the morning."

My head hits the pillow, and the relief of sleep coming soon washes over my tired mind. Then, like a freight train, it suddenly dawns on me. *I don't have any plans with Liam.* I haven't talked to him since Wednesday night. Since hearing about June's connection with my brother on Wednesday, I've neglected to call or text him. I wonder what he's doing tonight or who he might be with. *Damn it.* I roll over, closing my eyes, as I pull the covers over my head. I wish my life didn't have to be so complicated. *Weren't things more simple just a couple weeks ago?*

21
June

SATURDAY

Caroline and I both wake up late on Saturday morning. We're not usually early morning risers on the weekends, but eleven thirty is pushing it a little bit. I stumble into the kitchen to the sound of Caroline groaning as she looks in the refrigerator, no doubt finding very little to eat.

"I'm glad we're going to this baby shower today. I hope they have some real food at your parents' house."

"I'm sure my mom will feed you until your stomach bursts, but I can't wait until two o'clock to eat. Is there anything edible?"

Caroline pulls out a plastic container with what appears to be unidentifiable leftover meat. *Yum.*

"No, thanks. I'll just do coffee and some of these peanut butter crackers. We can head over there early if you want."

"Sounds good to me."

I make coffee while Caroline opens the blinds to let in some light. She sits at the bar and opens a magazine, waiting for her coffee to be served.

Last night, I felt like Caroline was avoiding something. Every time I attempted to talk about her job or recent love interest, she would turn the conversation back around to my problems. At first, I thought she was trying to be nice because of everything going on with me right now, but now that I think about it, she didn't give me any details about her life the entire night. Being the nosy person that I am, I can't stand not knowing what's going on with her.

"So, Caroline, is everything okay with your mom?"

"Yup," she says, not looking up.

"How about the rest of your family?"

"Fine. Why do you ask?" This time, her eyes break free from the celebrity gossip, and she appears to be concerned.

"No reason. I just remembered you were worried about your mom last weekend."

"Oh, well, I think things are okay. No one has said anything."

"Okay." I pour our coffee and add just the right amount of cream and sugar for both our tastes. "How about things with that guy from work? Is all that still going well?"

"No offense, but I really don't want to talk about it. I haven't talked to him in a few days." Her shoulders tense as she closes the magazine, and when she picks up her coffee mug, she grips the handle tightly. Then, she walks to her room and shuts the door.

Okay, I guess I pushed some buttons there. Note to self: Don't ask Caroline any more personal questions for the rest of the month. At least, I figured out the likely culprit of her bad attitude.

I take my coffee to my room and get dressed. When I'm done, I find Caroline ready to go. She's sitting on the couch, staring out the window. Something is seriously wrong with her, but I guess I won't get any serious details until she's ready to talk.

# # #

We get to my parents' house around one o'clock. The front yard looks like a pink elephant threw up all her babies. Alternating pink elephants and yellow baby bottles line the sidewalk leading to the front door. A large wreath made of pink, yellow, and purple ribbons with small baby animals interspersed between bows hides the entire front door. I look over to Caroline, smiling, but I realize her normal snide self is still missing.

"You know, we don't have to go in. We could go see a movie or go back home."

"No, it's alright. I'm fine. I'm sure we'll have fun," she says, giving me a less than halfhearted smile.

"We should at least get some good laughs."

Opening the front door is like entering a zoo. Stuffed baby animals are lying around everywhere. A large table with a pink tablecloth sits at the back of the living room, which is already full of baby gifts. A giraffe, almost double the height of my mother, towers in the corner behind the gift table. Thankfully, no children are coming today. The giraffe alone would have scared me to tears when I was young.

I reach into my purse, feeling like a complete loser, and I place my greeting card complete with a twenty-dollar gift card on the edge of the table. I plan to announce that the gift card will be useful toward diapers and other necessities, so no one blames me for being lazy since I didn't purchase a real gift.

"June, Caroline, you're early."

"We are. We thought we would sneak in and grab a bite to eat before the guests arrived."

"How perfect. We just put out all the sandwich fixings on the kitchen island. Go help yourself." She gives us both a quick hug, and then she and Addison begin to flitter around the living room as they fluff stuffed animals.

Caroline and I make a sandwich, and then we devour them in a matter of minutes.

Pretty soon after, people start to arrive for the shower, and we join the crowd sitting on the couches and chairs in the living room. The guest of honor, Mary, is having a baby girl in about two months, and she looks like she might be a little bloated instead of seven months along. I'm positive that every woman in the house is jealous of her genetic predisposition to perfection when it comes to carrying a baby.

All the guests ooh and aah over each item as they make Mary hold up every single piece of clothing, baby bedding, pacifier, and so on for pictures. I can only imagine how her cheeks must be burning from all the smiling, but she genuinely looks happy.

When all is said and done, the guests continue to mingle as they eat cupcakes and drink punch. I'm enjoying a red velvet cupcake when my mom stops me.

"June, can you girls come to the kitchen with me?"

"Uh, sure," I say. I look over to Caroline and shrug my shoulders.

I begin to walk toward the kitchen, and Caroline follows suit. We enter to find Addison and Mom hugging tightly.

"Hey, Mom. Everything okay?"

"Yes. Addison has something to tell you, and I didn't want to be rude to our guests."

"Okay. What's—"

Interrupting me, Addison shouts with excitement, "We're pregnant! Noah and I are going to have a baby!"

She runs across the kitchen and embraces me in a hug so tight that I feel my spine pop under the pressure. I hug her back, of course, but I have to admit that I have mixed emotions. Don't get me wrong. I'm happy for Addison.

She and Noah have always wanted to have babies, multiple babies. I think Noah would like to own a sports team one day, and he would be happy if he could have enough boys to stock the entire team. I know Addison will be a good mother, and with our mom's help, this child will not suffer from lack of attention.

The honest truth is that I'm dreading the nine months of nagging I'll get from my mother. *When will you find someone to marry? Have you found your Mr. Right? Maybe you should join a club, like a bowling league.* That's not my idea of enjoyable conversation.

"I'm so happy for you, Addie. How excited is Noah? How far along are you?" I ask, giving her a genuine smile.

"Oh, he is beyond excited. I'm only seven weeks along. He couldn't wait to tell his family though, so we decided to tell family only. We'll tell everyone else after twelve weeks."

"We'll keep your secret. Won't we, Caroline?" I say, squeezing Addison's hand.

"Uh-huh," Caroline states with little enthusiasm in her voice.

When I give her a stern stare, she adds, "I'm really excited for you, Addison. You'll be a great mom."

"Eeeee!" Addison squeals, hugging me again. "Okay, enough about me. We better get back out there, or Mary will wonder where we all ran off to."

Mom and Addison head back into the living room, giggling with excitement.

"That's pretty exciting, huh?" I ask Caroline, hoping she'll at least cheer up about a baby.

"It sure is. Do you think you'll be ready to go soon?"

"Whenever you are. I think they're done with everything."

"Alright."

Caroline walks out, and I'm left in the kitchen by myself. *Alone.* The happiness that began my week has quickly faded into something I wasn't expecting. I haven't heard from Cohen. My best friend is acting like she's upset about something, but she won't talk about it. And my sister is moving ahead with her perfect life.

Watching Addison's excitement along with all the happiness surrounding Mary and her baby makes me realize something. *I don't want a struggle.* The past week with Cohen was amazing, but the fact that he hasn't contacted me is frustrating. I need to put everything that happened between us behind me and move on. *If he calls, I'll be all business. Besides, I don't need anything distracting me from my work.*

After saying what feels like 200 good-byes, Caroline and I head back to the apartment. She is quiet the entire way home, and I don't push her to talk. Once we're home, she changes into her workout clothes and then heads out the door without a word.

22
Caroline

SATURDAY

With my earbuds in, I run my legs off on the treadmill. I know I'm being a complete bitch to June, but I don't know how to deal with everything that's going on. I haven't seen or talked to Liam since Wednesday. I know I could call him, but I feel like he should show some interest in me. Not to mention, it's the weekend, and he hasn't tried to make any plans with me. I was originally planning to go to the family dinner tomorrow with June, but now, I'm wondering if my fragile brain can handle being around both June and Liam for an extended period of time.

Suddenly, the music from my phone is interrupted. Looking to the screen, I see that I have a text message from my brother. After slowing the treadmill pace, I pick up my phone and tap the screen to open his message.

Sorry about last week. I'll be back in Houston on Monday.
Can we do dinner? —Cohen

Yes. Is everything okay back home? —Caroline

Not good but okay. I'll only be in town for a few days. —Cohen

Are you going to talk to June? —Caroline

We'll talk about it when I see you. —Cohen

Please text her and tell her you're okay. —Caroline

I don't receive any messages back from my brother, but at least I know he's coming back to Houston. I'm not sure what's going on back home. I guess I'll have to wait until Monday to figure it all out.

In the meantime, I'll have to find a way to be friendlier with June, or she's eventually going to freak out. I stop the treadmill and wipe off my sweat with a towel as I head to the weight machines. After I spend thirty minutes lifting weights, I decide to call it a night.

# # #

When I get home, I have every intention of spending some time with June, but as I walk in the door, I see she has fallen asleep on the couch. I take a quick shower and get into bed. I pick up my phone and decide to make a quick call to check on my mom.

"Hey, Care. Haven't talked to you in a couple of days."

"I know. It's been a crazy week. I was just calling to check on you."

"Check on me? Well, honey, I'm fine."

"Are you really, Mom?"

"Care, what are you talking about?"

"Why did you have to go to the doctor the other day? You didn't sound good. I've been worried, but I didn't want to say anything. Is everything okay?"

"I guess I should be honest with you."

"Okay." *Oh crap, maybe I shouldn't have asked.*

"I wasn't really at the doctor's office for me. Julie's been sick, so I was helping Laura get her to and from the appointment."

"Oh my gosh, Mom. Is she okay?"

"She is, but that's why your brother had to come home. Things aren't going well."

"How bad is it?"

"Let's just say that you might need to come home soon, too."

I feel tears welling up in my eyes. "Why didn't you tell me sooner?"

"Laura didn't want to say anything to CJ yet, so I didn't think I should tell you before he knew."

"That makes sense, but I still wish I would have known sooner."

"I know, Care, but there's nothing you can do. It's hard on

all of us. Just be there for your brother. I know he's returning to Texas soon. Spend a little time with him."

"I will."

"Alright, well, get some rest, and I'll talk to you soon."

"Bye, Mom. Love you."

"Love you, too."

We hang up, and I stare at the ceiling. I wonder what Cohen knows. *Should I call and talk to him now? Maybe it's better if I wait until tomorrow.* I glance over to the bedside table when my phone lights up.

Haven't heard from you. You going to dinner tomorrow? —Liam

Sorry. Been busy, I guess. Yes, I'll be there. —Caroline

I've been busy, too. See you soon. —Liam

I breathe a sigh of relief. At least, Liam seems to be acting normal. Tomorrow will be a new day, and I will find a way to act like I'm happy. Reaching over to turn out my lamp, I know the first thing I'll have to do in the morning is make up for my bad attitude with June.

SUNDAY

My back is killing me from sleeping on the couch half the night. I have no clue what time Caroline got home, but I know she saw me lying there because the TV was turned off when I woke up. Groaning as I roll myself out of bed, I hold my back and lean forward like an elderly woman. As I walk slowly toward the bathroom, I think that my senses must be teasing me. *I swear I smell bacon and coffee.*

"Good morning, June. I'm making breakfast, so hurry up and get dressed!" Caroline shouts from the kitchen.

What the crap? Did she just have a hint of cheer in her voice? I take a shower, running the hot water over my sore back and neck. After drying off and getting dressed, my body is already feeling better.

As I walk into the kitchen, Caroline appears to be back to

her old self. She's wearing cute pink pajama shorts and a matching top with a cooking apron tied around her waist.

"Holy crap! This looks amazing." I look over the plates full of pancakes, eggs, bacon, and cinnamon rolls. "How in the world are we supposed to eat all of this? Did you invite someone else over?" I ask, eyeing her bedroom door.

"Nope." She laughs. "Just you and me. I feel bad for how hateful I've been over the past couple of days. I'm really sorry, June."

"Oh, don't worry about it. You weren't too bad. Just don't let it happen again, or if you do, make sure to add chocolate milk to the list for breakfast."

Caroline smiles at me, and I feel like my world is beginning to return to normal. We eat breakfast and then go our separate ways to run some errands.

# # #

Meeting back at the apartment, we ride together to my parents' house.

So far, dinner is uneventful. Liam, being his typical weird self, chooses to sit at the opposite end of the table again. My mom and Addison are talking about all things baby when my dad interjects.

"Addie, you probably shouldn't do too much planning until you see the doctor. A lot of things can happen before your first appointment."

"What are you trying to say, Dad?" Addison asks. "Do you

think something might happen with the baby?"

"Leave her alone, and just let her be excited. Besides, the baby is just fine. I wouldn't worry a bit, honey," Mom says, obviously irritated with my dad's comment.

Dad shakes his head and takes another bite of chicken.

Caroline and Liam are chatting away about work and life in general. She seems to be in a happy place, and Liam has been genuinely listening to her. The more I see them interact, the more I wonder if I was wrong about letting them hook-up.

The night ends with an amazing double-layer chocolate cake with chocolate icing. I am so full that I can barely move when it's time to leave. I'm about to suggest that Caroline and I head out when I feel my phone vibrate in my back pocket. As I take it out, I wonder who could be contacting me because everyone that matters to me is currently in the same house together. Sliding my finger across the screen, I see Cohen's name. I close my eyes, feeling light-headed.

"Caroline, I'm going to the bathroom before we leave. I might be a minute."

I bolt for the bathroom and close the door behind me. Sitting on the closed toilet seat, I read the message.

Sorry for not calling. Back in Houston early this week.
Can we grab dinner on Tuesday? —Cohen

Should I answer? No, I'll let him suffer for at least a few minutes. I count the seconds tick by until I realize I'm being an idiot. Thinking back, I realize it's only been three days since I've heard from him. *I don't know why he had to head back home. Maybe he has a good reason for leaving quickly and for not calling. I should give him an opportunity to explain.*

Dinner would be good. See you Tuesday. —June

Although my recent emotions about Cohen have been flip-flopping, I can't let this go without first hearing him out.

The words from our last conversation run through my head every night. I know he was sincere when he said all those things, and the passion I felt was so intense when he placed his lips against mine. I can't fully explain it, but when our lips touched, it was like I could envision spending my life with him. I didn't want to say it then, and I probably shouldn't be thinking it now.

As he was pouring out his heart to me at dinner that night, I had the urge to tell him that he is worthy of love. Maybe it won't be me who will show him the love he deserves, but considering the strong feelings I already have for him, I know I have to give him a chance to see where this could go.

So, dinner it is, and after that, I'll see if I need to shut him out of my life.

24
Caroline

SUNDAY

Dinner with June's family is perfect.

Liam and I manage to talk to each other without any question of our motives. Since most of the discussion is centered around Addison's pregnancy and all the changes the new baby will bring, our side conversation doesn't draw much attention.

"I've been so busy at work this week," Liam states. "We're finalizing a new merger, and I've got several new projects to complete before that happens. I've been going in early every morning and leaving after five every evening."

"See, that's why I'm glad I get paid by the hour. At least my efforts would be rewarded if I worked overtime," I say.

"True. Salaried positions have their downsides. Overall, I like my job though, so it's all good. I just hope it slows down a little bit, so I can have more time for things I enjoy." Liam gives me a quick wink as he smiles.

"I hope so, too." I feel my cheeks blush.

Listening to Liam explain his busy week—and the fact that he felt the need to explain—makes me feel better about not hearing from him on Thursday or Friday. Not to mention, he basically said that I'm something he enjoys.

After dinner, I help June clear the table. As we're about to leave, I'm sad because I can only give Liam a simple wave good-bye, but then June rushes past me, saying she has to go to the bathroom.

Once she's out of sight, Liam gives me a sneaky grin before he pulls me by the elbow, guiding me to their guest room that's just past the living room. We walk in, and he closes the door behind us. Backing me up to the door, he presses his body against mine.

"Well, this is a familiar position," I say, giggling softly. "Will you always end up leaning me against doors in your parents' house?"

"We won't always be at my parents' house, but doors aren't such a bad thing, are they?" he asks with a look full of desire.

I begin to speak, but then his hips push into my body, halting my voice. His lips cover mine before I can find words. My hands travel up his arms and into his hair. I tug gently as his tongue caresses mine, and he moans into my mouth. I feel one of his hands slide slowly down my side, and his fingers slip under my shirt to touch the bare skin of my back just above my waist.

"Caroline?" June calls from behind the door. "Mom, have you seen Caroline?"

"Ugh," I sigh, blowing my hair out of my eyes as I look up at Liam.

"It's alright." He kisses me on the tip of my nose. "Can I take you out tomorrow night?"

"Actually, I have plans already. Maybe later in the week?"

"Sure," he says, backing away.

"I'll call you."

Cracking open the door, I peek around, and I don't see anyone close by. I slip out and close the door behind me. As I walk into the foyer, I find June with a confused expression on her face.

"Hey," I say, smiling.

"There you are. What the crap?"

"I just stepped out the back door for a little fresh air. Sorry."

"You ready?"

"If you are," I say, still smiling.

# # #

MONDAY

Although the weekend turned out okay, I'm still a little worried about what my brother will have to say at dinner tonight. I'm busy all day with a new client project, so when five o'clock rolls around, I'm not even near ready. I pick up my phone and send a quick text to him.

> *Running late. Where do you want to eat?*
> *I'll be at least another 45 minutes.* —*Caroline*

> *No problem. Why don't we meet at that same diner?* —*Cohen*

> *Sounds good. See you soon.* —*Caroline*

♯ ♯ ♯

Entering the restaurant almost an hour later, I scan the seating areas. He is sitting in a corner booth at the back, looking over the menu. I walk up to the table without him noticing.

"Hi."

"Oh, Care. Hey. Sorry, I didn't see you come in."

"You look horrible."

"Gee, thanks." He rolls his eyes and then looks back at the menu.

"Well, you do. When was the last time you showered and shaved?" I ask matter-of-factly.

He ignores my question.

My brother's messy brown hair is in full bed-head style. It's like he wore a hat all day, took it off, ran through a wind tunnel, and then tried to tame his locks by letting a bird nest in it. I know it sounds bad, but it really is that bad. His color is pale compared to his usual olive skin tone, and he has dark purple circles under his eyes.

A waitress comes to the table and takes our orders. I get a soup and salad with an iced tea, and Cohen gets water and a grilled cheese sandwich.

"That's seriously all you're getting?" I ask.

"I'm not that hungry," he says, staring at the table.

"Okay, spill it. What's going on?"

Cohen looks up, and when his eyes meet mine, I can see they are troubled and scared.

"Listen…I don't know. It's all so complicated. I went home because Julie's parents were worried about her. She hasn't been doing well lately, but she seems okay right now. It's hard to say what's going to happen. Mom and Dad say I should move on, but it's not that easy."

I am, from that instant forward, in caring sister mode. "I'm so sorry, Cohen. I know it has to be hard."

"It is, and meeting June on top of it all has me crazy in my head. I don't know what to do. I know I should have called June after I got to Seattle, but how was I supposed to do that while sitting around with our family? I know I need to tell her."

"Yes, you do." I pause, taking in my brother's frailty. "But I understand. You need to give June some credit though. She'll get it. Have you talked to her?"

"I texted her yesterday. She agreed to have dinner with me tomorrow."

"Well, that explains her attitude improvement last night." I laugh. "She's got a lot on her plate with work right now, so she doesn't need to worry about you. I think you need to be honest with her."

He places his face in his hands. "I don't know if I'm ready."

"I don't mean to be harsh, but you better get ready. I won't lie to her forever."

The waitress shows up with our food, and we take some time to eat in silence. My heart breaks for the tattered version of my brother sitting in front of me. I don't want to feel this way, but I wish things with Julie could just be over, so he could move on without guilt and regret.

Cohen sighs. "I'll be here until the end of the week. Do you think we can try and get together again before I leave?"

"Sure, if you promise to wash your hair next time," I say as I reach over and tousle his hair.

He smiles as he reaches up to push my hand off of his head. "Ha. Ha. You're so funny. I'll call you on Wednesday or Thursday."

At least I got one smile out of him.

We walk to the sidewalk in front of the restaurant, and after a quick hug, we head our separate ways.

25
June

TUESDAY

I'm not sure why I did it, but I got up two hours early, took an extra long shower, made sure my hair cooperated, and put on my good makeup. *Okay, that's a lie.* I know exactly why I put so much effort into getting ready. Today, I am supposed to see Cohen. Not only am I supposed to see Cohen, but we also have plans to go out to dinner. Once again, I'm unsure about what he wants to discuss, but this time, I'm trying not to make any assumptions. Also on the agenda, I hope to not injure him or myself while we're spending time together.

I walk into the office with my chin up and a big smile on my face. If he is already here, I want to look like I've been fine. I sure as hell don't want him thinking that I've been moping around and pining away for him since last Friday morning. Making my way through the maze of cubicles toward my office,

I see no sign of him. I let out a sigh as I step through my door. I place my workbag next to the desk, and I turn to glance at the clock.

Something moves in my peripheral vision. It scares me enough to make me jump back, causing me to fall into my large potted plant-tree-thing in the corner. To avoid hitting the ground, I sit cockeyed in the pot. My face is covered in limbs and large green leaves. Peeking through the human-eating plant, I can see Cohen sitting on the comfortable sofa with one hand held over his mouth. I don't hear any sounds, but from the looks of it, he's laughing. For some reason, my usual standoffish self takes a holiday. I launch myself up from my seat in the pot holding the plant, and I take brisk steps toward him.

"What are you doing in my office? Do you enjoy scaring the crap out of women and causing near catastrophes? Or is it just when you see me?"

His eyes grow wide, and those sexy wrinkles beside his eyes fade. *Thank God.* I don't think I could hold on to my angry attitude if he kept smiling.

"Mr. Hargrove wanted me to tell you that we'll be meeting in the conference room at eight thirty. I have to leave by the end of the week, so we need to get started on the rest of our project. I came to tell you, but you weren't here yet, so I made myself comfortable. I'm sorry if I scared you."

"Right. Okay. Well, you can go now. I'll see you at the meeting," I say, turning toward my desk.

With my shoulders back and head held high, I walk over to my desk chair and sit. Looking back at Cohen, I give him the meanest stare I can muster.

"See you there." He stands to leave, but then hesitates as if he wants to say something else. His mouth is open, but then he bites down on his bottom lip, holding back.

"Did you need something else?"

"Actually, I was just going to tell you that unless you enjoy the feel of sitting on bark, you should probably find a mirror and wipe off your skirt."

You have got to be kidding me!

He walks out of the office with the wrinkles by his eyes reappearing. I storm to the door and then quietly close it because I'm at work, and slamming doors here is inappropriate. Turning around and looking over my shoulder, I take stock of the damage to my rear end in the full-length mirror on the back of my door. Five large pieces of bark from my potted plant are hanging off from different places on my skirt. I even have two pieces on the back of my shirt. I was so focused on being mad at Cohen that I didn't even feel them when I sat down in my desk chair.

I brush the pieces to the floor. While I'm running my hand over my butt, it dawns on me that he must have been staring at my backside as I walked to my desk. *How else would he have noticed?* Well, I guess the chunks of wood on my rear end could have drawn his attention. Either way, he was looking at it. With this realization, a small smile creeps onto my face. I attempt to replace it with my frustrated stare, but the smile stays put.

At the meeting, our team comes up with a strategy for the rest of the week. Cohen puts in his two cents every now and then. I choose to keep my eyes focused on my notes, the presentation screen, or my coworkers. I look anywhere but at Cohen. The few times I speak up, I make sure to address my ideas directly to Mr. Hargrove.

When we break for lunch, I take mine in my office with the door closed. I need as much space from Cohen as possible if I'm going to be truthful and coherent when we meet for dinner tonight. After lunch, I remain in my office, returning emails and taking phone calls. The afternoon is going smoothly until I hear a soft knock on my door.

"Come in," I call out with a loud voice.

"Hey, it's Cohen. Don't be scared. I come in peace." He laughs. Placing just the tips of his fingers through the door, he waves them in slow motion.

"Shut up. What do you need?"

"It's five thirty. I was wondering if you were going home or if you wanted to grab dinner now."

"Are you serious? It's already five thirty?"

"Definitely serious."

"I guess we can just go now if you want."

"That would be fine with me. Go ahead and wrap things up, and then I'll meet you in the parking garage." Cohen leaves, closing the door behind him.

I sit frozen for a few moments. *Did I really agree to have dinner with him?* I have no idea what he'll have to say, and I have no idea how I'll react. I want to know why he left so suddenly last week and why he has to leave so quickly this week. It's none of my business, but I want to know. I finish up my last email for the day and then head out the door.

When I walk into the parking garage, Cohen is standing against his car, staring down at his cell phone. For the first time today, I take in his looks. He isn't as well put together as usual. His pants and shirt are obviously clean and ironed, but they are nowhere near neatly pressed. He appears more casual than normal with his sleeves rolled up to the middle of his forearms. His hair, although usually messy, is now in more disarray.

A little piece of frustration falls away as I realize something unsettling must be going on in his life. Normal people don't say they want to spend time with someone and then jump on a plane the next day—unless they're bipolar or schizophrenic. *I won't explore those possibilities right now.*

"You ready?" I call out from my car about three vehicles away.

When he glances up, I instantly see it—sadness. A dull ache falls on me as I watch his subdued expression.

"Yeah. I was thinking we could go to that burger place around the corner."

"That's fine."

"You want to meet there or ride together?" he asks.

"I'll follow you there," I say, not wanting to be distracted by his presence in the car.

During the drive to the restaurant, I think about what could be going on in Cohen's life.

As we walk in together, I start to twirl my hair around my

finger. Once we're seated, my focus is not on the menu. We tell the waiter to come back three times before I'm finally ready. After we order, we have to give up our menus, so we no longer have a barrier to hide behind. Cohen looks at me as I glance at anything on my side of the table—my fingernails, my napkin, my salad plate, my fork.

He finally breaks the silence. "I'm sorry," he says in a voice that sounds broken.

I just can't figure out why he is broken. "It's okay."

"No, it's really not. I should have called you."

"You left me a note, so I knew you were gone. You can't help when things happen in your life."

"But I can help myself from lying to you."

I think about that for a moment. *Should I push the obvious question? Yes, I think I should.* "What are you lying about?"

"June, there are a few things you don't know about me," he says, hanging his head.

"I'm sure there are. We've known each other for less than two weeks. There are lots of things you don't know about me."

As if trying to gain stability, Cohen closes his eyes and grasps the edge of the table with both hands. After watching him take several deep breaths, I contemplate asking if he's okay, and then his eyes dart open.

"The things you don't know about me could change how you feel."

"And how do I feel?"

"Before I left, I was sure you felt how I feel. I wanted a chance with you. I wanted you to give me a chance."

"Wanted? So, now, you don't want a chance with me?"

"I don't deserve that chance."

"What? Did you have to rush back for your court date? A court date where you were being charged for rape, murder, and armed robbery?"

"Really? You know the answer to that," he says, shaking his head.

"Actually, I don't, but I'm going to assume that means no. What could possibly make me change my mind about giving someone a chance? It's not like I'm agreeing to marriage. A chance is just that. I might get hurt. You might get hurt. We might miss other chances. That's the risk though. That's the chance you take."

"What if I told you that you probably don't want to risk it?"

"Well, I don't think that's your call. I'm guessing that if you choose to stop lying to me, then I could make a more educated decision, and we could move past this."

Our meal arrives, interrupting our discussion.

We both look down at our food, and I assume Cohen is thinking the same thing I am. The conversation has taken away my happy mood along with my appetite. We both pick around our meals for a little while and take sips of our drinks here and there. Cohen glances at me every once in a while. I peek at him less often than I wish I could.

In the end, I get tired of the silence and the apparent lies. "Here's the deal. I'm not old, but I'm not young. I want a real relationship. I want someone who cares about me, someone who can be honest with me. I think it's pretty obvious that I want someone who won't break my heart and who might trust me to not break his. I am willing to give you a chance, but if you can't let go of whatever is going on, then maybe you're right. Maybe this isn't going to work."

Cohen's eyes search mine. He looks worried. *No, he looks scared.* I can see he wants to say something, but instead, he sits there in silence.

"I'm done eating. Thank you for dinner. If you decide how you feel about me and how you want to deal with those feelings, give me a call. Otherwise, we'll be coworkers and nothing more."

"June, I'm so sorry."

"Cohen, if you are sorry and want something different, then you need to make it happen. I'm here right now because I'm willing, but obviously, whatever decision you are trying to make is too hard for you."

I push out my chair, and it takes all my courage to turn away from him. Walking slowly, I hope to hear his footsteps behind me. I want his voice to call my name. When I reach my car, I turn the ignition and sit for a minute or two. He doesn't walk out of the restaurant.

I drive to my apartment. He doesn't call me. I change clothes and lie down in bed. He doesn't text me.

Translation: He doesn't want me, or if he does, he's a coward.

Tomorrow is going to suck. Somehow, I'll have to find a way to put my emotions in the closet, so I can get through the day.

26
Caroline

WEDNESDAY

After my third close call with Liam at his parents' house on Sunday, I've decided that meeting in neutral territory is the safest thing to do until we decide to let out our secret. I couldn't see Liam on Monday because I had dinner plans with my brother. Then, Tuesday was crazy swamped at work for both of us. I am thankful that we can at least have lunch together today.

As I grab my purse, about to head out the door, Audrey catches me.

"Caroline, I need you to work some extra hours tomorrow night. The Pattersons are out of town, and they want their daughter's room complete before they return on Friday morning. Could you meet the painters and a contractor at their house at six?"

"Um, yeah. I don't see why not."

"Great. I'll send you over with some materials to finish up a couple of pieces. Wait until you see the room all put together. It's going to be beautiful."

"I bet it is. Little Stella is going to feel like a princess."

Audrey smiles. She turns around and begins to walk down the hallway to her office.

"I'm out for lunch. Be back in a little bit."

"Meeting that hot piece of…I mean, that guy from the charity event?" she asks, facing me again with raised eyebrows.

"Yes, I'm meeting Liam. I'll see you in about an hour."

"Take your time. I'll be overworking you tomorrow."

Audrey is a really great boss. I don't dare admit that decorating and painting are hardly considered overworking in my book.

I walk to the Italian restaurant where Liam and I first ran into each other. He already has a table, and it happens to be the same table from our last lunch date. I wonder if that's a coincidence. Liam smiles and stands as I walk toward the table. He hugs me, and his embrace is warm and comforting. After the past week of hiding the truth from my best friend, interacting with someone I don't have to lie to is a relief.

"So, how's your week been?" he asks as I sit across from him.

"Had better, had worse," I say without thinking first.

"Really? What's been bad?"

Well, I can't tell him about my brother. I'm trying to think on my feet, but nothing is coming to mind. Good lies require preplanning. Liam's stare holds my attention. *Look away, look away, or else he'll know you're lying.*

"Oh, nothing really. Just work stuff, you know?"

"I sure do." He leans across the table and takes my hand in his. "Everything at work has been so hectic. It's five o'clock before I realize it, and I still have five more hours of work I could do."

"Ugh, I'm so sorry."

"Oh, don't worry about it. It won't be like this forever. Hey, before I forget, I wanted to ask you if you might want to go to The Alley tomorrow night."

"The Alley?" I look at him confused.

"Sorry, it's a theater downtown. I forget you didn't grow up here."

"You know, I would love to, but I already have plans. Well, not really plans. My boss wants me to work late, like really late, tomorrow. We have to finish up a room at a client's house before they get home on Friday."

"Okay. No big deal."

The look on his face does not say the same.

"I'm really sorry," I say, trying to defuse the tension between us. "Can we make plans for Friday?"

"No," he says and then pauses. I'm about to say something when he starts again. "I have meetings all day on Friday, and I'll probably have to be at the office late that night. Maybe we can get together on Saturday?"

"That sounds really great. I wish our schedules weren't so tight lately."

"Me, too."

During the rest of our time together, we talk about other random topics. We both avoid anything to do with work or his family. I'm not sure when I should bring it up again, but we have to make a decision about when we're going to tell June and the rest of his family that we're seeing each other. Maybe after we have another real date this weekend, I can bring up the topic again. Then, hopefully soon, I won't have to keep lying about my brother, and all the deceit can be over.

27
June

WEDNESDAY

Today is turning out to be a fairly good day. Mr. Hargrove sent me on some errands in town, so I haven't been in the office much. This is great because it means I haven't had to worry about running into Cohen. It's about three o'clock when I walk back into my office. My phone rings just as my tail end hits the chair.

"Hello?"

"June. Could you come into my office? There are a few things we need to discuss."

"Sure."

Mr. Hargrove wants to see me? I wonder what this could be about. He didn't beat around the bush, and he sounded sort of serious. I'm heading toward his office when I see Cohen exiting just a few feet in front of me. He looks my way and nods, but then he turns and walks the other direction.

I walk into my boss' doorway and lift my closed fist, ready to knock.

"June. Come in," Mr. Hargrove says before my knuckles have a chance to meet the wood. "No need to knock. Close the door behind you."

I do as I'm told, and then I take a seat in one of the plush chairs in front of his desk.

"I bet you're wondering why I asked you here," he says with no hint of happiness on his face.

"Yes, I am curious."

"Some things have come to my attention. I was wondering if you could shed some light on them for me."

"Um…" I pause, not knowing where this is going. "I hope I can do that."

"First of all, where do you get off stealing the affection of one of our top client representatives?"

No way! He knows? What did Cohen say? I'm going to lose my freaking job, and then I'm going to kill him. I can't believe he would do this to me! Is he punishing me for the things I said? All because I wouldn't let him just string me along while he goes about living his normal life back on the West Coast?

My inner rant is continuing to ramble as my eyes venture to catch a glimpse of my boss again. *He's smiling? Wait, is he laughing?*

"Oh, June, you are too easy." He laughs.

"What are you talking about?"

"It's all good news, June. I just like to mess with you."

I think I just had a heart attack. My breathing has to be

irregular.

"Cohen and the group at Bushing have commended your hard work and dedication. In fact, Cohen just brought in a letter stating what an asset you are to their project. In light of all your recent success with this client, I've decided to give you a raise. I know you haven't been here long, but I want you to know how much we appreciate your organic style of thinking."

I sit, dumbfounded and speechless. Mr. Hargrove is still grinning in my direction. I stare at him, wide-eyed. I think I'm having another heart attack. *A raise?*

"Earth to June. Did you hear me?"

"Oh, um. Ye-yes. I heard you. Thank you so much. That is amazing."

"Well, you deserve it. We'll talk about all the details later. Until then, get back to work, and keep impressing the crap out of everyone you meet." He hands me a single piece of paper with some typewritten words.

Walking back to my office in slow motion, I read the letter. My face feels flushed by the end of the esteemed commendation. People in the office probably think I've been fired. The truth is that I've never seen a letter more full of positive attributes. They're all about me, and the letter is personally signed by Cohen.

The remainder of the day passes without any further surprises. I work until the clock strikes five and then head home. I'm looking forward to a warm bath and some relaxing tunes. Quite the celebration, I know.

THURSDAY

Elevators stress me out and make me claustrophobic. I thought elevators were supposed to be sexy. *Doesn't every book worth anything have an amazing scene where something happens in an elevator? And by something, I mean, a really hot kiss at least.* Of course, nothing that exciting is occurring for me at this moment.

Instead, I'm on my way up to work, standing in the front corner of the elevator with middle-aged men on every side. I can feel Cohen's eyes staring a hole in the back of my head. When I walked into the elevator, I noticed him toward the back. Paying him as little attention as possible, I positioned myself in the opposite corner and stared at the junction of the two metal walls.

I know it might seem ridiculous, but after our dinner on Tuesday, I need to put up some serious walls. *I will not let this guy think he can walk in and out of my life as he pleases.* And if he thinks giving me a good review—which I deserve by the way—is going to soften me back up, then he's got another thing coming.

When the elevator dings, several people file out. I stay stationary in my corner, not chancing a glance at Cohen. I'm feeling proud of myself for standing my ground when I hear soft footsteps coming toward me. My entire body stiffens, but nothing happens. The elevator dings again as it opens on our floor.

Attempting to be casual, I say hello to a few people on the way to my office, but I never stop walking in the direction I'm heading. Constant movement and lack of direct contact with Cohen will be my saving grace today. I close the door to my office, sit in my desk chair, and take a deep breath.

I shake the mouse, so my computer comes to life. I check my email and notice immediately that we have a meeting scheduled with Cohen and a few other associates at eight fifteen. I had some practice with ignoring Cohen yesterday, so I should be in good shape.

After gathering some needed items, I walk into the conference room with a smile on my face. I'm hoping my face yells confidence and happiness although I'm quite sure it just reeks of falsehood. Cohen is sitting at the far side of the table, clicking away on his laptop. He doesn't even look up when Mr. Hargrove and I start speaking to one another. I make an effort to position my chair, so I'm not tempted to look his way during the meeting. Now, I would actually have to crane my head around like an owl to catch a glimpse of him.

The meeting is going well. We've set up goals to accomplish many important steps. Then, I hear a small dinging noise, and a chair moves quickly. I'm about to turn to see the cause of the commotion when Cohen comes into view. He is frantically pushing buttons on his phone. Never once taking his eyes off his phone, he crashes into a chair and stumbles for a few feet before catching himself with one hand against the glass-lined wall. He gives a quick glance around the room as if he's just realizing that he's still in a meeting. His eyes are filled with a disconcerting look.

"Excuse me. I-I…need to make a phone call," he says, not waiting for a response before leaving.

Silence fills the room until someone cuts through the tension, picking up the discussion where we left off. I can't make myself listen. My mind is going over what would cause Cohen to act so erratically. Even though I'm not wasting my time on a relationship with him right now, his demeanor does have me worried. *What was he not telling me the other night? Does it have anything to do with his sudden distress?*

# # #

FRIDAY

Cohen never returned to the conference room, and I haven't seen him the rest of the week. Once again, my email and text messages are free and clear of Cohen's name. I don't ask Mr. Hargrove any questions. *If Cohen wanted me to know what was going on, he would tell me, right?*

As I'm leaving work on Friday evening, I decide to text Caroline, letting her know that we're going out tonight. *If Cohen isn't calling, then I'm going out. Why should I stop enjoying myself because he came into my life?* I'm not going to wait around for him to come to his senses.

Going out tonight. Put on your party dress! —June

Are you sure? I don't know if that's a good idea. —Caroline

Since when do you not like to party? —June

I've had a lot on my mind, but if you're up for it, I guess I could join you. —Caroline

It seems like Caroline might need a little cheering up as well. Her moods have been so extreme. *What's up with her?*

# # #

A couple hours and many tweezed hairs later, Caroline and I are walking out the door on our way to Club Red. I've heard from several different people that this is the place to go for a good time. Not to mention, they have free cover for ladies along with some awesome drink specials.

As I slide into the driver's seat, I decide to ask Caroline more about the guy she's been dating. "So, what's been going on with you and the mystery man? Will I get to meet him soon?"

"Probably not," she says, looking out the passenger-side window.

"You aren't thinking of ditching him yet, are you?"

"No, we've both been busy with work. You know, real life gets busy."

"Yeah, but maybe you should call and see if he could join us tonight," I say she'll say yes.

"We already tried to make plans for tonight. He has some

late meetings or something."

Caroline doesn't seem too interested in talking during the rest of our ride to the club. After I park the car, we stand in line, waiting to show our IDs in exchange for an invisible ink stamp.

Once inside, I take in the surroundings. Lining each side of the dance floor are round black booths situated around tall black tables. In the middle of each table is a bright red ashtray, illuminated by a small spotlight. There are people everywhere—dancing, drinking, talking, kissing. *Yes, Caroline and I could get into some trouble tonight.*

"Let's get some drinks, and then see if we can grab a table!" I shout over the music.

Caroline simply nods, and we walk toward the bar.

28
Caroline

FRIDAY

I wasn't too keen on going out tonight. I haven't seen or talked with Liam much since I had lunch with him on Wednesday. We're supposed to go on a serious date this weekend, but we haven't been able to nail down a time that is good for both of us. I know he's busy with work, so instead of focusing on him, I remind myself to have fun.

The crowd is crazy in this place. I'm trying to walk in between people without touching anyone indecently. It's quite a challenge. When we reach the bar stools, a small area opens, giving me a full view of the bar as it stretches out to our right. That's when I see him sitting casually on the edge of his seat.

Liam is drinking a clear liquid that I'm sure burns as it goes down his throat. His eyes brighten as she approaches. A leggy blonde with boobs the size of Alaska puts her hand on his shoulder as she throws her head back, laughing. *Could she be more over-the-top?* I can't hear their conversation, but it's obvious they're having a good time together. *He must enjoy her type.* Just when I think I couldn't be any more disgusted, a redhead appears behind him, and he turns, smiling at her. *Wow, just wow.*

Tears sting my eyes, but I can't let June see my distaste. If she found out my feelings for Liam now, I'm sure it would earn me multiple I-told-you-so conversations over the next few months. Not to mention, I would have to explain why I lied to her for the past two weeks. I wrinkle my nose a few times to ward off the wetness that threatens to land on my cheeks.

"Are you going to sneeze?" June questions.

"No, I just need to go to the restroom. I think the smoke is getting to my eyes. I'll be right back." I get up from my seat and make my way through the crowd.

I walk the long way around to the small hallway, so there is no danger of Liam seeing me. I don't want him to feel guilty for being himself. I should have known that nothing good would come from dating June's brother.

I push open the restroom door, find the first open stall, and throw myself against the back of the swinging door. *I will not cry. I will not allow him to make me feel this way. I am a strong, capable woman who does not need a man to make her feel worthy and fulfilled.* As I am chanting these sentences over and over in my head, tears are streaming down my face. I don't believe a word of it. I am, in fact, crying, and I do feel sad.

In this moment, I am weak, and suddenly, I'm scared of my next interaction with Liam and with June. I take some tissues from my purse and dab my eyes. I'm dreading what I will see in the mirror once I get the courage to walk out of this stall. As I pull open the door, the dark painted brick walls of the restroom come into view, and June is standing against the sink counter, picking at her nails.

When she looks up, her eyes instantly cloud with worry. "What the crap, Caroline? Are you okay?"

"Yeah, I just have a lot going on with work and everything. Plus, I think I got something in my eye, and I can't get it out," I lie.

She sees right through me. "Like I believe that for a second. I knew something was up when you were talking about smoke out there. This place is nonsmoking. Spill it. What's wrong?"

"Listen, do you mind if I go home? I'll take a cab. You stay and have a good time."

"Are you sure? I really don't like seeing you this upset."

"I just need to go home and get some sleep. I think I'm running on fumes at this point."

"I'm going home with you, and we'll make some hot tea,'" she says, eyeing me with caution. "I just ran into my brother at the bar. Let me tell him that we're leaving. I'll meet you at the car."

"No, really, June. I just want to have a moment of alone time. Tell Liam hello for me," I say as the tears threaten again. "I'll see you later at the apartment, okay?"

June wraps me in a hug. "Hey, it's alright. Whatever's going on will work out in the end."

I wish I could tell her I don't think that's true, but I keep my mouth shut.

I walk to the street, hail a cab, and slide onto the worn upholstery. As I tell the driver where to go, I lean my head back on the seat, close my eyes, and take a deep breath. My heart is erupting in my chest, begging for the release of a good sob, but I try to hold off until I get home. This is a perfect example of why I never gave my heart away in college.

After a short time, the cab pulls into the parking lot of my apartment complex. I slip the proper fare to the driver and get out of the car. I walk slowly across the sidewalk to the set of glass doors. Suddenly, a hand grabs the handle and opens the door wide. My eyes trace across the crisp white long sleeve up to his shoulders before I meet his gaze. My face instantly turns hot, but it's not from blushing. I am furious. Liam is standing beside me, grinning. *What the hell is he so happy about?*

I walk through the door with purpose, trying to leave him behind.

"Caroline, wait. Are you okay? June said you were upset, so I came over to make sure you were alright."

"No, Liam, I am not alright. I started off my night by trying to enjoy some time with my best friend, and instead, I got to watch her drunk brother flirt with hot girls at the bar. So, I would definitely say that I am not alright!"

He looks stunned. *I hope his face gets frozen in that position, so no other girl ever wants to give him the time of day.* When he steps toward me, I take a step back.

"Don't even think about touching me."

"Caroline, you have to listen. I'm not drunk. I was only drinking water. Have you ever seen me drink alcohol? Those two girls are just friends from work. I know it sounds like an excuse, but it's true. We had some great meetings this week, and things wrapped up a little earlier than we thought today. We just wanted to go out to celebrate for a little bit."

I give his statements some thought, but my anger is too loud for me to hear any logical reasoning. "Meetings? Right. Is that what you call them? Do you refer to all your dates as meetings, so you don't have to feel guilty about leading girls on?"

Liam closes his eyes and takes a deep breath. When he looks at me again, he speaks with a calm voice. "I wish you could have heard our conversation on the way to the bar tonight. For heaven's sake, all I talked about was you. I left the girls at the bar, so they had to catch a cab home. I drove like a madman to come and see what was going on with you."

"You need to leave," I say coldly. Turning away from him, I'm determined to make it into the apartment this time.

"Please, Caroline, don't do this. I care about you. I know June probably told you to stay away from me, but just give me a chance to explain. Give me a chance to show you how much I care."

"No, I won't do it." I know I sound immature, but to be honest, I need the resolve of a stubborn child to stand my ground. "You will not make a fool of me, and just so you know, I haven't said anything to June. I'm the one deciding to stay away from you," I say as I close the door in his face.

Rushing into my apartment, I run to my room, slam the bedroom door behind me, and then collapse onto my bed. I wish I had never given him a first chance, and I have never understood the point of second chances. *If it wasn't worth it the first time, then how could it be worth the risk again?*

I hear the muffled sound of my phone ringing, but I know it must be him. I close my eyes and try to sob as quietly as possible, so there's no way he could hear my sadness if he's still at the front door.

A few minutes later, my phone rings again…and again…and again. I finally get up and fish it out from the bottom of my purse. Before I turn it off, I take a quick glance at my missed calls. They're all from my mom and dad. *Why would they call me so many times?* My sadness quickly turns to fear as I return my dad's call.

"Caroline…"

There is an emotion in my dad's voice that I can't place at first. Then, before I can get any words out, I hear my dad crying on the other end of the line.

"Dad?" I say, scared to ask any questions.

"Care, it's your brother."

He's not just crying. I can barely understand his words through the tears.

"Dad, you need to tell me what's going on before I get in my car and drive all the way to Washington tonight. Where's Mom?"

"She's with your brother. They're waiting for the doctors."

"Oh my god! Is Julie okay?"

"Julie is very sick, but we're also worried about your brother. On Wednesday, he got a call that Julie wasn't doing well, so he flew home immediately. This morning, the Franklins brought Julie to the hospital, and CJ was driving here to be with her. I'm sure he hasn't been sleeping well with everything that's been going on, so I'm guessing he was tired. He had an accident on the way to the hospital."

"Is he okay, Dad?"

"It isn't good, Caroline. Your mom thinks you should come home."

I can feel the tears welling up in my eyes again. "Are you serious? Is he going to die?"

"We don't know."

The line is silent, except for my dad's uneven breaths. I can tell he's about to lose it again.

"Oh my God. I'll book a flight tonight. I'll send you my itinerary soon. Please tell Mom that I love her. I'll be there with you as soon as I can. I love you."

"We love you, too, Care. We'll talk to you soon. Be careful."

I hang up the phone and clutch it to my chest. My tears have dried, but I know they will come flooding back soon.

When I hear a knock on the front door, I walk over to let June in. *She must have lost her key again.* I unlock the door, open it slightly, and immediately turn, walking in the other direction, so June can't see my tear-streaked face.

"Caroline."

I stop abruptly. *Why is he still here?* I thought I made my opinion of him pretty clear. Tears prick my eyes again as I turn to tell him to leave, but instead, I take in his lean frame. His expression is filled with concern and worry. In one motion, I throw myself into his arms, sobbing uncontrollably. I remind myself that just a few hours ago, he mattered to me.

"I'm so sorry," he whispers lightly into my hair, his hand running over the back of my head.

"My brother," is all that comes out from between my lips.

Liam gently pushes me back, so he can examine me at arm's length. "What about your brother?" he asks, his brows furrowed with confusion.

"He's dying."

His face then fills with another emotion—pity.

We walk to the couch, and he sits, guiding me to lay my head in his lap. He pulls a blanket over me as I sob, soaking his khaki pants with my tears. Caressing my hair, he whispers what small pieces of reassurance he can find for a situation he knows little about.

I'm not only crying for myself. I am crying for my parents, for Julie, and for her parents. I am crying for June and for the way she will respond when I have to reveal everything about my brother. I dread telling her that the guy she has been falling for is now lying in a hospital bed.

As my thoughts run in circles, my eyes begin to feel heavy from crying until everything fades to an uneasy shade of gray.

29
June

FRIDAY

Caroline is acting so weird. I have only seen her cry a handful of times. Most of them had to do with snags in designer clothes or mean professors. This time, her crying was different though. It was heartbreaking. I wish I could do something for her, but she has been pushing me away more and more. *Maybe she's homesick.* I should call her mom and see if her parents could come for a visit. I resolve to find a solution after I get home this evening, but for now, I'll spend a little time hanging out with my brother.

"Hey, Liam."

"June, where is Caroline?" he asks, looking past me.

"On her way home." Liam turns his attention back to me. "Apparently, she has had a rough week at work. I haven't seen her this upset in a long time. I think something else might be bothering her, but I just can't put my finger on what it could be."

"She was upset? Did she mention what she was upset about?"

"I just told you that she said it had to do with work. Why?"

"No reason. Listen, I need to get going. I have a lot on my schedule tomorrow, and I should get home. Have a good time, sis."

With that and a pat on my back, he heads toward the door with long strides.

I stay and dance for a little bit, but I'm not enjoying myself. I don't know anyone here, and my mind keeps drifting back to Cohen. *Why can't he just freaking call me?* If he wasn't interested in me, then he should have just left me alone when he came back to town. And if he is interested, he has a really funny way of showing it. Then, there was the way he acted at the meeting earlier this week. *Maybe this guy has way too much baggage for me.* After about thirty minutes of upbeat music and depressing inner dialogue, I decide to head home and see if Caroline is ready to talk a little bit more.

The drive home is ridiculous. Traffic is horrible, and I'm left alone with my thoughts. Instead of dwelling on Cohen again, I decide to turn up some music, roll my windows down, and sing at the top of my lungs. After getting a few laughs from other drivers, I decide it's best to dial back my singing.

When I finally pull into my assigned parking spot, I notice that someone has parked in our visitor spot. It looks like my brother's car, but I know it couldn't be him. He's never said anything about knowing anyone in our apartment complex. *Some idiot must have parked in the wrong spot. I swear that people have no respect for rules.*

When I get to the door, I slip my key in the lock, but as I turn it, I realize it's already unlocked. *That's strange.* Caroline is normally a stickler about safety. Ever since some pervert tried to crawl in her window when we were in college, she has always made sure that all windows and doors are locked. When we moved in, she even wanted to put sensors on all the entry points.

When I step into the living room, my mouth almost hits the floor as I take in the view of my brother with Caroline in his lap. She appears to be asleep, and he brings a finger up to his lips, signaling for me to be quiet. I watch as he picks Caroline up, cradling her in his arms. He carries her down the hallway into her room.

My feet are stuck to the floor as I try and process the scene I just witnessed. A minute or two later, the light in her room is turned off. My brother closes Caroline's bedroom door and walks back through the hallway toward me.

"What the hell are you doing here?" I whisper.

He looks down. "Listen, don't get upset. We should have told you before, but we agreed to wait a little while before we let people know."

"What are you talking about? You and Caroline are not…" I trail off, realizing that the guy from work Caroline has been dating is actually my brother. "Liam, what did you do? Did you hurt her? I swear to you, Liam, if you hurt her, I will kill you."

"I didn't mean to. She saw me with my coworkers at the bar tonight, and she thought that I was dating one or both of them. She was crying in the restroom because of me. When you told me she was upset, I had to come and see why, but when I got here, she wouldn't even listen to me," he says, his face full of sadness.

"Then, why are you here? I've never seen her in such a deep sleep. Did you drug her or something?"

"God, June! No, I didn't drug her. I'm your brother. Remember me? You act like you don't know me, like I'm some guy off the street. I was sitting outside the door, waiting for you to get home, so I could explain everything to you and see if you would talk to her for me. Then, I thought I heard her crying, so I knocked on the door to check on her. She opened it and then turned around before seeing who it was. When she let me in, she must have thought it was you. After she realized it was me, she started crying again and said something about her brother dying. Do you know anything about that?"

"What did she say? Oh my god. Do you know what happened?"

"All she said was, 'He's dying.' I don't know anything else, but I think she needs to go home. When she wakes up, can you let her know that I'll get her a ticket to leave early in the afternoon tomorrow?"

"Sure. See if you can get me a ticket, too."

"Alright. I'm going to head out. I'll talk to you both tomorrow."

"Okay. Liam?"

"Yeah?"

"Do you really like her? I mean, are you and Caroline serious?"

Liam's face transforms into a grin I don't think I've ever seen before. It's a soft smile and sincere in every way.

"I hope so. She's perfect, June. She broke my heart when she told me to go away tonight. I was trying to find the best time to tell you about us, but I was scared you would convince her that I wasn't worth it."

I smile up at him. "I don't think you understand my relationship with Caroline. She rarely listens to me, especially when it comes to men. Honestly, I would have been just as concerned that she'd drop you on your ass as I would about you leaving her high and dry. Maybe the two of you are meant to be.

"Thanks, June Bug. Good night."

After my brother leaves, I lock the door, get ready for bed, and sink down against my headboard. *What have I been missing over the past week?* I was so caught up in my time with Cohen that I didn't even notice my best friend was dating my own brother. It would explain how easily they seemed to get along at dinner last weekend.

When did Caroline find out that her brother is dying? Have I really been that horrible of a friend? Instead of worrying about myself, I decide to place all my focus on my best friend over the next few days. She's going to need someone to help her through this. I'll have to find a way to forget about Cohen.

30
COHEN

SUNDAY

When I was ten years old, I got a trampoline. My first thought wasn't about how it would impact my life. I thought about the special tricks I could learn, like bouncing my friends higher than any sane adult would allow. The moment I ripped through that wrapping paper, I was ecstatic as I stared at the picture of three happy kids jumping with their limbs flailing through the air. The box was gigantic, but I found a way to hug that box with more emotion than any other hug I had ever given.

Of course, my dad had to put it together right away. We sat in the backyard with metal pieces and tools surrounding us. The large round fabric was spread out, obscuring the grass from the sun.

Two weeks later, when I was happily jumping up and

down, the unimaginable happened. One moment, I was free as a bird, flying through the air, and then falling, bending the fabric toward the ground. As I took my next flight, I could have never predicted what occurred next. When my feet left the trampoline, I raised my hands out from my sides with a huge grin across my face. While my body was in the air, I glanced toward the front of the empty house next door, and suddenly, my world changed.

A petite young girl with blonde hair flowing around her shoulders slid off the seat of a moving van. She was smiling and laughing as she ran up the sidewalk. My body descended, but my heart was still floating above. Then, it came crashing down moments after my eyes lost sight of her.

My young mind had no words for the emotion that planted its seed that day. I should have known then that I would fall in love with Julie Franklin. Instead, with everything in my being, I fought against loving her for the next three years.

# # #

On my thirteenth birthday, I decided to have a party at my house rather than a lame bowling or miniature golf get-together. My dad, being a friendly guy, decided to invite Julie since she lived next door.

"Dad, seriously? I don't want her to come."

"Could you try and be a little friendlier, son? Mr. Franklin has been really helpful to me on several occasions. It wouldn't hurt you to have his daughter come over and enjoy some cake."

"She probably won't know anyone here. We don't have the

same friends."

"She's a nice girl, and her parents are always kind. It's only for one day."

"It's supposed to be my day."

"I know, son, and having Julie here won't take away from that."

As he walked away, I knew I had no further say in the matter.

Being around Julie made me nervous. It felt the same as when a teacher would call on me in class, and I wouldn't know the answer to the question. I didn't like that feeling. I had no clue what I would say to Julie or if I could even look at her, so I decided that I would avoid her at all costs. When my friends started to arrive, I tried to forget about Julie.

My party went off without a hitch, and Julie didn't show up. *Thank God!* It was basically like any other day at my house, except we had cake, presents, and a few extra people.

After the party, I was lying on my trampoline, throwing a baseball in the air. When I felt the trampoline give on my left side, I glanced over through pieces of my long hair, and I saw Julie smiling shyly at me. I sat up quickly as she slid an unwrapped gift box toward me.

"Hey," is all she said.

"Hey." I nodded.

A minute or two went by as we awkwardly looked at each other. It was just an awkward stare.

"Happy birthday," she finally said.

"Uh, thanks."

"I'm sorry I couldn't make it to your party."

"That's okay."

"Well, open it." She motioned to the box.

"Oh yeah. Okay."

I opened the box and found a cupcake decorated to look like a baseball.

"I made it for you." She looked down at her hands fidgeting in her lap.

"Wow. Thanks, Julie." Without thinking, I placed my hand over hers, not knowing what had possessed me to touch her.

"Do you want to come in for dinner? My dad's ordering pizza since it's my birthday."

Julie came in for dinner that day and then practically every day after.

A few weeks later, Julie's parents invited my dad and me over for dinner. They were beginning to miss having her at home.

# # #

When I turned sixteen, I was sure Julie was *it* for me. I never left her side, and she was always there for me. We had the picture-perfect high school sweetheart story.

On graduation day, I proposed to Julie with a simple gold band. It wasn't much since I bought it with the money I had saved from my part-time job. Our parents thought we were too young to get married, but we wouldn't listen to anyone. We chose colleges in the same town and knew that we could handle leaving home as long as we had each other.

We got married two weeks before starting college in Seattle, which was eleven hours away from our families. When we informed our parents that we would be moving, they all decided to up and move with us. Although it might seem very strange, Julie was an only child, so her parents couldn't stand the thought of being that far away from her. My dad didn't mind moving back, especially since it meant he would get to see more of Caroline. Everything just worked out. Her parents and my dad were even able to find homes just down the street from one another.

Julie went to culinary school. After just two years, she opened a bakery shop, specializing in cupcakes. Her mom helped her out in the shop a few days a week, and both my parents were frequent customers. Julie loved running her own shop, and she was passionate about making baked goods to complete someone's special occasion. No day was complete unless I found her covered in flour.

College took me an extra year because my dreams kept changing, but Julie never complained. She was always supportive of my dreams. Even when I had to request extra student loans, she just joked about how a few extra cupcakes could pay the bill. After I graduated and attained my dream job, we started to make plans for a family.

Then, things changed. Everything was destroyed. I never thought my feelings for Julie could be swayed. Of course, if our path hadn't veered, I would still be in love with her, still longing for the life we planned together.

# # #

Some days, the guilt overwhelms me. As I'm lying in this dark hospital room, staring up at the ceiling tiles while listening to the beeping sounds from the medical equipment, I wonder what I will say to Julie.

My head is killing me, and my back is aching. I could really use some pain medication, but I don't dare move a muscle because I don't want to disturb my mother sleeping in the uncomfortable recliner next to my bed. She won't leave my side, and the least I can do is let her get some sleep.

When I am able to leave this room, I have to go find Julie. I don't know what I'll say, but I have to tell her that I've met someone and that I want a new life.

31
Caroline

SATURDAY

The pain in my head feels like a thousand little needles are pricking against the outer edge of my brain. I roll onto my side and reach for the drawer of my nightstand where I keep an extra bottle of Tylenol handy for mornings like this. Feeling constrained in my clothing, I realize that I'm still wearing my outfit from the night before.

Memories come flooding back. *Holy crap.* My brother could be dying. I feel my breath being stolen from my lungs. I toss the painkillers onto my bed, and feeling sicker than any hangover I can remember, I quickly run across the hallway to the bathroom. The kinds of drugs needed to eliminate my pain are illegal and highly addictive, but I would suffer the consequences just to feel anything other than what I am right now.

"Caroline?" June's voice is soft and accompanied by an

even softer knock on the bathroom door.

I rest my head against the wall, keeping the toilet bowl within reach. I close my eyes and try to imagine a restful place. My attempt to find peace is interrupted by another knock, and although my arms don't feel like part of my body, I convince one of them to unlock the door. After I drop my arm back to my side, I lie, unmoving, against the cold tiled floor.

"Oh, Caroline, Liam told me your brother is hurt. He said he would get you a ticket to fly out this afternoon. I can help you pack or call your parents or..." She trails off as she turns to me with a warm washcloth in her hand while tears are streaming down her face. "I'll do whatever you need, Care."

If she only knew everything, she would realize that I don't deserve her tears right now. *How can I tell her now?* After last night, she must know something is going on between Liam and me. *How can I tell her that my brother was about to break her heart? How can I tell her that the man she was falling for is now lying in a hospital bed, dying?*

The warm moisture of the washcloth steadies my thoughts. *I won't tell her anything.* I have to leave and be with my family. I have to forget that any of this is happening. I can't worry about Liam. I can't think about my best friend. I have to think about my parents and how they might be losing a son. I have to deal with the fact that my brother might be gone soon.

"I need to call my mom," I say without looking at June.

"Okay, I'm going to shower and start packing. Let me know what you need."

I know I should ask her where she's going, but I just don't

care.

I call my mom, who is unable to talk without sobbing, so I end up talking with my dad.

"Hey, Dad. How's CJ?"

"He's stable for now, but I think you should still come home. Did you get a flight?"

"Yeah, sorry I didn't call last night. I'll be leaving this afternoon. June is taking me to the airport."

"Alright, Care. Be careful and, we'll see you soon."

"Thanks, Dad. Love you," I say before hanging up the phone.

Trying to pack, I walk around my room in a daze, remembering my brother. I know I shouldn't be thinking of him as if he's already gone. *But what if he is?*

My brother was...scratch that...he *is* the kindest person. At least, I thought he was before this whole thing with June came up. He is my big brother, my biggest cheerleader, and my number one encourager. I don't know if I'd be able to get through life without him.

He married his high school sweetheart. They fell in love, began their careers, and were living the happily-ever-after they both deserved. I can still hear him chastising me for dating so many guys when I was in high school.

"Caroline, don't you want the feeling of missing someone when they're not around?"

"Why would I want to miss someone when I could just enjoy the next person in line?" I answered.

"One day, you'll begin to miss someone without realizing it.

When that day comes, I want you to call me and tell me all about this magical boy who somehow made you fall in love."

I will never forget his smile as he talked about falling in love. For him, it was a fairy tale that would never end—until, of course, it did end.

June's voice breaks into my thoughts. "Caroline, we need to leave in about thirty minutes. Liam emailed me the itinerary. Are you about ready to go?"

"I'm ready."

June takes my luggage to her car as I spend a few minutes pulling up my hair and washing my face.

# # #

The ride to the airport is a vague blur. After June parks the car, she gets out and begins to pull the luggage out of her trunk. My door opens, and I look up into Liam's caring eyes. He pulls me to my feet and surrounds me in the warmth of his arms. He doesn't ask if I'm okay, and he doesn't tell me that everything is going to be alright. He just holds me for a moment. I glance to the ground behind him and see a dark green duffel bag sitting near his feet.

"Is that yours?" I ask.

"Yes. We're going with you."

"We?" I look at him, puzzled.

"Yes, you don't need to do this alone," June says from behind me.

"No, no, no! You have lives that need to be attended to

here. You can't just drop everything and take off to Seattle." I am starting to panic inside. *June cannot get on that plane. She can't find out the truth this way. And Liam? Didn't I just try to kick Liam out of my life last night?* He can't think this will erase what I was feeling before my life came tumbling down around me.

"You don't have a choice. I've already bought our tickets, and our luggage is packed. We're here for you," Liam says, holding my hand and leaning down to pick up his duffel bag with his free hand.

I have no energy to fight this battle. Maybe this is the way things were meant to happen. By the end of this trip, it's possible that I might lose my brother, June could hate me, and Liam may realize that settling down with me comes with a lot of baggage. This flight marks the beginning of the end of my life, and there's no need to delay the inevitable.

32
June

SATURDAY

We walk into the airport together. While Liam is handling Caroline's luggage, I'm barely handling my emotions. This morning, I witnessed my take-charge best friend crumble into despair. I have no clue what has happened to her brother, and at this point, I don't think she could manage answering any questions. Her flawless face is surprisingly emotionless while my brother is leading her through the motions of checking in and going through security.

Although it is one of the most depressing things I have witnessed in my life, I am shocked at my brother's caring nature with her. I mean, it's not like he isn't a nice person. He just normally ditches girls the minute anything serious happens. I would say a possibly dying brother, requiring a last-minute flight to Seattle, counts as serious. Instead of running away, he has stayed by her side.

When I told him she wasn't able to talk on the phone this morning, he wanted me to make sure Caroline knew he was taking care of all the travel plans, so she wouldn't worry. As I watch him guiding her, it warms my heart. Although I know I would be here for her even if he weren't, I'm glad that she has someone strong to lean on.

My mind wanders to the last time I was in an airport security line. Cohen seemed like a gentleman. I just don't understand what went wrong. It's been seventy-two hours since I have seen or talked with him. This time, he left without a note or any kind of message.

Why hasn't he called me or just sent a simple text? I feel insensitive thinking about Cohen right now, but at least it keeps me from crying every time I look at Caroline's face. In my head, I replay all the words he said to me when he poured out his feelings at dinner. I think about his soft kisses against my lips as they made me feel more emotion than I thought possible. Then, I remember him confessing that there are parts of his life he isn't willing to share with me. *Why would he tell me he's interested in getting to know me and then fall off the face of the planet?* Whatever he's hiding, it must be a secret worth keeping. Sometime this week, when I get the courage, I'll have to pick up the phone and call him out on his less than gentlemanly behavior.

After we make it through security without any trouble, Caroline, Liam, and I sit on a long blue bench to put our shoes back on. Caroline wore a pair of slip-on flats, so she's done before Liam and I can tie our tennis shoes.

"I need to go to the restroom," she states, her voice flat.

"Alright, Care. Do you want me to go with you?" I ask.

"No, thanks."

Liam and I are left sitting on the bench as people rush back and forth past us. *It's funny how life around you can seem to move so quickly while you feel stuck in the moment.* When I glance over at Liam, I see a rare emotion. He looks overwhelmed. He's rubbing his forehead with his thumb and middle finger, pulling inward from his temples to the middle of his forehead and back.

"Liam, why are you going to Seattle?" I ask, curious about his intentions.

"I don't know." He stands, staring down at his feet, and he kicks the corner of the bench. "I guess I didn't want to her to go away and decide that whatever drama we had yesterday was too much to deal with. I want to be there for her."

"So, you're saying that you like her?" I laugh and punch Liam in the leg.

"Yeah, yeah. Shut your hole. I don't know why you didn't think about introducing us earlier." He gives me his goofiest smile.

"You should be glad I waited to let you two meet. Two years ago, you would have broken her heart and missed out on the love of your life."

"Or I would have settled down sooner."

"Did you just admit that Caroline is the love of your life?"

"And what if I did?" he asks confidently.

"I'm going to go check on Caroline." *This conversation is getting crazy. Now, my brother is in love with my best friend?*

I walk into the restroom and find Caroline leaning over the sink.

"Hey, are you doing okay?" I ask, laying my hand on her shoulder.

She looks up with tear stains on her cheeks. "I don't know, June. God, I don't know." She sobs, folding herself into me.

"Oh, Care, I don't know what's going on, but we're here for you."

"June, I need to tell you something. I just can't have you mad at me when we get there."

"Don't worry about any of that now. If you and Liam want to be together, then I say go for it. I think it's great. Really, I do."

"No, it's more than that."

"Well, whatever it is, it can wait. All that matters is getting you to Seattle, so you can see your brother."

Caroline pulls away, wets a paper towel, and cleans up her makeup. I'm not sure what's going on, but I don't want her to worry about me.

# # #

We board the plane. Caroline sits in the window seat, Liam slides in beside her, and I take the aisle seat. Not only is the aisle seat normally my least favorite, it also gives me yet another reminder of the flight with Cohen.

Soon, we are taking off, and then we're in the air. I close my eyes, trying to fall asleep, as I attempt to keep my mind off of the fact that I'm thousands of miles in the air. Unfortunately, once I'm asleep, my dreams bring memories of Cohen. I wake up with about thirty minutes left in the flight. I am starving, and I missed the in-flight meal.

When I look toward the window, Caroline looks sad, Liam looks worried, and I feel helpless. Thankfully, we're almost there.

33
Caroline

SATURDAY

We step off the plane into the familiar hustle of the Sea-Tac Airport. Finding our way through the crowds to the baggage claim is a chore by itself. People are everywhere—pulling along their luggage with their children, standing in the middle of the walkways as they talk on their cell phones, and making a beeline for the restrooms.

I follow closely behind Liam. Ever since last night, the world around me has faded to a harsh blur. The faces of the people around me don't quite come into focus. I'm staring at Liam's hand, his fingers entangled with mine, as I'm wondering why he's here. *Why does he care?* I didn't ask him to come with me. In fact, I was pretty sure he would run the other direction after I yelled at him last night.

June and Liam got a little sleep on the plane, but there was no way I could find rest. Instead, I thought back to my fight with Liam last night, and I decided he was probably telling the truth. After all, I've never seen him take a drink of alcohol. I was upset because he was out at a bar when he said he was busy, but he could be just as upset with me since I was out at a bar as well. *I should probably drop it.* After all, our disagreement will likely pale in comparison to the issues that will crop up while we're here in Washington.

As we reach the baggage claim area, Liam motions to the chairs. "Sit down, and we'll wait for the luggage." I place my purse in the seat beside me and watch as he walks toward the carousel with June.

I take out my phone and send a quick message to my mom, letting her know we made it. It isn't long before my phone rings. I don't feel like talking, but I pick up anyway.

"Hey, Mom."

"Caroline, I am so glad you made it safely. June is with you, right?"

"Yes, and Liam."

"Liam?"

"Her brother came, too."

"Oh...well, okay."

"I'll explain later, Mom. Just tell me, do we need to come straight to the hospital?"

"You should go home first and drop off your things. Let June and Liam settle in, and then you can bring over John's car."

"How is he doing?" I'm careful not to say my brother's name in case June is within earshot.

"He's doing better, but he's pretty banged up. The doctor thinks he's out of the woods now, but he's being watched closely in the ICU."

"Alright. I'll call you when we leave the house."

When we hang up, my heart feels a little lighter, knowing that my brother will probably be okay. I won't have complete relief though until I see him myself. If those television shows about crazy medical dramas have taught me anything, it's that doctors try to give you the best outlook until the time comes when they have to tell the truth. For all I know, my mom could be saying he's fine when he might actually be unconscious with tubes coming out of every part of his body.

As I watch Liam and June load our luggage onto a big cart, I realize how lame I'm being. I stand as they walk toward me. I step to the back of the cart and take hold of the shiny bar. June raises her eyebrows to Liam as if I'm not standing right next to them. We're already close to the exit, but at least it will look like I'm trying to help. As we near the exit doors, Liam places his hand on the cart, stopping us in front of a rental car counter.

"We can just take a cab to the house and then use my stepdad's car," I say, trying to save him a little money. I never even thought about asking him how much the airline tickets cost.

"It's okay. The company discount I get is pretty awesome."

"Yeah, it's called 'I get tickets and car rentals for free.'" June rolls her eyes.

"Free?"

"Well, not quite free, but it doesn't cost very much. Did

you forget I work for the airlines? The flights weren't too full, so we flew standby, and I can use some points I have for a rental car. No worries."

"Okay, but you should let me pay you back."

"Don't worry about it. It really isn't a big deal," he says, giving me a small hug before turning to talk to the rental car attendant.

# # #

The drive to the house is quiet. The car came with GPS, so I don't have to give Liam directions. I'm sure June and Liam have no clue what to say. I should tell them that my brother is doing okay, but I don't feel like talking right now. I'm too busy trying to figure out what I'm going to tell my parents when they ask why Liam came with us.

Liam and I haven't had the chance to talk about what happened last night, and with June here, I'm not sure when we'll have any time alone. It should be the last thing on my mind, but I know my parents will ask. Maybe I'll just tell them he tagged along to see some sights in Seattle. I know they won't buy it, but it'll give me some time to talk with him before I tell them we're dating.

Next on my list of concerns is June finding out about my brother. I picture the decor of each room in our house. Thankfully, my mom isn't one of those people who has a picture of each member of the family from various significant life events in every room. She has photo albums, but I can't think of any framed pictures in the main areas.

The only places I'll have to keep June away from are my mom's office and bedroom since she keeps a few family pictures in those rooms. That shouldn't be a problem though because my mom normally keeps her office locked, and there's no reason for June to go into my mom's bedroom.

There might be a few pictures in the basement, too. When my brother would come to visit, he would always claim the basement as his man cave. Last time I checked, it still held some of Cohen's memorabilia and photos. I'll have Liam stay on the couch in the basement, and when I show him the way, maybe I can move around a few pictures.

My fingers begin to feel sore, and I realize I've been running the tips of them over and over again across the black material of the car door. I clasp my hands together and set them in my lap, trying to keep myself from fidgeting constantly.

Then, it hits me. *What about Julie?* I didn't even ask my mom about Julie. I couldn't be more insensitive. I wonder if she's going to be okay. I know her parents must be sad and worried. If Cohen is awake, I can't imagine how he must feel. I hope he's been able to see her. I just need to get to the hospital, so I can get the whole story.

As we pull into the driveway, I close my eyes and take a deep breath. I feel Liam's hand rest on my thigh, and I'm surprised when his touch calms me. Opening my eyes, I meet his gaze and give him a half smile. It's all I can give right now.

We all get out of the car. Liam stretches his arms over his head, and for the first time, I catch a glimpse of his perfectly sculpted abs. When he sees me staring, he gives me a goofy grin, which sends me into a fit of laughter. June comes around the back of the car with her luggage in tow. After we all make our way into the house, I take them on a quick tour of the main level.

"June, the guest room is over here."

"Alright, I'm going to go change clothes real quick," June states, taking her luggage to the guest room.

"Liam, if you don't mind the couch, you can stay in the basement down there," I say pointing to the stairs.

"I don't want to impose on your parents. Maybe I should just get a hotel room," Liam states with a questioning glance.

"My mom would never have that. You have to stay here."

"You won't hear me argue with that. I'd rather be close to you."

When he turns toward the stairs leading to the basement, I stare after him. I can feel the empty space he left behind, and a slight ache fills me. *I have got to put these emotions on hold and take care of business.*

We discard our belongings in our respective rooms and then meet back in the kitchen. It's getting late, so we decide to head to the hospital before visiting hours are over.

# # #

When we arrive at the hospital, I purposely place June in between Liam and me. I'm dreading what I might find when I see my brother, and I don't feel up to answering questions about my new relationship just yet.

The halls of the hospital are long. Staring down the last distance to the ICU, my eyes adjust to the bright fluorescent lights, white ceiling tiles, white vinyl floor, and white walls. I see my dad sitting in a chair outside the waiting room with his head in his hands. I have to stop myself from running to him like a lost child who is seeing her parent for the first time in months. It's a struggle to keep my steps steady and measured as I try to act normal. As we get closer, my dad lifts his head, and I can see his tired eyes and his sad face. When he recognizes us, his mouth turns up into a small smile.

"Care! Oh, I am so glad to see you. June, thank you for coming." He hugs us both. "You must be Liam. Vivian told me you were coming also. It's nice to meet you."

Dad and Liam shake hands. For a moment, I forget about everything around us, and I'm proud to see them together. I feel like they would get along, like they might understand each other. *Maybe I will have a chance at love.*

"Dad, can I see him?"

"Sure, the ICU staff is only letting family in, so you two will have to stay here. I'm sorry," he says to June and Liam.

"That's alright. We'll just sit tight," June says, giving me a quick hug.

I follow my dad to a phone on the wall. He picks it up and announces his name and then my brother's name. I glance back quickly to see that June has already entered the waiting room, so she's out of earshot. *Thank God.* A couple seconds later, the large double doors swing open, and we walk side by side into the ICU. Nurses are walking back and forth between patient rooms and the main nurses' station. I can hear a soft hum and several different patterns of beeping from the machines. I don't know how patients get any rest in here.

As we walk through the hallway, I can see visitors gathered in patient rooms. I catch sight of one woman, probably in her fifties, crying into her hands without a sound, and I wonder what kind of news she might have gotten. It saddens me to think that many of the patients in this unit have family members who are full of worry.

Dad stops in front of two large sliding glass doors, and my mom is leaning against the hard metal of the door frame with her eyes shut. The curtains are closed, blocking the view of the inside of the room. A large number 8 is on the door.

"They were finishing some dressing changes," Dad informs me.

Hearing his voice, my mom opens her eyes. When she catapults herself into my arms, I have to brace myself to keep standing upright.

"Hey, Mom. Good to see you, too."

The curtain flies open, and a nurse opens the door. "You can go in. I just gave him some pain medicine, so he should be feeling better soon."

"Thank you," my dad replies in a kind tone.

I reach my hand around the curtain and pull it back a little more. My brother is sitting up in bed. *He looks...good.* I can only see one tube that is lying across his upper lip with small pieces going into each nostril. It's connected to a gadget on the wall and appears to be providing oxygen. He's wearing a loose hospital gown, and a blanket is covering his lower body. *Thank God. He's okay.*

As I walk past the curtain, he opens his eyes and a huge smile erupts on his face.

34
June

SATURDAY

I've never dealt with death. I've never even stepped foot in a hospital. When the revolving doors of the main entrance came into view, I felt sick at my stomach. I know that good things happen here and people do get better, but all I ever see when I look at a hospital is death.

I keep praying this won't be true for Caroline's brother. She still hasn't said anything about what happened to him. I don't know if he has a disease or if maybe he was involved in an accident. *Hell, I don't know that much about him.* Maybe he's a drug addict and overdosed. I keep thinking I should ask, but I can't come up with a polite way of saying, "Hey, Caroline. So, what's your brother dying from?"

As Caroline and her dad walk through the ICU doors, Liam and I walk into the waiting area. It's a strange space. All four sides are glass walls. Two sides meet with other waiting areas. Each area is about half full of people. In one waiting area, pallets of blankets are on the floor, and a coffee pot is sitting on a counter. I think about how tough it would be to have to spend nights in the hospital waiting room while wondering if a loved one would make it through the night or even through the next hour. My heart is heavy for my friend and for all these people.

"June, are you doing okay? I know you hate hospitals," Liam says, pulling me into a hug.

"I'm okay. I'm just sad, and I want to know what's going on."

"Yeah. Me, too. Caroline has been really quiet, and from what I know of her, that's not normal."

"No, it's not normal at all. I'm guessing she's just scared. I hope seeing her brother will help."

"Maybe when she's done, we can go grab some food. I don't think any of us ate much on the plane."

"That sounds amazing. I didn't want to say anything until she got to check on him, but I am starving."

♯ ♯ ♯

We sit in the waiting room for another thirty minutes before Caroline and her mom come out, smiling. *That's a good sign.*

"Hey, guys. June, you've met my mom, Vivian. Mom, this is Liam, June's brother."

"Good to see you, June, and it's nice to meet you, Liam." Smiling, she places her arm around my waist and kisses me on the cheek. "Thank you for coming to be with my baby. She has good friends."

"So, how is he doing?" I hope I'm not making a mistake by bringing it up, but I just can't stand not knowing anymore.

"He is doing great. They said that he hit his head pretty hard, but he shouldn't have any permanent damage. He has some bumps and bruises, but he should be out of the ICU tomorrow, and then he can go visit Julie. She is down on the fifth floor, and I know her parents are anxious for them to see each other."

"That is so great," I say.

"Yes, it is. Listen, I know you kids must be hungry. You should get out of here before you get desperate enough to eat in the hospital cafeteria. John will be here soon. He's going to stay here with me tonight. Your dad will be heading home soon."

"Alright, Mom. Call if you need anything or if something changes even if it's in the middle of the night," Caroline says.

"I will. I love you. I am so glad you're here."

Caroline gets one last hug from her mom, and then we head out to find some food.

# # #

At Caroline's request, we pull through a fast food restaurant and then head home. I know I'm tired, so she must be really pushing it to keep her eyes open at this point. Even though we got good news today, I'm still feeling a little down from our visit to the hospital.

We sit on stools around her kitchen island and eat our food. The first few minutes are awkward. I look at Liam. Liam looks at me. Liam looks at Caroline. Caroline looks at me. Then, I can't help it. I giggle once and look at Caroline, grinning. Caroline tries not to smile without success, and then she starts howling with laughter. Of course, Liam, being a man, has no clue what's going on.

"What's wrong with you two?" Liam asks.

"Don't you ever have those moments when things get so chaotic you have to laugh?" Caroline asks, still chuckling.

"No, I don't, but whatever works for you," he says, throwing a french fry at her face.

This one small act incites a thirty-minute food fight with every piece of food we can get our hands on. At one point, I feel like I'm sliding into home base as I slip on some mustard, spin past the kitchen island, and land on the floor. When it's all over, we are covered from head to toe in disgusting amounts of food as we sit side by side with our backs against the refrigerator.

"Well, now that we've gotten that off our chests, maybe we should get some sleep before we all decide to go toilet paper the neighbor's house," Caroline says, out of breath.

"Probably a good plan. I call dibs on the shower," I say.

Caroline gathers a towel and other items, so I can take a shower. I start the water, get undressed, and throw my dirty clothes into a plastic bag. Giggling at the absurdity of what we just did, I step into the shower and let the water soak my body.

The laughter of tonight brings back thoughts of my time

with Cohen. I don't understand why I can't stop thinking about him. I start to consider that maybe I should text him and just say something, anything, to try and get him off my mind.

I dry off, throw on some pajamas, and pick up my phone. Sitting on the floor in the bathroom, I contemplate what kind of message I should send. I want to be rude and say something like, "Thanks for the fun time. Don't ever call me again," but instead, I settle on a generic message.

Haven't heard from you since you left. Wondering how you are. —June

Now, if he doesn't respond to that, I'll delete him from my phone. It's as simple as that.

35
Caroline

SATURDAY

Visiting with my brother was a huge relief, but to be honest, standing in this pile of ketchup, flour, and who knows what else is probably one of the best feelings I have had in the past twenty-four hours.

"I guess we should wait in here until June's done in the shower. I wouldn't want to track this stuff all through your house," Liam says, taking off his shirt.

I walk to the sink to wash my face and hands. "That's a good idea."

Liam leans against the counter next to me. "Funny how my favorite moments with you all happen in the kitchen."

"Uh-huh." I'm not sure what to say to him right now. For one, I can't talk because he has his shirt off. For two...well, he has his shirt off.

"Hey, I'm really sorry about your brother. I hope that I'm not making it harder by being here," he says, misreading my silence.

Finding my voice, I finally speak. "Listen, I know things were kind of crazy last night, but I really appreciate you setting up my flight and coming with me. I know I've been a little reserved, but I was just worried."

"So, you're not mad at me?"

"I wouldn't go that far. I still think we need to talk about it all, but I'm pretty sure I'll forgive you if you're really nice to me."

"I can be nice," he states in a low voice.

I notice when the sound of the shower stops down the hall. "I'm sure you can be nice. Why don't you go take a shower in the basement? I'll get cleaned up, and then I'll come down, so we can talk."

"Okay, I'll see you down there," Liam says as he heads toward the stairs.

Having the self-control to just have a talk with him is going to be a challenge.

# # #

When I walk down the hall, June is already out of the bathroom. The guest room door is closed and the lights are off, so I assume she's already lying down. After heading into the bathroom, I grab a towel, set the water to a comfortable temperature, and step into the shower. For a few minutes, I let the water run over me to get the food mess out of my hair, and then I run a bath, so I can soak my tired body.

As I lie in the bathtub, I think about June finding out about my brother. I know it's bound to happen, but I don't think I'm ready for the fallout. Every scenario I play out in my head ends with June storming out of the room as she shouts some version of, "Never talk to me again," or "I thought you were my friend."

When my bathwater starts to turn lukewarm, I decide to get out and go have my talk with Liam. I get dressed in a blue tank top and gray cotton shorts, thinking about what I'll say to him. Although I'm glad to know he cares about me, I have to get to the bottom of what happened Friday night. Maybe I did handle things in an impulsive manner. June surely wouldn't have been so nice to him in front of me if she thought he had done something wrong.

As I come down the stairs, I can see Liam sitting on the couch. His back is to me, and I can tell he has his shirt off again. *Is he trying to break my resolve?* I attempt to walk without making a sound, but when I reach the twelfth step, it creaks. *That stupid step has gotten me caught since I was in second grade.*

Liam stands and walks toward me. "Hey."

"Hi."

"I saved you a seat," he says, motioning to the couch.

"Gee, thanks."

"Can I talk first?"

"Sure."

"I need to tell you that nothing was going on with those

girls. They both work with me, and I've known them for at least a year. We were just out celebrating work stuff. When I said I talked about you nonstop, it was true. I wish you would have come up to the bar and said hello, so they could meet you. They kept telling me that you had to be a figment of my imagination. They said that no girl as perfect as you sounded would go for a guy like me. When June told me you were upset when you left, I had no clue it had to do with me. I was so worried that something was wrong with your mom or with your job. I had to find you and make sure you were okay."

I can't take it. I don't want to hear him talk anymore. I place my finger to his lips. "Shh, take a breath," I whisper. I lean toward him and lay my lips softly against his.

"I was so worried."

I kiss him again.

Pulling away, he looks into my eyes. "I know what you thought, but you have to know that you are all I can think about. I don't want anyone else."

"I know," I say just before I crash my mouth into his.

As I moan against his lips, he pulls me onto his lap. Wrapping my arms around his neck, I lean my head back as my fingers gently tug at his wet hair. His lips touch the soft skin around my collarbone. He lingers there for several kisses, and then he slowly drags his tongue to the side of my neck just below my ear. My body is humming, and I am panting with uneven breaths. His kisses are tender and loving as his hand runs down my sides to my hips.

Within a few minutes, Liam sets me back onto the couch

and takes my face in his hands. "You wanted to talk, didn't you?"

"Yes," I say reluctantly.

"So, talk to me."

I close my eyes and take in a few deep breaths. When Liam releases my face, I instantly feel his absence. I open my eyes, slide closer to him, and lay my head against his shoulder.

"Seeing my brother today was really great. I really appreciate you taking care of everything."

"It was no problem."

I'm debating on whether I should tell Liam the truth about my brother. I mean, June is his sister, so I would understand if he got pissed. After I go through the possible scenarios of the aftermath in my mind, I decide to lay it all out there. It's killing me to keep this secret from everyone. At least this way, it won't be my secret alone.

"I know he still has some level of recovery ahead of him, but after everything that happened with Julie, hearing that he was in an accident was gut-wrenching." I go on, wanting to tell Liam about Cohen's wife. "Julie is my brother's wife. He was actually driving to the hospital to see her when he got in his accident. She has been ill recently, and she was just put in the hospital this week."

"Wow. That's pretty crappy. I am so sorry your family has had to go through all of that."

"Well, that's not the whole story."

Liam sits in silence, waiting for me to continue. *I can still turn back. I don't have to tell him.* I am freaking out inside. My heart is racing. *What if he gets really mad and doesn't want to see me anymore? He could go upstairs right now and tell June everything.*

"I'm going to tell you something, and I hope you can understand."

"Hey, if you can let go of the misunderstanding with the girls at the bar, then I think I can let go of whatever you're about to say."

"I'm not sure about that. You see, my brother works for a company here in Seattle, but he travels a lot for work. For the past two weeks, he's been back and forth to Houston for business."

"Well, that's interesting," he says with a little sarcasm lingering in his tone.

"Yes, but here's the bad part. My brother's name is Cohen. He met June at the business meeting she went to in New York. They met again in Houston two weeks ago, and since then, he's taken June out on a couple of dates."

"Wait, are you saying that your brother..." He pauses, staring at me with his brows furrowed.

"That's exactly what I'm saying. The guy she talked to you about the other night, the one that took her to the museum and out to dinner, the one she kissed—that's my brother...my married brother."

"Wow. And you didn't think telling her would be a good idea?"

"I didn't know right away. After I figured it out, I discussed it all with him, and he promised he would talk with June. Then, he got in this accident, and I was so angry with you. I didn't know what to do. Actually, I still have no clue what to do."

"Well, you're in quite a predicament. Do you plan to tell her soon?"

"I want to, but I have no idea where to begin."

"I don't think it matters where you begin or end as long as you're telling the truth. Give June some credit. With everything that's been going on, I think she'll understand. You're her best friend. She knows you wouldn't intentionally hurt her. Now, on the other hand, Cohen might want to stand a few feet away when he tells her he's married."

"There is actually more to that story, too. Selfishly, I hope you're right about her reaction to my part in it all. Cohen will have to explain his side of the story."

"Hopefully, you can talk to June tomorrow and get it all sorted out. She's going to find out everything eventually. You might as well get it over with." Liam kisses the top of my head. "For now, let's get some rest."

I lie down in front of him, and he wraps his arm around my waist, pulling me against him. I close my eyes and drift to sleep easily.

36
COHEN

SATURDAY

"Sweetheart, are you awake?" my mom asks, placing her hand on my shoulder.

"Uh-huh, just resting my eyes a little bit."

"I don't want to upset you, but the Franklins are worried about Julie. They've asked your doctor to let you see her now."

"Oh, okay. What did the doctor say? Can I go?"

"Yes, but you have to stay in the wheelchair, and you can't be gone long. Your nurse will come with us."

"Can I put some pants on?"

"Sure, baby."

As my mom leaves the room, my phone vibrates on the bedside table. I decide to ignore it as I get dressed. I can't think of anyone I need to talk with right now. I saw Caroline tonight, and I'm sure she has told June everything by this point. I've been worried about facing June with the truth, but she probably doesn't want to have anything to do with me now.

I push my call button, and within a few seconds, the nurse is in my room with a wheelchair. We meet my mom in the hallway and head down the elevator. I have rehearsed this conversation in my head so many times. I need Julie to know everything. I need her family to understand. I want to be there for her and for them.

When the elevator doors open, Julie's mom is waiting for us with her arms wrapped around herself.

"Cohen..."

When she begins to cry, I try to get up from the wheelchair, but the nurse places a firm hand on my shoulder. I reach out my hand instead. Her grip is soft, and her fingers feel fragile.

"Laura, I'm so sorry."

"Let's just get you in there to see her," she says without looking at me.

My mom steps closer to her and places an arm around her back. It's obvious that Laura needs the support. As I release her hand, she crumbles into my mom's shoulder, still crying.

This whole scene is breaking my heart. I can't imagine what will happen when I enter Julie's room. I'm glad it's late, so at least, a lot of family or friends won't be in the room. When we round the corner and pass a nurses' station, several of the nurses look up at me with eyes that tell me they know our story. I used to see those eyes a lot when Julie was in the hospital before.

"I'll stay at the door. Just push the call button if you need anything," my nurse says kindly.

"Thank you."

My mom wheels the chair into the room and then leaves me alone—alone with Julie. It has been so long since we were alone in a room together. It almost feels unnatural.

Julie is covered with a sheet and several blankets up to her shoulders. She must have been cold. Her face is pale, but she's still as beautiful as a bright sunrise. I stroke her cheek lightly and run my hand softly across her golden hair. It has lost much of its shine, but her long locks still make me smile. She used to spend hours trying to get a certain curl just right. It drove me insane, and it made us late anywhere we went.

I start to pull my hand away, not wanting to disturb her, but then I realize she won't be waking up. My mom already told me that she hasn't opened her eyes in days. I hear a faint beep and look up to see her feeding tube has run out. I reach up and turn the dial, placing it on hold, so no one comes in to interrupt us. She has two IV lines in her right arm. Being careful not to tug on any of them, I lay my head against her chest and squeeze her frail body. The fact that I'm aware of the purpose of all these tubes and lines is sad. At the age of twenty-seven, I shouldn't have this much knowledge without being in the medical profession—but I do.

"Hi, Julie. My sweet, sweet Julie, it's Cohen. I'm here, baby. I know you aren't going to answer me, but I pray you can hear me. I'm so sorry you are sick. The doctors are taking good care of you, and all your family and friends have been coming to visit you. I had a little accident, but I don't want you to worry. They say I'm going to be just fine."

I don't deserve to be fine. I don't deserve to be sitting beside her as she lies in a hospital bed. I should be in a bed right next to her. Better yet, I should be the one in her state while she is awake and living her life. I put aside my self-pity. I know I need to tell her. I'm just not sure how to do it.

"You are so beautiful. I know I've always told you that you were as beautiful as the cupcakes you made. That sounds ridiculous now, but I loved the smile on your face when I would say it. The truth is that you are so much more beautiful than that. You are gorgeous from the inside out. No one could ever say anything negative about you. Your beauty, your compassion, your love for life—they are all perfect pieces of you.

"I wish I had your same passion for friendships. I know you always hated how I didn't like to go out or have people over. I'm sorry I took that away from you. We should have gone out to dinner more. We should have had date nights with our friends. We should have invited more people over and enjoyed their company."

I need to stop making small talk and just say what I came to say. I've run through the words a million different ways, but I know our families are outside the room and probably listening in, so it makes it that much harder to say.

"Julie...oh god, Julie. I should have talked to you about this sooner. Please understand. To be honest, I never thought I would need to talk to you about this. I never thought I would find love again. You were it for me, Julie. You know that. You stole a part of my heart before I was old enough to know I could give pieces away. I miss you. I miss you every day, every damn day. But I have to do this."

I find her cold and limp hand wrapped underneath all the blankets, and I cover it with mine. I hold it to my chest and hope she can feel my beating heart.

"You have to know that this woman I met is wonderful. You would like her. She is kind and sweet and fun. She has ambition, like you, but she is so different from you, too. I want you to know that if you were here, I would love you forever. Even when you are gone, I will continue loving you. But since you are leaving and you won't be here any longer, I need to move on. I need to love again. Please, please understand."

I feel the first tears stream down my cheeks, and then they are followed by countless more. I sit and watch Julie's chest rise and fall. She doesn't respond. She doesn't squeeze my hand. She lies motionless, except for her breathing.

After a few minutes, my mom walks into the room. I can see her out of the corner of my eye, but I don't acknowledge her presence. She comes to the side of the bed and gives Julie a kiss on her forehead.

"We love you, Julie. We will always think of you," she says.

Is she trying to kill me? The sobs rush out of me, and I begin to cry out, throwing my hands over my face as my elbows rest on the bed. *My life is not supposed to happen this way.*

"Oh, Cohen. Baby, I am so sorry."

Soon, I am surrounded by my mom and dad and Julie's parents. They all look at me lovingly, and I want to slap them. *This is my fault.* I continue to cry as that night crashes back into my mind.

# # #

Julie needed some ingredients to finish baking something. I didn't even know what she was baking. That was how much attention I was paying to her that night. She told me she wasn't feeling well, but she looked fine to me. I said I was tired and needed to finish up some research for work, so she left by herself.

I went to the bedroom and got comfortable on my side of the bed. I fell asleep with my laptop open to my personal email. I woke up hours later to a call from the local hospital. When they told me what had happened, I felt an instant panic. I knew I would never forget that phone call.

While Julie was driving the four-mile trip to the grocery store, something happened that caused her to cross the median into oncoming traffic. She was hit head-on by a school bus—a school bus of all things. A symbol of innocence and childhood fun was the vehicle that destroyed my life. The police never figured out what caused her to cross the median, but they assumed she either passed out or swerved to avoid something in the road. The bus driver was fine, but Julie suffered injuries to many parts of her body, including her head, and she was never the same. We all held out hope for a long time. The doctors even said she had a chance for a meaningful recovery, but when it came down to it, her brain was too damaged.

For those first few weeks, I spent every waking moment at the hospital. I was at her side, making sure I never missed a doctor's visit. I was exhausted, but I felt like if I left, then I was giving up on her.

After about a month, her parents and I agreed to have the feeding tube in her nose replaced with one in her stomach, so she could get nutrition more easily. Julie and I had never discussed if she would want this type of thing, but she didn't require any other kind of life support, so we all thought a more permanent way to provide nutrition was for the best.

Once Julie was medically stable, the doctors said we had to figure out where she would be taken care of after she left the hospital. Her ability to control her bodily functions was so limited that she was unable to participate with therapies, so she couldn't go to a rehabilitation facility. Her parents didn't want her to live in a nursing home, but I couldn't quit my job, and with our insurance, I definitely couldn't afford in-home care.

Neither of us had the forethought to get disability or life insurance. We hadn't thought it was important at our young age. I wasn't even sure what I would do with her bakery and all the accrued medical expenses.

Since I couldn't care for her in our home, her parents were adamant to have her home with them. Julie's mom stayed with her, and they hired a caregiver to come in a few days a week.

For several weeks, I would go visit, but I would only stay a few minutes. The guilt of what I had done was too hard to bear. Julie would keep her eyes open, but she didn't seem to know when someone was in the room. Loud noises would startle her, but she wouldn't even respond to her name. *I did this to her.*

Days turned to weeks, and then months turned into two

years. During those two years, I had started to get back into the routine of my new life. I woke up, went to work, went to bed, and then started over again the next morning.

As time passed, people grew less and less interested in how I was holding up. I was still dying inside from losing her, but I had to pretend like I was moving on.

# # #

Sitting now beside her bed, I look into our parents' eyes, and I am scared. When she dies, that will be my fault, too. As if reading my mind, Julie's dad comes to my side. Kneeling next to me, he takes my face in his hands.

"It's okay, Cohen. We know you loved her with your whole heart. You gave her the best years of her young life. She loved you so much, and she would want you to move on. She wouldn't want you to feel this guilt. You didn't do anything wrong. You aren't doing anything wrong now."

With the exception of a few sniffles, everyone is quiet for a few minutes. I know I need to go back to my room, but leaving her side for possibly the last time creates an emptiness in my chest. I feel this deep hollowness in my soul, like a dark cavern without an exit, and I begin to wonder if it will ever be filled again. I can't speak another word tonight.

The nurse wheels me back to my room. My mom and dad say good night, and I curl up into a ball on my hospital bed. I click the button to turn out the overhead lights. My phone vibrates on the table next to me, and without thinking, I grab it to see who it is.

June? Why would she want to talk to me? I don't read the text. I'm afraid of what it might say, afraid that I have ruined yet another wonderful thing in my life. As tears fill my eyes again, I close them, hoping to shut out my life.

It doesn't work.

37
June

SUNDAY

I wake up early to the quietness of Caroline's house. I know things were weird and tough yesterday, but I'm hoping that Caroline will come out of her funk since she saw that her brother is doing okay. I rub my eyes and yawn so big that I feel like my jaw might unhinge. *Why do we yawn?* Unless they serve a purpose, I find unnecessary things to be annoying. Yawning is one of those things. If someone could tell me the point of a yawn, I might reconsider my frustration.

I walk down the hall and open a door. I thought I was walking into the bathroom, but when I open my eyes and they begin to focus, I realize I must be in Vivian's office. Bookshelves line every wall, overflowing with books of all sizes and colors. I walk toward one of the shelves and admire the worn covers. I wonder what Vivian would think if she knew I was in her office. Some people are freaks about other people entering their space, but surely, she would have locked the door if it were that important to her. I turn and place my hands on the back of her large leather chair.

Vivian is a successful realtor in the Seattle area. I never thought having a realtor in my corner could be helpful. *Boy, was I wrong.* When Caroline and I were ready to get our own place at college before our sophomore year, Vivian was on top of things. She contacted several realtors in the area and made sure we got a wonderful place in a clean neighborhood with a landlord who wasn't a total pervert. She also made certain that things like lawn work and household repairs were included. I would never have thought of all the things she did. Of course, when we moved to Houston, she helped us out there, too.

Glancing over her clean desk, I see several pictures gathered at the far right corner. I sit down and lean forward on my elbows, gazing over the pictures of Caroline on vacation in different beautiful locations. I notice a younger man sporadically included in these photos. *He must be her brother.* I pick up a dark wooden frame in my hand, and after staring at it for a second, I almost drop it to the ground.

If these are family pictures, then what is Cohen...*he has to be a family friend, right?* I pick up another frame showcasing four smiling people. Cohen is wearing a cap and gown as he stands beside Caroline. Caroline's parents flank them, and as I look at the proud smiles plastered across their faces, I realize they're not just Caroline's parents. I place the photo back on the desk and sit in a daze. Everything in front of me is a blur of confusion.

All at once, I am moving with purpose down the hallway. I storm into Caroline's room and find it empty. *She and Liam didn't waste any time making up, I see.* I rush down the steps to the basement, moving so quickly that I almost lose my balance toward the bottom. I catch myself against the banister, making a loud thud, before I flip on the lights.

"Rise and shine, everyone!" I say, feigning happiness.

"What the crap, June?" Liam says with a groan.

"I think we should save the what-the-crap questions for our good friend, Caroline. What do you say, Caroline?"

"June, what are you talking about?" She goes from a sleepy-eyed look to a more concerned demeanor in moments, revealing she already has some idea of what this is about.

I don't feel like beating around the bush. "What's your brother's name?"

I stare at her, holding her gaze, until she looks down to her feet. I see another framed image of Cohen on a shelf in front of me. I pick up the frame and shove it into Caroline's lap, so she can't avoid my question or the obvious answer. Sitting up from the couch, Liam looks at me and shakes his head. I am contemplating his look of frustration when Caroline finally speaks.

"Cohen," she says, her eyes focused on the carpet fibers.

The room is silent. I didn't think this through very well. I knew, coming down here, that I was mad. I feel even angrier now, but I'm not sure how to respond. I thought she might try to lie or maybe try to explain why she hadn't told me.

"How long have you known? Did you know he was leading

me on?"

"Since Wednesday, the night you came home from the museum, and of course not."

"Why didn't you tell me? I went on three separate dates with him and flew all the way to Washington on the same plane with you while freaking out about this guy not calling me." I'm pacing the floor in front of them as I throw my hands in the air every once in a while. "You knew the whole time why he couldn't call, but you chose not to tell me."

"It didn't happen exactly like that."

"Well, why don't you tell me how it really happened? Were you planning on never telling me? Were you just going to let me believe that this perfect guy came into my life and then left me for no apparent reason? You didn't think it was important to tell me that he had an accident? I've been thinking horrible thoughts because I thought he just dropped me on my ass. I even texted him last night, and I was pissed that he didn't respond. They probably don't even let him have his cell phone in there."

"There's more to the story, but I think Cohen should be the one to tell you. He didn't come home for anything work-related, and he got into the accident on his way to the hospital to see Julie."

"Oh, that's right. And who the hell is Julie? Your mom talked about her last night like she's part of the family. Do you have a sister you would like to tell me about?"

"June, you need to lay off. If Caroline doesn't think she should tell you, then maybe we should go to the hospital and let Cohen tell you," Liam says, looking a little annoyed.

"Are you really sticking up for her? I guess that makes sense, considering the two of you have been lying to me about your relationship for God knows how long."

"Get a grip. We weren't lying to you. We were trying to get to know each other without interference," Liam says.

"Without interference? Well, why don't I afford you that opportunity? I think I'll catch the next flight back to Texas, and you can let me know how everything goes."

"Please don't do that. I know my brother would want to see you. I'm so sorry it all came out this way. I had no idea you were seeing Cohen until the night you told me about your kiss. You seemed so happy, and I didn't want to ruin your excitement. I texted Cohen that night, and he promised he would talk with you. I talked with him again, and I thought he was going to talk to you about everything sometime this week. Then, I found out about the accident. When you told me you were coming to Washington, I tried to tell you not to come, but you were both so adamant about being with me...and honestly, I needed you. Then I tried to tell you at the airport when we were in the bathroom, but you were so worried about me. It was selfish, and I understand that you're mad, but at least come to the hospital and talk to Cohen."

I contemplate saying no, but a part of me wants to know who this Julie person is. I'm curious about why she's in the hospital and why she matters so much to Cohen and to their family.

"Fine. I'm getting dressed," I say before turning and stomping up the stairs.

⸕ ⸕ ⸕

We drive to the hospital in silence. I'm tired of all this awkward space. When we pull into the parking lot, my stomach is already tied in knots. *I feel sick.*

"You know, on second thought, maybe you could just have Cohen call me when he feels like talking."

"I doubt he'll want to say what he has to say over the phone," Caroline says with a serious look on her face.

She and Liam get out of the car and stand, waiting for me to follow suit. After a couple of minutes of positive self-talk, I open the car door and walk into the hospital with them. We find out that Cohen has been moved out of the ICU and into a regular room. Caroline's parents and stepdad are in his new room, but he is nowhere to be found.

They tell us that Cohen went to see Julie. By the looks on their faces, it's obvious that they're all very sad. Up until this point, I have successfully avoided coming up with scenarios to explain who Julie might be, but in this moment, I know she is someone special.

"We should go find him and see if he needs anything," I say without thinking about what's coming out of my mouth.

"Are you sure?" Caroline asks.

I nod, but I don't know what else to say. After Vivian tells us Julie's room number, the three of us take the elevator down one floor, and then walk through several long hallways before we come to another nurses' station. We approach Julie's room slowly, and I can see Cohen sitting in a chair with his head lying on the bed. He is talking quietly, and I can barely make out what he's saying.

"Julie, I'm so sorry. I know that you wanted us to be something others would envy. I wanted that, too. I wanted it all. I love you so much."

I can see that the woman in the bed is young. Her skin is pale, and she doesn't move or give any response to Cohen's words. He continues lying still with his head resting next to her body, and then I notice he is working something small in between his fingers, moving it back and forth. When it catches the light, I realize it's a ring—a simple gold band. Julie's arms are folded across her stomach, and I see a similar gold band on her ring finger.

The truth comes crashing down on me. *This can't be happening. How did I not know? Why didn't he tell me? Why didn't Caroline tell me?* They're married. *Cohen is married.* She is his wife. There's no doubt in my mind. I don't need to ask anything. His love for her is obvious. It pours off of him, filling the room, as it suffocates me with guilt. *I can't break up a marriage. I have to leave.*

I turn around to find Liam and Caroline gone. They must have left, thinking Cohen and I would need time to talk. I can't imagine why Caroline would encourage me to talk with Cohen, knowing he is married.

Before my thoughts can settle on an answer, I walk down several long corridors until I reach the main elevators. When I arrive at the front lobby, I ask for a cab to the airport. Within a few minutes, the cab pulls up. I look back and wonder if I'm making the right decision, but I can't think of any better option. I take out my phone and send a quick text to Liam.

Headed home. Need to be at work tomorrow morning. Tell Caroline I'm sorry. —June

I shut off my phone and stare blankly out the window as the buildings rush by. *Soon, I'll be home, and I can move on with my life. I refuse to fall for a married man who is clearly in love with his wife. I can't believe Caroline would keep that from me.*

38
Caroline

SUNDAY

We left June outside Julie's hospital room, hoping she and Cohen would find a way to talk about what's happening. I know the talk they are about to have will be hard and awful, but I can't be the one to tell her. Maybe I'm just being a coward, but I have no clue what to tell her. I haven't had the chance to talk with my brother about his feelings for June. I don't know if he's willing to pursue a relationship or if he thought he found someone who could help him forget things for a moment. I can't tell June that my brother might have been using her. *What if he wasn't using her? What if he's really interested in her?*

Liam and I are sitting side by side on the uncomfortable sofa in my brother's room. My parents were gone when we got back, and I'm beginning to wonder if we should call them. Then, Liam's phone vibrates in his lap. He picks it up, reads a message, and hangs his head.

"What? Who is it?"

After a few moments of silence, he says, "June."

"Well, what did she say? Have they already talked? That was quick."

"No, I don't think they talked. She's heading home, and she says to tell you that she's sorry."

"Are you kidding? Call her. She couldn't be too far yet."

He pushes a couple of buttons and then puts the phone to his ear. As quickly as he lifts the phone, he brings it back down to his lap, shaking his head. "She must have turned it off. It's going straight to voice mail."

I stand quickly. *She can't leave. They have to work this out.* "We have to go find her. We can't let her go. What about my brother? I know he's going to want to talk to her."

Still sitting in the exact same spot on the sofa, Liam rests his hand lightly on my arm. "Just let her go, Caroline. Don't push her. If they're meant to talk and work this out, then they will. Just leave her be."

"Leave who be?"

We both look up to see my brother walking of his own accord into the room.

"Cohen! I am so glad to see you!" I run to my brother and hug him tightly.

"Whoa. Be careful, sis. I'm still a little sore."

"Sorry." I scrunch my nose in apology, hoping I didn't cause him too much pain.

"That's alright. Who were you talking about?"

"Um, no one. We were talking about a friend, a friend of Liam's." I look to Liam who is faking a grin unsuccessfully. "Did you see any visitors while you were up in Julie's room?" I ask, trying to sound indifferent.

"Her parents were there for a little bit, but no visitors. They're trying to keep it pretty quiet, and I think they wanted to give me some more time." Cohen turns his attention toward the sofa. "Hey, I'm guessing you must be Liam," he says, offering his hand.

"Hi. Glad to see you're up and around, man."

"You're telling me. I hate that you all came up here, and I wasn't really hurt too badly. Mom and Dad sort of exaggerated from what I've heard. They meant well."

I nod in agreement and give him a light punch in the arm. "I think you just scared the crap out of them, and with Julie being in the hospital, they weren't sure what to do."

"Uh-huh." Cohen sits on the edge of the bed, looking at the floor.

"Liam knows," I say, trying to ease his discomfort.

"Oh," he says, looking up with concern in his eyes. "Does she know, too?"

"No, I didn't tell her. She was here, but I think she's leaving."

"She was here? Like in the hospital, here? Why didn't you come find me?"

"We took her up to Julie's room to wait for you, but she must have decided that she didn't want to know. I don't know, Cohen. She was standing right outside the door."

Cohen stands up from the side of the bed. The look on his face is a mixture of disbelief and frustration. "Are you kidding me, Caroline? There's no telling what she could have heard me say. You should have gotten my attention before you left her there. She probably thinks I'm a total creep."

He walks to the bedside table and retrieves his phone. As he dials a number, his footsteps trace a path back and forth across the worn floor in front of his hospital bed. Just as Liam discovered, his call to June must go straight to voice mail. Rearing back, he throws his phone with full force onto the unmade bed. It bounces, falls to the floor, and slides under the sofa. No one makes a move to find it.

"Has she been in town this whole time?" Cohen asks, still pacing with quick steps as he links his fingers together behind his neck.

"Yes, she came with us on Saturday. You need to calm down," I say.

"Are you serious? Why didn't you tell me or bring her to me earlier?"

"You could only have family in the ICU, and I didn't want to be the one to tell her. She must have seen a picture of you or something at the house this morning. She came barreling down the stairs before she started shouting at me. I didn't tell her anything about Julie, but you should consider explaining everything to her. It's obvious you care for her. She'll understand."

We are all silent for a few minutes. I'm not sure what Liam and Cohen are thinking, but I know my mind is racing, trying to figure out a way to make sure June doesn't stay mad at me for life. I lied to her about Liam. I lied to her about Cohen. I let her travel all the way to Washington without coming clean. She was right to be upset, and I can't blame her for leaving.

I think back to fights we had in college, but nothing this serious comes to mind. The biggest fights we had were about leaving dishes in the sink or eating each other's groceries. She might have more difficulty in the forgiveness department on this one.

"I'm going to the restroom, and then I'm getting a snack. You guys want anything?" I ask.

They both shake their heads without saying anything. I get up and leave the boys to their silence. This whole situation is driving me crazy.

39
Liam

SUNDAY

When Caroline walks out of the room, I immediately feel the tension increase. Cohen has taken a seat on the bed across from me. He's staring at his feet as he alternates lifting the toes of one foot and then the other. I stand and walk to the window. The view isn't the best as I look out to a brick wall and a few window washers. I can see how people who are stuck in the hospital for a long time could get depressed.

I decide to speak up. "Are you really interested in her?"

Cohen is silent for a moment or two. I begin to wonder if he even heard me. As I turn around, his eyes meet mine, and I see they are glazed over with tears.

"Yes. I mean, it's hard, but I really do care for her."

"I know Caroline is going to tell you to call her. She'll probably try and call her for you a few times, but I know my sister. You need to leave her alone."

Cohen hangs his head again. "I understand if you think I'm not good enough for her. I know I screwed up."

I've never felt such pity for a guy in my life. In most situations, I would tell a guy to suck it up and move on. Unfortunately, I don't think something like that would be appropriate for a guy I barely know whose wife could die at any moment.

"I don't think you get it. I like you, Cohen. I think you're a pretty good guy. Caroline would probably be pissed if she thought you were leading June on or purposely trying to hurt her. It's not like you've done anything wrong. I'm not sure I would have done anything differently. You can't change what has happened over the last few weeks or anything else in your past. Julie had to come first.

"If June knew the whole story, she would understand, and she would respect you for that decision. As it is, who knows what she thinks? What I'm trying to tell you is that if you push her too far, too fast, then you'll never have a chance. Just leave her to her own thoughts, and if she has any feelings for you at all, she'll show up."

Cohen looks up, giving me a slight nod, just before Caroline walks back into the room. She walks straight into my arms, and I pull her in tightly.

"Hey, Cohen, I ran into Mom downstairs. It sucks you're in the hospital because she's taking Liam and me out to that awesome Italian place by the house."

When she sticks out her tongue, Cohen laughs.

"Joke's on you. This hospital has a gourmet chef," he says with a serious face.

"No way."

I can't believe she fell for that. God, I love this girl.

# # #

A few hours later, I am showered and dressed for dinner with her parents. As I walk up the stairs from the basement, I catch a glimpse of Caroline rushing past in a purple dress. When she passes by, some pieces of the dress float behind, making her look like some kind of fairy. I reach the top of the stairs, and she starts to fly by again. Catching her around the waist, she shrieks as I tickle her sides gently.

"Liam, stop! I need to finish getting ready."

"What could you possibly still need to do? You look amazing," I say, leaning down to kiss her.

We stand there, pecking kiss after kiss across each other's lips. As I start to run my hands across her back, I'm wondering if we can ditch dinner. Then, I hear the front door open, and we each take a step back with our faces clearly looking guilty.

"Caroline, sweetie, are you both ready?" her mom asks, giving me a look that says we weren't fooling anyone.

"Sure, Mom. Are we all riding together?"

"Actually, John had to go into the office to finish up some things, so he probably won't make it. Your father is meeting us there."

Caroline grabs her purse, and we all head out the door.

When we reach the car, I climb into the backseat, expecting Caroline to sit up front with her mom. When she slides into the seat next to me, I give her leg a quick squeeze. I start to feel nervous, like I'm going on my very first date in high school again. Caroline's mom, Vivian, looks back at us a few times through the rearview mirror, and each time she gives a sweet smile.

We arrive at the restaurant just as Caroline's dad, Peter, pulls in. He walks right over, and I present my hand. He gives me a wink, taking my hand in his, before he pulls me into a hug.

"Dad, would you be normal, please?"

"What? A guy can't hug another guy? Am I embarrassing you?" he asks, pulling back and looking to me for an answer.

"Oh, uh…no, sir. My family hugs quite a bit, too."

"Good, good. My little girl deserves a lot of hugs."

"Dad!" Caroline gives him a glare as she slaps him across his arm.

We sit down to eat dinner, and we enjoy various conversations related to every topic we could think of—from Vivian's realty business to Peter's obsession with baseball to college degrees to dog breeds. I'm beginning to think we'll never have a need to get together again because we've covered it all tonight. We are all laughing about a funny golf story Peter just told when Vivian speaks up.

"Caroline, how is June doing? She left so suddenly. I didn't get to see much of her."

With that, tension fills the space between us at the table.

Caroline wipes her mouth with her napkin and sighs. "I'm

not sure. I've tried to call her several times, but her phone must still be turned off."

"I can't imagine why she would leave without saying good-bye. Do you think everything is okay with your family, Liam?"

"Oh, yes, I talked with my dad this afternoon. She made it home okay. I think she felt a little overwhelmed with everything. She isn't used to hospitals and all that."

"I see. Well, how did Cohen seem when you left him today?"

"Okay, I guess. Well, as okay as a heartbroken man can be," Caroline says.

"What he's going through just kills us," Peter says, looking at me.

"I couldn't even imagine," I say.

"You know, when he went to see Julie yesterday evening, he mentioned being interested in dating again. It was the first I've heard him talk about it. Do you know anything about this girl?" Vivian asks.

Caroline looks to me, biting her bottom lip, and I give her a slight shrug.

"Caroline? Are you keeping something from me?"

"No, Mom."

"You know, you never were a good liar," her dad states, smiling.

"Alright, fine. Cohen is interested in June."

"What? Did you say June? Like *our* June?"

Caroline raises her eyebrows and a small smile appears on her face.

"How is that possible? Did they meet sometime while you were in college?" Vivian asks.

"No."

Her dad tilts his head to the side and gives us both a confused look. "I think there might be a story they need to tell us, Vivian."

Caroline sighs again and begins to explain how Cohen and June met. She mentions how we both think they would be wonderful together, but then June found out about Julie before Cohen could tell her.

"I don't know how much she knows about the situation. Cohen said he didn't even see her outside of Julie's room. Something must have happened to make her leave so quickly, but I'm hoping once she has some time to think about it, she'll give him a chance to explain everything."

"Oh my. Well, that is quite the dilemma. Caroline, I think we need to come up with a plan," Vivian says, tapping her finger against her chin.

"A plan?" Caroline asks.

"Yes. June is such a sweet girl. She would be wonderful for Cohen. We'll have to find a way."

"I don't know if that's the best idea," I state.

"Why not?" Vivian asks.

"Well, June doesn't respond well to being pushed in one direction or the other."

"Oh, we won't be pushing," she says, smiling at Caroline.

Caroline gives me a sheepish grin.

We finish up our dinner and head back to Vivian's house.

Cohen is doing really well and should be getting out of the hospital tomorrow, so no one stays with him tonight. Caroline spends the rest of the evening upstairs with her mom, devising a plan to get June back to Washington. *If nothing else, this will at least be interesting.*

40
June

MONDAY

I get back to work and sit at my desk. I'm going through the motions, but I know my attitude could use a major adjustment.

"June, glad to have you back. Hope everything is okay with your family."

"Yes, Mr. Hargrove. Thanks for asking."

"Sure. Now, I have a few new projects for you. Since you've been doing so well with your work with The Bushing Company, I thought I would float a few more of their projects your way. You and Cohen seem to work well together," he says, giving me a knowing smile.

Any other time, I would see this as a big pat on the back, but today, it feels like a cinder block being thrown against my chest. I do my best to hide my discomfort, but the confused look that falls on his face tells me I'm unsuccessful.

"Are you okay today, June? You look a little pale."

"I'm fine. I'm just tired from traveling."

"Okay. Well, let me know if you have any questions."

"Thanks, Mr. Hargrove."

After he leaves my office, I hurry to shut the door. I throw myself into one of the large cushioned chairs in front of my desk, and I start crying. After the embarrassing amount of tears I shed on the plane ride back to Texas and the car ride home, I would think there wouldn't be any tears left. Yet, here they are again, soaking my cheeks as they fall into my hands covering my face.

How did I get involved with a married man? Am I that pathetic? I mean, it's not like I ask those kinds of questions on a first date. I guess it's another thing to add to the list of failures I've achieved. My mother would be so proud.

When I hear a soft knock on my door, I dry my tears with a tissue, check myself in the mirror to make sure I'm presentable, and then open the door. Two deliverymen are standing on the other side with large vases of peonies. *You have got to be kidding me.*

"Those can't all be for me."

"Are you June?"

"Yes."

"Well then, they are all for you."

I direct them to set one on my desk and the other on a small table against the wall. Before they leave, one of the deliverymen hands me a small envelope with my name written across the front. Sitting back into the chair, I debate on whether or not I want to open the card. It has to be from him. *What could he possibly have to say? Sorry, I didn't tell you I'm a married man. I'm sure sorry things didn't work out.* Anger builds up inside me, and I crumble the envelope in my hand. He couldn't possibly think this would make anything better.

Slouched in the chair, I sit and stare at the flowers, thinking about Cohen and what I saw. *Is it possible that I'm wrong?* I can't believe Caroline would hide all this from me, and Liam knew, too. He could have told me. Holding the crumbled envelope and card in my hand, I need to know what it says. I decide to open the card.

June,

We appreciate you coming to Washington with Caroline. You are such a good friend. I'm sorry I didn't get to see you before you left. I hope these flowers remind you of our sincere love for you.

Vivian

She couldn't possibly know that these were the exact flowers in the exact colors that Cohen sent to me after our first meeting in New York...or maybe she could. *Someone must have put her up to this.*

TUESDAY

I'm going through a file drawer and organizing paperwork just to pass the time. My office phone rings, and I see my mom's number flash across the screen.

"Hi, Mom."

"June, I only have a minute. I was wondering if you were busy tonight."

"Not really. Caroline's still out of town, and it's a weeknight."

"Oh, good. Addison and I are hoping you might join us for dinner."

"I guess so. Is everything okay?"

"Yes, everything is fine. We just thought it would be fun to have a girls' night. We'll pick you up at six."

"Okay. See you then."

My day is filled with nothing worth mentioning. Around four thirty, I tell Mr. Hargrove that I'm headed home for the day, and he is packing up to head out the door as well.

# # #

Mom and Addison are right on time, which is unusual, and they decide they want to eat at my favorite Mexican place.

"So, have you heard from Caroline?" my mom asks.

"No. Can we talk about something else?"

"Um, sure," my mom says.

We sit in silence for a few minutes. Glancing around the

restaurant, my eyes stop at the booth where Cohen and I sat on the first day he was in Houston. Now, a couple is sitting in the same booth, having dinner, as they laugh and hold hands across the table.

"How is the baby doing?" I ask Addison, trying to make small talk to get my mind off Cohen.

"Really good. We heard the heartbeat at the last appointment. It was amazing."

"I bet it was."

"You know, we're going to be done here pretty early. There are a couple of museums with new exhibits. How about we go check one out?"

Did my mom just change the subject from baby to museum? "I don't know, Mom. I'm pretty tired."

"Come on, June. You're young. It'll be fun."

I reluctantly agree. She pays the cashier, and we head out.

# # #

When we pull into the parking lot, I realize we are at the Museum of Fine Arts. Tears prick my eyes, but I close them quickly. *Why, after only knowing Cohen for two weeks, does everything remind me of him?*

We walk through the museum slowly, and each corner we turn brings back another memory. Even the silence of the museum reminds me of our laughter when we were here.

When I finally get home after spending the evening with my mom and sister, I am exhausted. My legs feel tired from walking, and my mind feels tired from feeling. As I lie in bed, I try to shut it all down. My legs already feel better, but my mind continues to race through all my moments with Cohen. I can tell it's going to be a long night.

WEDNESDAY

Two meetings take up the whole day. Mr. Hargrove sends me home with several loose ends to tie up on a big project due on Friday. I stay up most of the night before finally getting some sleep.

THURSDAY

I walk into my office without luster. This week feels as if it's passing by with the speed of a slug making his way through molasses. If the boredom sets in early today, I might run screaming through the hallways for some excitement. With several meetings to prepare for, I'm feeling like today should be better. As I sit down at my desk, my office phone begins to ring, and I see that it's my boss.

"Good morning," I say, trying to sound like my usual self.

"Good morning, June. Listen, I need you to send a potted plant for me right away. I just got a call that Cohen's wife has died. I had no idea he was even married, but apparently, she was sick for a while. They're having the funeral Saturday, but I would like to send a plant to their house."

Blinking my eyes, I try to focus on what he just said. *Was he talking about Julie? She can't be dead.*

"June, are you there?"

"Yes, sir. Uh, where did you need me to send that plant to?"

He gives me the address, and I scribble it down on a bright yellow sticky note. Just as I hang up the phone, it rings again.

"Yes, sir?"

"June?"

I haven't been answering my cell phone since I left Washington. I turned it off on the ride to the airport, and I didn't turn it back on until I got home later that night. I have kept it on silent, and except for calling my parents, I have avoided even looking at my phone. I have fifteen voice mails and I don't how many text messages, but I can't bring myself to listen or open any of them. It's not that I am angry necessarily. I mean, a part of me wishes that Caroline would have come clean earlier, but I can understand not wanting to throw your brother under the bus. The main reason I haven't answered the phone is because I have no clue what to say.

"June?" Caroline says again.

"Yes."

"Hey."

"Hi. How are you?" I ask, trying to sound more confident than I feel.

"If you want the truth, I've been better."

We sit in silence for a moment before I hear Caroline sigh loudly.

"June, I'm so sorry. I didn't mean to hurt you."

"I know," I say, wanting this conversation to end already. "I'm okay. Really, I am. I just needed some time to think."

"How is the thinking going?"

"Not good, but I'll be alright. When are you coming home?" I ask, knowing she will have to stay for a funeral.

"Actually, that's why I called. I didn't mean to be pushy with all the phone calls and text messages, but I need to talk with you. We won't be coming home until Sunday at the earliest." She pauses and then takes a breath. "Julie passed away yesterday, and the funeral is on Saturday."

"I heard."

"Cohen's been a mess, June."

"Well, I am sure he has. His wife died."

"No, June. That's not what I mean. You really should talk to him."

"I don't think that's a good idea. He needs time to grieve."

"Just come be here with me and with Liam this weekend, and maybe you'll understand a little better."

"Caroline, it's not going to happen. I have too much work to do, and Liam can use his work perks for flights only so many times during the year. I don't want to use them all up for a pointless trip where I will just end up with my heart broken again." *There. I said it.*

"But—"

"Just drop it! My office is sending a potted plant to Cohen's house, and that is as close as I'm getting to the situation."

"Okay," Caroline says, sounding defeated. "I guess I'll see you late Sunday."

"Alright. Give Liam a hug for me. I'm glad he's there for you."

"Okay."

I hang up the phone and plow through my day. As expected, meetings and conference calls fill my schedule and help the afternoon pass quickly. It's after six in the evening when I finally wind things down for the day.

# # #

When I get to the apartment, I go through the motions of getting ready for bed, and then I throw myself onto the couch. I turn on some music and allow the melody to pass through my body as I close my eyes. The lyrics pierce my mind as a husky male voice sings to me about giving things another chance. I quickly hit the shuffle button, hoping for something more upbeat. I am successful with the upbeat sound, but I still find the lyrics pressuring me to think about my decisions. I turn off the music and decide to go to bed. Surely, my dreams will leave me alone.

# # #

I wake up in the middle of the night, sweating and tightly wound up in my sheets. After untangling my limbs, I walk to the bathroom and splash some cold water on my face.

My dream was vivid and impulsive. I was running and running, quickly coming to the edge of water. It was either a large lake or maybe the ocean. The sun was setting on the horizon. It was beautiful…until I saw a wooden box floating in the distance. The box was long and deep. It floated effortlessly toward the horizon.

As I looked around, several people stood at the edge of the water. They looked like they had been standing for some time as their feet were buried in the sand while the water washed in and out around their calves. They were all waving. Their faces showed varying emotions—some sadness, some happiness, and some even indifference.

As the box reached the horizon and appeared to drop over the edge, everyone began to smile and turn away. I stood there, staring at the thin line drawn between the water and the sky. The box was gone, but I was still there.

In an instant, I realized the sun was no longer present, and I was standing alone in the dark. I slowly turned away from the water only to find the sun rising directly behind me. A figure was standing before me, shadowed by the striking light. He walked, placing one foot carefully in front of the other, as did I. As we inched closer to one another, I could make out his face. I blinked my eyes, attempting to focus, and then he was gone. The rest of my dream was spent in a feverish search, running through the sand, as the sun blinded me.

Dreams. Who knows what they mean?

I change my soaked T-shirt and go back to bed, trying in vain to achieve more sleep.

When my alarm clock goes off, I'm still awake, and I don't feel like going to work.

41
Caroline

SATURDAY

This has been the saddest week of my life. After Julie passed away, Cohen spent most of his time planning the funeral with her parents. Yesterday, I went with him to help finalize a few last details. I wanted to be there in case he broke down and needed someone. I still can't believe that she's gone.

I sit on the bed in my childhood room with clothes splayed out in front of me. It was hard enough figuring out what to wear to my grandma's funeral. She was ninety-four years old, and she lived a good life. She had children and grandchildren. Heck, she had great-grandchildren. Absolutely nothing was missing from her life.

This funeral is a stark contrast. *How do I figure out what's appropriate to wear to the funeral of a twenty-eight-year-old woman?* Since Wednesday, I've been wondering what people will say about her today. *She was a beautiful person. She made really good cupcakes and cookies. She knew everyone because she cared about everyone.* But she had no children. She was still missing pieces of her life—important pieces that weren't guaranteed.

Standing from my bed, I choose a long black dress with beautiful black lace and a gray sweater to wear in the cold church. *Julie would want me to look pretty.*

I hear a soft knock on my door. "Come in."

"Are you decent?"

"Yes, Liam." I smile.

He has been here with me all week. Even when I begged for him to go home so he wouldn't have to miss work, he just pulled out his laptop and claimed he could work from anywhere. When my parents found out everything Liam had done to get me to Washington safely and quickly, they fell in love with him instantly. We've had several talks about our relationship now, and I feel good about where we are. Although we're not in the best of circumstances, I've been able to see a wonderful side of Liam through it all.

"Need any help getting indecent?" He grabs me around the waist and pulls me into his chest.

"No, I don't think that would be appropriate with my parents down the hall."

"Damn. I always forget about the parents." Leaning down, he kisses me softly on the lips. "I just came up to tell you that your brother is here."

"Oh, okay. Well, I should be ready in a few minutes. Just tell them that I'll be right down."

"Alright."

After he walks out of the room, I sit back on the bed. My thoughts linger on my brother's comments about missing someone I love. *Do I really miss Liam the moment he walks out the door?* My smile spreads across my face.

Once I'm dressed, I walk down the stairs and head into the living room where everyone is gathered.

My dad immediately embraces me in a hug. "You look wonderful, Care."

"Thanks, Dad."

Glancing around the room, I see my brother sitting on the loveseat in the corner. I walk over and take a seat next to him. For a moment, we just sit. The silence is good. His fingers are intertwined as he repeatedly rubs one thumb roughly against his palm. I rest my hand on top of his and give him a small smile. I know his nerves have to be on edge. His shoulders visibly relax, and although he doesn't smile back, at least his frown is a little less depressing.

After June left, we talked about everything that went on between the two of them in Texas. I found it hard to believe that he didn't think about the possibility of her being my roommate and best friend. *Come on, how many Junes are there?* He said he just didn't think about it. *Such a man excuse.* His story of their first meeting in the airport and then again in New York was adorable. Knowing how June felt during that time, hearing his version made it that much better.

I did confront him for not being honest about Julie. His reasoning made sense, but it wouldn't make it any easier for

June to understand. He kept saying that it was difficult to bring up the topic. First, he struggled with whether to tell her his feelings because they work together. Then, he thought if he started off with, "Hey, I'm actually married, but my wife can't communicate with anyone or eat on her own," things probably wouldn't go too far. Add those two issues to the fact that my brother still blames himself for Julie's accident, so he doesn't feel worthy of finding love again, and I can see why it might have been difficult.

I tried to call June all week to see what made her leave. When I finally got in touch with her yesterday, she obviously knew my brother was married, but it was difficult to get any more information out of her. I'm just hoping that when I get home she will open up about the whole situation. She said she's not mad at me, but I wouldn't blame her if she stayed upset for a while. I still think I did the right thing, but sometimes, the right and the wrong solutions don't give very different outcomes.

Feeling a hand rest on my shoulder, I look up to see Liam smiling sweetly down at me. "You ready? I think it's time to go," Liam asks.

"Sure. Cohen, do you want to ride with us?"

"No, Julie's parents should be here soon. I'm going to ride with them. I'll see you there."

I give his hand a quick squeeze and then he shakes Liam's hand. Liam and I walk out the front door and head to the vehicle with my parents. We sit in the backseat of my mom's car. He holds my hand the whole way, and I am lost in bliss. I do feel a tinge of sadness that Julie will never meet Liam. She always wanted me to find someone special.

42
COHEN

SATURDAY

Riding in the backseat of Julie's parents' car reminds me of our first date.

We called it a *real* date although her parents were with us the whole time. They even sat next to us during the movie. Our hands rested on the cup holder in between us. We eventually got up the nerve to hold hands, but no other portion of our bodies touched during the entire movie. Our palms were sweaty, and I had to drop her hand to wipe mine on my jeans several times.

It's hard to say whether my nerves would have been better if her parents had at least sat on a different row. As I wipe my sweaty palms on my black slacks now, I look over to the empty seat next to me, remembering the love Julie and I shared. It was wonderful and short-lived, but it was worth every minute.

We pull into the parking lot of the church. Laura leads me

to a side door where the minister greets us. I give him a quick handshake and head into the small hallway. Flowers and potted plants line the room, and I wonder why they haven't placed them in the church. As I walk around the corner, the sanctuary comes into view, and I quickly realize that there is no more room. Colorful flowers, potted plants, small figurines, teddy bears, and cards fill the front area. An easel, holding a large picture of Julie, sits beside her casket.

I stop in my tracks, staring at the open lid. *Can I handle this?* I close my eyes, bend my neck from side to side, and take in a series of deep breaths.

"Son, you don't have to go right now. We can just sit," Julie's dad says to me, placing his arm around my shoulders.

Even after everything, he still calls me son. After the accident, I often wondered if he would stop referring to me as his son and begin using my given name again. If I were to tell the truth, I thought they would disown me completely. At this point, I'm not sure what value I bring to their lives, except for pain and suffering.

We sit on the second pew, reserved for family, and I continue to stare at the open lid. All at once, it beckons me and disgusts me. I have been through every emotion since Wednesday. After we realized Julie wouldn't be recovering, I went through the stages of grieving, but a therapist once told me that I would likely go through them again when her death became final. I wonder what stage I've returned to now.

After forty-five minutes of staring at the open lid and feeling people file in around me, I decide to see her again. I walk alone, placing one foot in even steps before the other, to the front of the sanctuary. Why this room can't have a different name during sad events, I'm not sure. This room is nothing like a sanctuary to me. I have no peace and no rest. It doesn't provide me with shelter or refuge. Instead, in this moment, I feel like an animal being viewed from a distance. I can feel everyone's eyes on my back as her face comes into view.

She is pale and beautiful with her golden hair falling softly over her shoulders. They have chosen to put her in a white-and-yellow gown as if she were just sleeping. Her favorite color was yellow. The gold band that I gave her when I proposed still fits around her ring finger although it's very loose.

As I look down to my left hand, I realize I didn't wear my ring today. Closing my eyes, I try to push out the thoughts of what others will think. They will just have to understand. If they want the truth, I haven't worn my ring consistently for over a year.

I reach out to Julie's face and brush my hand against her cheek lightly. Once I feel that I have gazed at her for long enough, I return to my seat and continue staring straight ahead.

Soon, the service begins. We have it all planned out. The preacher speaks, music plays, and people sing. Then, it's time for the part I am dreading the most—they call on me to speak. I stand tall and walk up the steps to the podium. When I adjust the microphone, it squeals loudly for a moment. I see a few people cringe at the sound, but most people just continue to look at me with what I see as mixed emotions of pity and distaste.

Placing my notes on the flat wooden space, I begin. "Julie was my wife for ten years."

Breathe.

"From the moment she entered my life when I was ten years old, she captured me."

Breathe.

"When I turned sixteen, she missed my birthday party, but later, she brought me a cupcake decorated like a baseball. Many of you have had her cupcakes, so you know that from that moment on, my heart was hers."

I don't look up to see a reaction. *Breathe.*

"We got married young and struggled through college together. Well, I guess she plowed through school and started a career while I struggled through college. She was always supportive, always giving of herself. She loved her job. She loved making something that people could enjoy during special times in their lives."

This next part is going to be hard to say out loud. I close my eyes and steel myself against the hurt. "A little over two years ago, her accident was the worst night of my life. I don't think I could ever apologize enough to her for letting her leave the house alone that night. I loved her very much. I loved her with my whole heart. I will miss her smile and gentle attitude for the rest of my life. I know you share in this loss, and I thank you for giving your time to honor her memory."

I have three more paragraphs written on the paper, but instead of going on, I fold it up and begin to walk off the stage. I chance a quick look through the crowd as I step down the stairs.

She's here. Instantly, my shoulders relax, and I find a small smile to send her way.

43
June

SATURDAY

My eyes are filled with tears as he speaks. Between Texas and this pew, I have questioned why I decided to come here a million times, but for some reason, my body just kept moving forward. To avoid any fuss over my arrival, I didn't call Liam or Caroline to tell them I would be here. Selfishly, I wanted to hear his good-bye to her, so I could know a little more of the truth.

As he begins to speak, I can hear his voice shaking. His words are succinct and to the point. He adds no unnecessary meaning to anything. He gives tribute, apologies, and thanks. Then, he is done. He never looks up from the podium as he speaks, and I am fairly certain he won't see me. When he nears the final step, he lifts his head a fraction of an inch and instantly catches my eyes.

My body goes warm, and I wish there was a way to hide the

blush that is creeping up my body to my face. His shoulders straighten slightly, and I think he's smiling. I give a weak grin, worrying about what others around me might think if they notice his gesture. After all, we are at his wife's funeral.

I can see the back of Caroline's and Liam's heads. They don't turn. After a few more songs, a slideshow begins. While I know I should probably stick around and at least say something to my best friend and my brother, I see this as a good time to get away since everyone is focused on the beautiful pictures of her beautiful life.

I slip out of the back pew and walk into the restroom. I'm staring at my image in the mirror, trying to accept the knowledge of what I now know. His wife was hurt over two years ago, and she died last week. He wasn't wearing a ring when we met, and he didn't wear a ring today. He loved her. I could see it in his eyes. He adored her. *But then, why me? Why did he want me if he loved her?*

I can hear the voices of people as they leave the sanctuary. I want to avoid running into anyone, so I leave quickly and head to my rental car. While stepping into the driver's side, I begin to think about why I came here. I didn't come to simply attend a funeral and then run away. I came to take a chance, hoping that Cohen might be willing to tell me his side of the story.

Looking down to the funeral program in my lap, I turn it over and find the address to where family and friends will be gathering to visit after the service.

Sitting in the car on the side of the road outside of her house, I start to wonder what I was thinking. I turn on some music and let the sounds and lyrics wash over me as I decide what I should do.

After about forty-five minutes, I see Cohen get out of a car with a man and a woman who I assume are Julie's parents. Not too long after, Caroline and Liam arrive and walk into the house.

Is it wrong of me to be here? Will people think I'm being disrespectful? Maybe I should go back to Vivian's house and wait for Caroline and Liam there. I close my eyes and lean my head back against the headrest.

"June?"

I hear a soft knock on the glass. Opening my eyes, I see Vivian. "Oh, hi. I was just leaving. I'm sorry."

"No, no. Please come in and eat with us. I know Caroline and your brother will be glad to see you."

I agree and begin to get out of the car. My legs feel shaky, and I'm more nervous than I've ever felt in my life.

She walks me around the back of the house. Leaning in close to my ear, she says, "Cohen will be glad to see you, too. Why don't you sit in one of the patio chairs on the deck? I'll go find Caroline and Liam."

No one is outside, but I can hear people talking just inside the doors.

I sit for what feels like an eternity before I see the door begin to open.

Cohen steps through the doorway, holding a glass in each

hand. He blinks at me a few times, as if trying to make sure his vision is clear. After a few moments, he extends one glass to me, and I sit there, my body frozen.

"It's just iced tea," he says.

"What are you doing out here?" I ask.

"What are *you* doing out here?" he asks in return, placing the glass on the small table beside me.

"Well, um…I-I don't know."

"You flew across the country, and you don't know why you're here?"

I shrug in response, and he moves to sit in a chair a few feet in front of me.

"Please tell me you came to let me explain." His expression is soft and hopeful.

"Sort of," is all I can say.

We sit for a few minutes, sip our tea, and look out on the perfect backyard of Julie's parents' house. I'm beginning to feel a little awkward with the setting when Cohen speaks.

"I know we haven't known each other long, but I want to tell you everything." He pauses, closes his eyes, and takes in a breath. "I want your forgiveness and understanding. I know I don't deserve those things, but I want them because you are the first woman that has made me feel like love is a possibility again."

"I'm so sorry about Julie. You obviously loved her. I just don't understand why you didn't tell me. Why were you so sure you wanted to pursue me but so unsure about sharing this with me?"

Cohen sighs heavily and leans forward with his elbows against his knees. He looks down at the wood planks of the deck. "My wife was a shell of a person after her accident. She never spoke a word, she never engaged with anyone, and she required care around the clock. Julie never responded when I kissed her or told her that I loved her. She never reached out for a hug when I walked in the door. She died during that accident, and from that moment, I grieved the loss of my wife.

"For more than two years, I have blamed myself for that accident. I allowed Julie to leave the house that night. I was the reason the accident happened. I talked myself into believing that I lost my chance at a lifelong love because of what I had done...until your eyes met mine at that airport. With every page of the magazine that hit me and then with the force of your body against mine on those steps, you revived my heart. I began to see past what I had been through, and now, I can look forward to what could be."

"So, why did you leave before explaining any of this to me? Why didn't you tell me you were Caroline's brother?"

"I don't know how it got past me, but I didn't make the connection that you were Caroline's friend at first. When I did realize, I wasn't sure how to tell you without sharing everything...and I wasn't ready to share it all. Then, I got the call that Julie was sick. I felt like I needed to tell her and her family that I was ready to move on. I needed to have her blessing even though I knew she wouldn't be able to hear or understand me."

We sit again in silence. I'm contemplating everything I

know now, and I'm trying to make sense of how I feel about it all.

"So, what does this mean?" I ask.

"June, I haven't allowed myself to feel many happy emotions. Like I said, I grieved the loss of my wife over two years ago, and it feels like the grief owned me the whole time. If you'll let me, I want to let go of that grief and try to find something happy with you," he says, standing and pulling me to my feet.

As he cups my cheek in his hand, I lean into his touch.

"I don't know, Cohen. It's so much to take in, and you still live across the country."

"I can be anywhere. Don't let the distance be what stops us. Please…just give us a chance."

I close my eyes, and feel him pull me into his embrace. My hands surround his waist, and I bury my face into his chest as tears begin to fill my eyes. I'm full of so many emotions— sadness for the loss of Julie, happiness that Cohen and I might find a second chance, and nervousness about how all this will work out.

We stand this way for a few minutes, enjoying a new moment together.

When I hear the back door open, I try to pull away, but Cohen holds me tightly. Over his shoulder, I see Caroline and Liam walking onto the deck.

"June, I'm so glad you came," Caroline says, smiling.

"Me, too," I say, reaching my hand out to her.

She runs to join our hug.

Liam also comes toward us, and when he steps behind me, I feel his hands rub my shoulders gently.

"Um, Caroline…I can't breathe," I say, laughing.

"Oh, sorry." She releases her arms and takes a small step back.

She smiles at me as Liam returns to her side, and I can't help but smile back.

"We better get inside before people start to wonder where I am," Cohen says, still holding me to his side.

Hand in hand, Caroline and Liam walk back into the house. I tug at Cohen's arm, keeping him outside for a moment longer.

"Are you sure you want me here?"

Cohen pulls me in front of him and places his hands on my cheeks. "I don't want you anywhere else but near me. I should have never let you leave my side after the first day you crossed my path, and I don't plan on letting it happen again."

Our journey to this point hasn't been easy, but I'm starting to think easy might be overrated. I smile up at him, and together, we walk into the house.

Epilogue
COHEN

FOUR MONTHS LATER

It's November. I'm wearing short sleeves, and it's freaking hot out here. Running my hand through my hair several times, I close my eyes, trying to get a handle on my anxiety. With my other hand, I begin tugging on the bottom of my button-up shirt. *I have to get rid of this nervous energy. Just walk forward, put one foot in front of the other, and walk up the steps. It won't be that bad.*

I've visited Houston several times to see June, but this will be my first time meeting her parents. Caroline told me about their Sunday dinners, so I flew in a day early to make sure I could be here. Knowing her entire family is aware of the difficulties we faced during the first few weeks after we met doesn't help to calm my nerves.

After another few seconds of delay, I force my legs to move. I step up to the front door and press my finger against the doorbell. Before I have a chance to swallow the lump forming in my throat, the door swings open to reveal a woman. She's smiling at me as if I were presenting her with a check from the Publishers Clearing House.

"You must be Cohen!"

She rushes to where I'm standing and embraces me in a hug.

"Um, yes, and you must be Mrs. Deckert."

"Don't be silly. Call me Karen. Come on in." She continues smiling as she steps through the open doorway and gestures into their home.

"Cohen!" June exclaims.

When she throws herself into my arms, I pull her in tight to my chest.

"I'm so glad you're here," she whispers in my ear.

"Me, too." I smile down at her, and for a moment, it's as if we're alone.

During the past few months, we've taken the time to get to know each other better. When I've been able to, I work in Houston, and when I have to be in Seattle, we talk on the phone or video chat. Things haven't been easy with our busy schedules, but we make time for each other. For me, it's been worth the sacrifice. So far, she seems to feel the same way. It still amazes me every day that she decided to give our relationship a chance.

Caroline breaks into my thoughts as she gives me a hard pat on the back. "Hey, brother. It's about time you got here. I'm starving," she says, walking toward the dining room.

"Hello to you, too." I laugh at her obvious comfort in

June's parents' home.

Caroline and Liam have been seeing each other for about five months now. I couldn't have chosen a better fit for my sister. Liam is a great guy. He even got Caroline interested in sports—something I had never been able to accomplish. Somehow, they found each other at just the right time. I don't know that either one of them really settled the other one down. I think they both came to the realization that finding someone to spend a lifetime with is worth a little effort.

June and I follow closely behind Caroline. When we walk into the dining room, three people are already seated at the table. My nerves come flooding back. June must notice because she gives my hand a tight squeeze.

"Cohen, this is my sister, Addison, and her husband, Noah."

"Hi." I smile and give a simple nod in their direction. *At least they're smiling back.*

She immediately turns me to face the head of the table. "And this is my dad."

"Nice to meet you, young man," her dad says, standing to his feet as he offers me his hand.

"You, too, sir. Thank you for having me." I reach out and shake his hand.

"Well, let's not keep the pregnant one waiting." Noah lovingly glances at Addison as he nudges her with his elbow.

As everyone laughs, the tension I felt before begins to ease again.

Once we all sit down, food dishes start traveling around the table. I'm holding a basket of rolls when Liam begins to speak to me.

"It's about time you joined the weekly family festivities."

"Yeah, I wish I could have come sooner, but you know how busy work schedules can be," I say, trading the basket of rolls for the bowl of potatoes he's passing my way.

"No further explanation needed," he says, shaking his head.

"How is your work going?" June's dad gives me his full attention.

"Very well. Actually, there are going to be some changes soon, and I think things at work will get even better over the next few months."

I've been waiting to tell June the news for a few weeks, but I can't hold it back any more. This seems like as good a place as any to share. "The Bushing Company has decided to open an office in Houston. They want me to move here next month to get things up and running by the first of the year. After that, I'll have a permanent position here."

June's eyes grow wide, and a smile erupts on her face. It's like none I've ever seen from her before, and my heart swells with excitement.

She shouts, "You're kidding, right?"

"Don't really think I would tell a joke like that at your parents' house."

She launches herself toward me for another hug, knocking over our glasses of tea in the process. Everyone on our side of the table jumps up from their seats to avoid getting wet. I never knew it was possible for clumsiness to be so endearing.

"Oh crap. I'll go get some towels," she says, looking at me with glistening eyes.

"I'll help you." I slide ice and liquid off the edge of the table into one of our glasses, and then I follow the path she took into what I assume is the kitchen.

As the swinging door opens, I see June standing at the sink with her hands braced against the edge of countertop. The light from the evening sun is shining against her skin, and I stand there for a second, admiring her beauty. She's staring out the window with a distant look on her face, and my heart sinks a little. *Maybe she's not happy about this after all. Maybe I should have waited to tell her when we were alone.*

"Hey, are you okay?" I ask in a soft whisper as I walk over to her. Placing my hands on her waist, I turn her to face me.

"Yes," is the only word that comes out of her mouth as a tear begins to fall down her cheek.

"June, what's wrong? Are you upset?" I grab a napkin from the counter behind her and dab her eyes gently.

"Nothing…absolutely nothing is wrong. I'm not upset. I'm in shock. I can't believe this is really happening. You're really going to move here?" Her expression reveals a mixture of hope and concern.

"You can believe it. It's really happening." I gaze into her beautiful eyes for a moment, getting lost in their subtle green hue. "I love you."

Did I just say that? We haven't said those words to each other yet. They just came out of my mouth before I had time to think about them, but it doesn't matter. I would tell her a million more times just to see her eyes sparkle the way they are right now.

"I love you, too."

When she lays her head on my chest, I place a kiss on her soft hair.

After a couple of minutes, she leaves my embrace, grabs a few dish towels, and then links her arm in mine.

"We better get the table cleaned up," she says, her face more at ease now.

We walk back into the dining room just as June's dad is finishing up a story, and the room erupts in laughter. As I glance around the table at June's parents, her sister, her brother-in-law, Caroline, and Liam, I breathe in the love filling the room. It wasn't long ago when I decided the path my life had taken seemed unfair, and I was certain I was unworthy of finding another love. When I look down at June, her affection for me is evident in her smile. I know now, in this moment, that my path has led me here for a reason—to find a place of healing where a second chance at love is possible.

ACKNOWLEDGMENTS

Grandma and Mom—Thank you for instilling a love of reading in me at a young age. It was one of the best gifts you've ever given me!

To my husband—Thanks for watching the boys while I spent time making a dream come true. I never could have done this without your support.

Beta Readers: Amanda, Ashley, Christina, Jennifer, Julie, Kevin, Lainee, Megan, Tara, and Tera—I appreciate every single piece of advice you gave me during this process. From the initial idea to the finished product, your imprint will forever be on this book.

Alexandra Woods—My fellow author, encourager, and friend. Thanks for the advice, honest opinions, and all the laughs. This journey wouldn't have been the same without you.

Jennifer Roberts-Hall—A simple thank you.

Ozarks Romance Authors—My Missouri writer friends.

I'm so happy to have a group where I can share my passion. We all come from different walks of life, but at the end of the day, it all comes down to words on a page shared across a table. You have each played a part in helping me grow in skill and in confidence. I can't say thank you enough.

# # #

Sarah Hansen—You made my cover shine brighter than I could have imagined! Thank you!

Jovana Shirley—You've made my first experience with an editor painless. I'm so thankful I found you.

Sometimes I stare at my book cover and tear up. Or I get an email from Jovana and wonder how I got here. I'm so blessed.

# # #

When I began writing this book, I had no clue what would come of this experience. Over the past year, I've been welcomed with open arms into a community that was not my own. The world of indie published authors is growing, and I'm so glad I joined in.

To The Writers Club and Indie Gals Connection groups—Without your constant encouragement and your persistence to complete your projects, I would not have had the wherewithal to finish this book. I am proud to be included in these groups with many talented authors.

To the readers who promoted my debut novel, trusting that the synopsis and small excerpts I'd posted would bring a book to fruition—You are a blessing. I hope you enjoyed my completed work.

And finally, to the bloggers who spend their free time reading, writing reviews, and promoting independently published books—I simply have no words worthy enough to describe my level of gratitude to you. Thank you for all you do!

www.ingramcontent.com/pod-product-compliance
Lightning Source LLC
Chambersburg PA
CBHW031248170626
46807CB00001B/44